The Sword and the Spirit

Book One

~ EWAN ~

Glossary and Author Notes

Bothy – a small unlocked shelter found in the remote mountainous areas of Wales, Northern England, Northern Ireland, and Scotland. They have been used by travellers and hikers for centuries and are still in use today.

Skamelar – a sycophant or lackey.

Sasunnach – Gaelic word for English.

Wedding Liturgy – taken from traditional Roman Catholic/Anglican sacraments.

'A Templar Knight is truly a fearless knight, and secure on every side, for his soul is protected by the armour of faith just as his body is protected by the armour of steel. He is thus doubly-armed and need fear neither demons nor men.'

De Laude Novae Militae (In Praise of the New Knighthood)
Bernard de Clairveaux, French Abbot, 1090 - 1153 AD

For John, my son, who makes me proud every single day.

PROLOGUE

With a shuddering groan, the stallion crashed to the sun-baked earth like a boulder, breath exploding from his mighty lungs.

"Melchior!" Ewan cursed and clenched his teeth as the dead weight of his mount pinned his left leg to the ground. The Templar charge was within reach of the Mamluk arrows, but Ewan saw no evidence his horse had been struck. Yet the beast lay silent and unmoving amid the chaos of battle, his magnificent white coat already turning to rust as the dust settled upon him. To drop lifeless, mid-stride, implied the animal's courageous heart had likely failed.

"Melchior," Ewan repeated, this time in anguish as the loss of a brave and noble friend became absolute in his mind. Choking on dust, he set his sword aside, and bent to grasp his trapped leg at the knee. All around him, the Templar charge continued. A horde of hooves thundered past, shaking the ground and raising clouds of Syrian sand.

If that were not enough, enemy arrows rained down from above.

"Damn their Saracen bones," Ewan bellowed and sucked dust-laden air through his slatted helm. At any moment, he was apt to be trampled to death or skewered. To die fighting in Christ's name was a great honour. But this... this was death by misfortune. And it did not sit well with him.

"Come on, you bastard!" Ewan's lungs burned as he tugged at his trapped limb. As the last of the Templar chargers moved past, the hail of arrows moved with them, many finding their targets. The cries of man and beast joined the cacophony of hooves and war drums.

Enveloped in a thick swirling cloud of sand and grit, Ewan could neither see nor breathe. Near suffocation, he pulled off his helm and cast it aside, coughing till tears tumbled down his cheeks.

The continued sounds of combat saturated the air. Still gasping, Ewan squinted into the sandstorm of battle and cursed his helplessness.

"*Baucent!*" came the familiar cry from the Master. Ewan roared his frustration as battle-fever pushed the blood through his veins. He placed his free foot against

Melchior's back, gritted his teeth again, and pushed till his head throbbed. All to no avail.

Then another cry went up, spreading across the battlefield like a rash. "Fire pots!"

A terrifying and familiar shriek filled the air as the burning missiles rained down all around. Another shout, close by, found its way to Ewan's ear. "On your right, Brothers!"

Still blinded by dust, Ewan continued his struggle for freedom. He did not fear death, but he was not yet ready to surrender his life. "Come on," he cried, tugging on his trapped limb, tears of sheer effort washing the dirt from his eyes. At that moment, something hit the ground nearby with a muted thud, and the surrounding air seemed to glow as if alight. Then he felt an impact against his mail coif on the side of his face by his left eye. At first, he barely flinched. The blow had been soft, like being hit by mud.

A moment later, fumes of burning pitch made his eyes weep and his nostrils flare. The viscous, flaming tar leached through the loops of his mail coif and bit into his flesh like white-hot teeth. The coif, meant to protect, now served as an instrument of torture. Ewan let out a howl and clawed at it, writhing as he struggled to peel it off. At last, it came away, taking burnt flesh with it, yet still his skin blistered as flecks of embedded pitch gnawed at his face like fiery leeches. Blinded and half-mad with pain, Ewan rolled over. He twisted his trapped leg and pressed his face against the dry earth, seeking to suffocate the terrible heat. But the agony remained, and that, combined with the stench of burnt flesh and hair, made him retch.

The shout went up again. "*Baucent.* Templars, to me!"

As the sounds of battle faded away, Ewan turned his head and looked to the dust-laden sky. Veiled by that devilish fog, the harsh, Syrian sun appeared as a perfect, fiery sphere. Yet Ewan felt cold, as if death had already taken him in its embrace. An arrow fell from the sky and thudded into the earth beside him. Then another, and another. He was a captive target, he realized, and crossed himself.

"I commend to your keeping, Lord," he whispered, "the soul of your servant."

No sooner had the words been spoken than the cloaked figure of a man loomed up, the sun forming a golden halo around his head. The man spoke, his voice blessedly familiar, yet somehow mystifying. "Not today, Brother," he said. "Not today."

Ewan tasted salt on his tongue and breathed in a lungful of cool, sweet air. As delirium pulled a merciful curtain across his consciousness, he thought of a land far away and capitulated to a blessed darkness.

Chapter One

Templar house

Port of La Rochelle, France.

Wednesday, October 11th,

Year of the Lord 1307

Ewan slid his sword from its sheath and tilted the blade toward the candlelight to better examine its honed edge. His keen eye sought flaws—small anomalies that marred the burnished steel. None were visible. Hardly a surprise. The weapon had not seen battle in a good while.

No matter. He would administer to it anyway. The grind of stone on steel was a gratifying sound. If nothing else, the exercise might at least help to smooth out his mild feeling of angst. Perhaps the summons meant nothing. Perhaps he worried for naught. And perhaps his instincts were wrong.

As Ewan lifted the whetstone from its place on the shelf, the sudden trill of a cricket broke the evening silence. The distinctive song was rare this late in the year, an anomaly that drew Ewan's gaze to the open window and the twilight beyond.

"The warm weather has undoubtedly aroused the little creature," said a sober voice from the other side of the room. "In the Orient, its song is considered to be a sign of good fortune. A foolish, heathen belief. And Hammett should be the one sharpening your sword. Where is the lad?"

Ewan threw a fleeting glance at his companion, who sat, quill in hand, at the writing desk, no doubt recording the day's events as was his habit.

"He's away with Jacques on a wee errand." Ewan settled himself in a chair by the empty hearth and bent to his task. "I'm no' above sharpening my own weapon, Brother. 'Tis a soothing way to pass the time, I find. After I've done mine, I'll hone yours too, if you wish. 'Tis likely in need."

"My blade, I can assure you, is without blemish," came the firm and somewhat piqued reply. There followed a soft sigh and the scratch of a quill on parchment.

Ewan smiled to himself.

His cohort, Brother Gabriel Fitzalan, was said to hold a crucifix in one hand and a sword in the other. Pious and disciplined in matters of faith. Deadly with a blade. Attributes befitting a Knight of the Temple.

What he lacked in totality, however, was a sense of humour—a deficiency that Ewan tended to exploit without apology. After all, who could resist hurling a stone into calm waters simply to watch ripples spread across the surface?

Not Ewan. Especially since Gabriel's veins ran with noble English blood. By virtue of birth alone, the two men should have been sworn enemies. Ewan, being the second-born son of a Scottish laird, was surely obliged, then, to ruffle his friend's *Sasunnach* feathers once in a while.

And friends they were, despite and above all else. Brothers-in-arms. Each ready and willing to die for the other and for the Brotherhood, if called upon to do so.

Ready and willing.

Ewan slid the whetstone along the edge of his blade and awaited Gabriel's anticipated question. A moment later, the scratching of the quill ceased.

"What errand?"

Ewan smiled to himself. "The Master sent a summons while you were at prayer. Only one of us was required to respond. Jacques took it upon himself to do so and took Hammett with him."

A brief pause ensued. Then, "My instincts tell me things do not bode well for the Temple."

"Your instincts and mine." Again, Ewan tilted the sword to the light and squinted along its edge. "The Brotherhood will, however, endure. Of that I have nae doubt."

Gabriel grunted. "But in what capacity, I wonder?"

The cricket ceased its singing, and Ewan lifted his gaze to the open window. "Methinks we're about to find out."

*

"Nay, I cannae believe it. 'Tis some kind of unholy madness." Ewan sprang to his feet, thrust his sword into its scabbard, and glared at the Templar brother who stood before him. "I'll no' do it, Jacques, do you hear? I'll no' run off with my tail 'tween my legs, like a kicked dog."

"Nor will I," Gabriel said, the sombre tone of his voice not quite hiding his indignation.

"To refuse is to disobey a direct command from the Grand Master himself." Jacques Aznar's dark, Basque eyes flicked from one man to the other. "Believe me, I share your anger and your desire to stand and fight. But this is not a battle to be won on some foreign field. This is not even a foreign enemy. This is a planned persecution by the crowned head of France. This Friday, Philippe will execute his royal edict and demand a widespread arrest of our Templar brothers. Others, besides us, have been similarly forewarned and ordered to seek refuge beyond the French borders. Though, in truth, we are few."

"But why us?" Ewan gripped his sword hilt as if seeking support. "Why have we been singled out for exile?"

"I voiced the same question." Jacques gave a grim smile. "And it is simply that we are better suited for it. We have each proven ourselves courageous. We're still relatively youthful, strong in body and heart." He gave Gabriel a pointed look. "We are also literate, able to read and write—important if we need to record our actions and communicate with others in the Order. And we each speak at least two languages."

"So, the reward for being an exemplary knight is a command to forsake the rest of our brethren." Bile rose to the back of Ewan's throat. "It goes against the code, may God forgive us."

"The Order must prevail, Ewan." Jacques heaved a sigh. "Its future now rests upon those who are able to elude Phillipe's oppression."

"Last year the Jews were targeted," Gabriel murmured. "This year, the Soldiers of Christ. Remove your creditors. Eliminate your debt."

Jacques gave a solemn nod. "Undoubtedly Philippe's motive, although he would surely deny it. According to our source, we stand accused of blasphemy, heresy, and all manner of unsavoury rites."

"I'm aware of the falsehoods spoken against us," Ewan said, "but to scatter like chafers into the night… I tell you, it turns my gut to even contemplate such a thing."

"Consider it a tactical manoeuvre, Brother." Jacques gave a half-shrug. "Not all battles can be fought with a sword, and I suspect we're facing our most formidable challenge yet. A sacrifice that demands the greatest courage from those chosen to take it."

Ewan failed to see the courage inherent in a retreat, and Jacques' words weighed heavy on his spirit. He knew the mighty heartbeat of the Order, a sound that had echoed throughout Christendom for two centuries, had faltered in recent years.

Pray God it does not fall forever silent.

"Where, then?" Ewan asked, without enthusiasm. "Where are we commanded to go?'

"England, I should imagine," Gabriel said, leaving his perch to move to Ewan's side. "We have a strong presence there."

"Nay, not England." Jacques kept his gaze locked with Ewan's. "We're unsure, for the moment, of how much influence Philippe might have over the English crown. This damnable persecution may yet traverse the Narrow Sea. Our destination is England's hostile neighbour. A less vulnerable and more distant shore."

"Scotland," Ewan muttered, realizing what lay behind the odd glimmer in Jacques' eyes. "You mean Scotland, aye?"

Jacques inclined his head. "Personally, I'd have preferred to take my chances in Andalusia, which also offers refuge, but Scotland has been chosen as our destination. All other reasons aside, it seems your ancestral home has long had an affiliation with the Order and has a standing promise of refuge. I understand your grandfather, Calum MacKellar, fought with the brothers at La Forbie, and was one of the few Templars who survived that terrible day. Your sire is named for him, I believe."

"My ancestral home?" Ewan frowned. "Are you referring to the country now, or the MacKellar family seat?"

"Your family seat," Jacques replied. "It is to be found on the western coast, is it not?"

"Aye, but…" Ewan shook his head. "We cannae go there."

Jacques raised a brow. "Might I know why? Does your grandfather's pledge to the Temple no longer stand? We're not asking for charity, Ewan. Your clan will be well compensated for giving us refuge."

Ewan grimaced. "'Tis no' a question of money, Brother. 'Tis more the fact that my sire and I dinnae see eye-to-eye. I left on bad terms. I doubt very much he'll raise a welcome banner for me, or any who travel with me."

Jacques gave him a bemused look. "But surely these differences can be set aside. Are you not his only son?"

Ewan shook his head. "Nay, I'm the second-born. Ruaidri is the elder by nearly three years, and heir to the seat. My mother died when I was born, and my father remarried. I also have a half-sister." An image of vivid red curls and wide blue eyes slid into Ewan's mind, and he felt a wistful tug at his heart. "She was but a wee lass when I left."

Jacques grunted. "Which was twelve years ago, yes?"

"Almost." Ewan shifted on his feet, unsettled by memories of his angry departure.

"I would also question their willingness to welcome me," Gabriel remarked. "As you said, they are hostile to the English, which makes me an enemy. And besides, there are other known Templar holdings in Scotland. Can we not find refuge with our own?"

"We have been ordered to disperse," Jacques replied, "which means, for now at least, we must seek refuge outside of the Brotherhood. And as a Knight of the Temple, Gabriel, you do not serve the English king. You answer to the Holy See in Rome and serve only Christ. In this capacity, you are a brother to Ewan and to me. If necessary, this will be made clear to Laird MacKellar upon our arrival."

Ewan huffed in frustration. "Perhaps you didnae hear what I said, Jacques. I'll no' seek refuge at Castle Cathan. I swore I'd never return to the place."

"An unfortunate vow. One made in pride and haste, I suspect." Jacques squeezed Ewan's shoulder. "I cannot force you to change your mind, Brother, but I urge you to do so. To set out from these shores without a definitive direction only adds to the sense of… of…"

"Desperation?" Gabriel's lip raised in a sneer. "Like rats abandoning a sinking ship."

"I prefer to think we're seeking survival by means of an ark. One that is making ready to sail as we speak." Jacques glanced at the window. "Destination known or unknown, we must leave on the dawn tide, so I suggest we begin preparations without further delay. We possess certain items that must not be allowed to fall into the king's hands. I'm sure I don't need to explain further. And, since we're likely being watched, discretion is essential. Needless to say, we'll be taking the tunnels down to the harbour."

Ewan muttered a curse in his native Gaelic. "Call it what you will, this entire thing has a bitter taste. What of our squires and sergeants? Are they aware?"

"All those beneath this roof will be made aware of our departure, but they will not be told the reason for it," Jacques replied. "Only Hammett will be coming with us, although I merely told him to prepare for a journey. He was not present for the meeting, so knows naught of what was said. I wanted to tell you first."

Ewan gave a bitter laugh. "So, we must add the shame of betrayal to the shame of retreat. May the good Lord forgive us."

Jacques heaved an audible sigh but said nothing.

"What of our horses?" Gabriel asked.

"Two each," Jacques replied, "and an ox to pull the wagon once we make landfall. The ship is being readied to carry them."

Ewan removed his hand from his sword hilt, unaware, till that moment, of how tight his grip had been. A mild pain tugged at the back of his eyes as he stepped over to the open window and gazed up into a clear autumn night.

"I cannae quite wrap my head around this nonsense," he murmured, furling and unfurling his stiff fingers. "Is there any doubt at all about Phillipe's intentions?"

There followed a moment of solemn silence before Jacques gave his grave reply. "None whatsoever."

"Then may God help us," Ewan turned and regarded his two comrades, "and guide us safely to Castle Cathan."

From somewhere outside, the soft trill of a cricket once again rose into the air.

*

The nameless, unmarked cog left the port of La Rochelle in that darkest of hours before dawn, tugged into black, open water by three, oar-driven longboats. As the sun rose behind a grey belt of cloud, it aroused a brisk breeze that ruffled the sea. The crew adjusted the ship's single, large sail, and the hull soon ploughed unerringly through the white-tipped waves, heading north.

It was an unadorned vessel; rudimentary, but large and solid. A single, open deck covered a compartmented storage and sleeping area beneath. Half-a-dozen horses and a hefty ox had been penned beneath a canvas roof toward the stern of the ship. No doubt unsettled by the movement beneath their hooves, the animals jostled each other, ears back and eyes rolling. Hammett stood with them, muttering words of calm that appeared to be having little effect.

Another hefty canvas covered the contents of a two-wheeled cart anchored to the deck by strong rope.

Ewan had slept little the previous night. The salt air whipped through his hair as he stood at the bow watching the distant coastline of Brittany disappear into his past. His thoughts were more turbulent than the surrounding waves, and the pain in his head persisted, like a tether around his skull.

Ten years as a Templar knight had changed him. Reshaped him. He no longer recognized the tempestuous young warrior he had once been. Beneath the white mantle of military discipline and piety, however, Ewan's veins still ran with hot, Gaelic blood. The thought of returning to Castle Cathan naturally stirred dormant memories of his clan.

And the unresolved conflicts he'd left behind.

Gabriel's voice drifted into his ear. "Have you had any contact with your family at all since you left?"

Ewan lifted his gaze to a seabird soaring overhead. "Nay."

"So, it should be quite a homecoming. You are their lost son and brother. The prodigal, returned at last."

Ewan narrowed his eyes against the breeze as he regarded the distant coastline once more. "I'm the unwanted son, Gabriel. The one who killed his mother on his way into the world."

Gabriel fell silent for a few moments before speaking again. "Castle Cathan," he said. "Does the name have a meaning?"

"It is named after Saint Cathan," Ewan replied. "'Tis said the man spent the night there while on his travels. He was taken by the beauty of the place and gave it his holy blessing."

"Cathan," Gabriel repeated, his voice ponderous. "I'm not familiar with this saint."

"He's been dead many centuries and is little known beyond Scotland." Ewan shrugged. "And there's naught sacred about Castle Cathan when the winter winds come screaming out o' the north. As you'll soon find out."

"With God's merciful grace, aye," Gabriel said. "You mentioned your sister's name with some fondness earlier. I must assume, then, that your relationship with her was pleasant enough."

"It was, aye. Children dinnae judge others till they are taught to do so." Ewan turned and met Gabriel's gaze. "I warrant she'll take one look at the ugliness I bear and turn her eyes away, as most folk do."

A slight frown settled on Gabriel's brow. "I'm certain she'll see beyond it, Ewan, as most folk do when they come to know you. It is a mark of courage, not ugliness. And one acquired while fighting in Christ's name."

"'Tis no' the scar which bothers me so much, nor the reactions of those who see it. 'Tis the fact that I didnae get the chance to fight that day." Ewan gave a wry smile. "Maybe that's why the battle was lost."

"I assume you jest. And besides, our fight is ongoing."

Ewan pointed his chin at the French coast. "Over there, perhaps, but no' out here, on this damned vessel. We're in exile. Nay, worse, yet. We're in retreat."

"Knights of the Temple do not retreat." Jacques stepped up to them, his sober expression offset by a gleam in his eye as he gestured over his shoulder. "Not while the *Baucent* still flies."

Ewan looked back along the deck and felt his heart quicken. There, supported between two, twelve-foot poles amidships, the piebald banner of the Templar Order fluttered beneath the invisible touch of the wind.

Blood racing, Ewan dared to turn back and look north, where his future now lay. Despite the declarations of courage and the pledges to endure this trial, a harsh truth remained. He was returning to a world that had become foreign to him. A world where he didn't belong. How could he even begin to prepare heart and head for such an undertaking?

Twelve years.

It seemed longer. By all things sacred, it felt like a lifetime. A somewhat blurred recollection of his brother arose in his mind. Ruaidri had been the double of their sire, with wild hair the colour of horse-chestnuts, and a square, stubborn chin. Not a tall man, but he'd been strong in body and mind, his quiet demeanour belying the fortitude of his spirit.

If their father had succumbed in Ewan's absence, Ruaidri would now be laird of Castle Cathan.

Ewan drew a slow, deep breath as he considered the possibility of his father's demise. What he felt about it could not quite be determined. Such events were mere imaginings, anyway. Fabricated assumptions that served little purpose. In truth, Ewan knew naught of his family's circumstances. They knew naught of his, either.

All that, God willing, was about to change.

"What is to become of us?" he murmured.

Overhead, the seabird let out a mournful cry, tilted his grey wings, and turned toward the distant shore.

Chapter Two

Castle Cathan,

Western Scotland,

Friday, October 13th

Year of the Lord 1307

Morag MacKellar shivered at the rattle of the wind against the shutters and tugged her shawl about her shoulders.

"I fear you'll be blown clear across the glen, horse an' all," she said, watching her brother fasten his sword about his hips. The lightness in her voice belied the weight of dread that sat like a lump of clay in her belly. Those she loved kept leaving Castle Cathan, and some of them had never returned. "Maybe you should delay your departure a wee while. See if the weather settles. I'm sure Alastair MacAulay will understand."

Sword in place, Ruaidri MacKellar shook his head and reached for his green, fur-lined cloak that had been tossed over the back of a chair. "The ceremony is set for Sunday, Morag. Alastair MacAulay is to meet me at the bothy tonight. There'll be no delay, especially for a wee bit of a breeze."

"A *wee* bit?" Morag glanced at the shuttered window. "Are you deaf? Do you no' hear it?"

"I hear it." Her brother settled his cloak around him and fastened its heavy, silver pin at his left shoulder. "Sounds worse than it is, no doubt. You can badger me all you like. It'll no' make any difference."

A burning tallow hissed and snapped, startling Morag. She cursed her stretched nerves and rocked on her heels. "You've no' seen the lass since she was a wee thing," she said, conjuring up an unlikely image of her brother's future bride. "What if she has a face like a pig's arse? Will you still wed her?"

"Her name is Elspeth, and MacAulay assures me she's bonny to look upon." Ruaidri lifted a canvas saddlebag from the same chair. "But the answer is aye, I'll take her to wife, face like a pig's arse or otherwise. I'm no' wedding her for her looks, but to strengthen the alliance 'tween our two clans."

Morag snorted. "'Tis a lacklustre reason to wed."

Ruaidri sighed. "You ken fine well how things are. 'Tis a way of keeping the wolves from our gates."

"Or maybe you are inviting them in, no?"

He cast her a stern glance. "That'll do."

"Sorry." Morag wrinkled her nose. "But I dinnae quite trust Alastair MacAulay. His eyes are set too close together, for one thing."

"Which means naught at all, you bampot. The man is a bit of a wily bastard, aye, but he wants this alliance as much as I do. More, yet."

Something in her brother's voice didn't quite ring true. Morag tilted her head and regarded him. He looked tired, she thought. Burdened. Or perhaps the shadows, cast by firelight, gave that impression.

"Still, you must wonder if your future bride is bonny or no'." A sudden rush of emotion caught her by surprise. "I hope she's bonny, Ruaidri, both in looks and character. I really do. You deserve a bonny lass."

"She'll be well suited, I'm sure." Ruaidri smiled and tugged on one of Morag's copper braids. "I have to go. Will you come and bid me Godspeed?"

Morag shifted her gaze to the flames, trying to shrug off the persistent sense of foreboding that troubled her. The lump of fear still sat in the pit of her stomach, but she could find no reason for its presence.

"Please take me with you." She blinked away a prickle of tears as she turned back to him. "I promise I'll no' get in the way."

"We've been through this, and my answer is the same," Ruaidri replied, his voice firm. "Besides, you're needed here. And in truth, you made a good point about the weather. 'Tis nae the season for traipsing around the mountains, and I can do without having my wee sister to worry about. I'll be back in a few days, I promise."

Morag pouted. "'Tis nae fair," she said, not caring about the petulant whine in her voice. "I'm your sister. I should be present when you marry. As should others in our clan."

"We'll have another celebration when I return. You can arrange it while I'm away." Ruaidri hoisted the bag over his shoulder and held out a hand. "Enough griping. It doesnae suit you. Come and see me off."

∧

Perched on a jagged promontory overlooking the Sea of the Hebrides, the castle walls of Castle Cathan were rarely free of the wind. On this damp and chilly October morning, it hurtled in from the northwest, snatching at Morag's skirts and nipping at her cheeks as she stepped into the courtyard. The smell of rain wrapped around her, and she glanced inland, where Ruaidri's direction lay. In the murky light of dawn, the distant mountains appeared grey. Colourless.

Ominous.

Morag tried to reason with herself, but the inexplicable sense of fear still sat in her belly. Ruaidri, however, apparently paid little regard to the dismal conditions. He strode past Morag and headed for the castle gate where Goliath, his handsome bay gelding, stood saddled and ready.

"The sky is sagging with rain and about to burst." Morag ran to keep up with him. "'Tis folly to travel the mountain pass alone in such weather. What if you get into trouble?"

"I could travel the pass blindfolded, rain or not. Besides, I told you, Alastair MacAulay is supposed to meet me halfway, and he's also providing the escort for our return." Ruaidri turned and grasped Morag gently by her arms. "Cease your worrying. I'll be fine, I swear it. Just keep an eye on things for me while I'm away. And make sure the place is ready for Elspeth's arrival. I'll leave you in charge."

Morag huffed. "Tell Duncan that, will you? He'll be ordering me and every other poor lackey about afore you even reach the end of the causeway."

Ruaidri chuckled and released her. "Dinnae give the man a hard time. He means well. And speaking o' the Devil..."

Morag glanced over her shoulder to see Duncan, the clan steward, scurrying across the courtyard, cloak flapping like wings. He blew out a hearty breath as he reached them and tugged his woollen bonnet down over his ears. "By Odin's hairy arse, 'tis a raw day," he announced, rubbing his hands together. "Are you all set, Laird?"

"Aye, I think so." Ruaidri hoisted the saddlebag onto Goliath's back. "I—nay—*we* should be back by Wednesday next."

"Very good." Duncan bobbed his head. "I shall look forward to welcoming our new lady. Dinnae worry about a thing here. I'll take charge of everything as needs it."

"What did I tell you?" Morag folded her arms and frowned up at Ruaidri. "Tell him."

Brows raised, Duncan flicked his gaze from sister to brother. "Tell me what?"

"Never mind. Just dinnae kill each other while I'm gone." Ruaidri sighed as he clambered into the saddle. "Bar the gates after me and let no strangers in, 'less you ken for certain they dinnae pose a risk. Do you hear?"

Morag huffed as Duncan's head bobbed again. "I hear you well, Laird," the steward said. "Castle Cathan will still be sound when you return, as will those within its walls."

"Good." Ruaidri shook a lock of chestnut hair from his eyes and gathered up the reins. "I dinnae want any surprises."

"God keep you safe." Morag forced her voice over the sudden tightness in her throat. "Please be careful. Promise me."

"Have nae fear, wee lass." Ruaidri gave a casual salute, pressed his heels to the horse's belly, and rode toward Castle Cathan's gates, his departing words sailed past them on the wind. "I'll be back soon!"

*

The shuttered windows of Castle Cathan's great hall did a fair job of keeping the autumn winds at bay, but they also denied entry to daylight. Consequently, the hall's lime-washed walls shimmered with the flicker of a half-dozen reed torches that snapped and hissed in their iron sconces.

Atop the tables, several skinny candles also burned, their fragile flames dancing as people moved about. The peat fire in the central hearth pulsed like a fiery heart as it warmed the air. A vein of smoke leached from it, snaking upwards to escape through the slatted opening in the roof.

If not for an hour-candle, the lack of daylight would make it necessary to guess at the hour. At that moment, though, Morag didn't need to guess. Till a short while ago, and for most of the day, she'd been atop the gatehouse, gaze fixed on the causeway leading to and from Castle Cathan. As the sun sank behind a curtain of grey, Morag's hopes sank with it. Capitulating to the chill of the wind, she'd been driven indoors.

Another day almost gone, this being the fifth in succession with no sign of Ruaidri and his new wife.

"Something is wrong, I tell you," Morag said, clenching her hands as if in prayer, fear and frustration knotting in her gut. She stood beside Duncan, her back to the hearth, soaking up the heat from the fire. "He said he'd return Wednesday. Today is Thursday. He should be back by now."

"Without other considerations, I'd be inclined to agree." Duncan grimaced and scratched his head. "But a day or two beyond what he said isnae unreasonable, given that the laird just got himself wed. That doesnae happen without something of a celebration. He's likely lingered awhile longer 'cause o' that. Or it might be the weather. It has barely stopped pissing here this past sennight, an' I reckon they've had the same at Dunraven. Aye, and it's turned to snow on the hills."

Morag scoffed. "Miserable weather never stopped Ruaidri before."

"He never had a wife to worry about before." Duncan shrugged a shoulder. "Could be the lass didnae wish to travel till things cleared."

"What Highland lass is afraid o' rain?" Morag countered, although she grabbed onto a measure of comfort in the steward's reasoning. Still, her unease persisted. "I'm worried, Duncan."

"I ken you are, lass," Duncan said, gentling his tone, "but I really think you worry for naught. We'll give it one more day. If the laird doesnae arrive on the morrow, I'll dispatch a couple of men to go look for him."

Morag opened her mouth to respond but found her gaze drawn to sudden movement in the doorway. She frowned as Brody, one of the men-at-arms, approached them.

Something in the urgency of his stride snared her attention. His expression also aroused her fear to fresh heights. The man looked as though he'd seen a ghost.

"God help me," she murmured, stomach churning as she clutched at the small, gold cross that hung around her neck. "What now?"

Brody stopped an arm's length away and drew a breath. Morag drew one also and held it.

"Mil…," Brody's voice faltered, and he cleared his throat. "Milady, we have visitors at the gates requesting entry. Three men, armed. And a lad."

"Strangers?" Duncan asked.

"Er, nay." The man grimaced. "That is, one of them isnae. I mean, I… I cannae be certain."

Duncan blinked. "What the devil are you blabbering about, laddie? Are they strangers or nay?"

Morag released her breath. "Do they have news of my brother?"

"In a way, aye," Brody replied, and cleared his throat again. "But 'tis nae something I care to repeat. I think it best you come with me, Milady, and hear it for yourself."

Chapter Three

Approach to Castle Cathan,
Western Scotland
Thursday, October 18th,
Year of the Lord 1307

It might have been a memory, but it felt more like the realization of a prophetic dream. In any case, the sombre image of Ewan's ancestral landscape, despite the passing of the years, had not changed. Its mirrored likeness still remained clear in his mind. Even the clouds looked the same as they skittered across the darkening sky, herded along by the eternal whistle of the wind. Salt tingled on his tongue as he breathed in the rich smell of rain and damp earth. The sensation of it stirred a dull memory, one forged in the depths of battle. Or perhaps it had merely been a dream. Ewan had never been quite sure.

He filled his lungs again, savouring the sweetness. Above him, gulls wheeled through the air, mocking each other with their cries. And then, of course, there was the castle itself.

On the cusp of nightfall, Castle Cathan appeared as a hard, grey silhouette, emerging from the coastal crag as if born from it. The main keep—an unadorned, rectangular tower—rose up at one end of a protective curtain wall. The backdrop of fertile pasturelands and distant mountains blended into the twilight, creating an ancient tapestry. In contrast, to the west, the sea stretched out to a horizon still aglow from the sunset. Below, the waves lashed incessantly at a rocky shore, stirred into a perpetual frenzy by the tides and winds.

Conflicted, Ewan tussled with his feelings. Part of him wanted to turn, dig his spurs into his horse's belly, and flee. At the same time, he felt the inexorable pull of the past, both curious and fearful to know what had become of his family. In addition, the disciplined Templar knight he had become still grappled with feelings of betrayal and anger aimed at the French king.

Their exodus to Scotland had not been without problems. Rough seas had forced them to drop anchor in a sheltered Scottish bay for two full days before continuing on to their destination port. On the way, they had lost one of their horses to sickness. Upon landing, they continued the journey north, through terrain both majestic and unforgiving, seeking shelter and sustenance where they could.

The Templar mantles had drawn some curious glances, but the Order was well enough known in Scotland, and the men had journeyed unchallenged. Given the remoteness, Ewan knew it would likely be a while before news of Phillippe's edict reached these northern climes.

"It's a fine bastion," Gabriel said, drawing Ewan from his musing. "A birthplace befitting a warrior such as yourself."

Ewan eyed said birthplace and grimaced inwardly. "Aye, well, I cannae say what kind o' welcome we'll receive. If any."

"I hope they don't turn us away," young Hammett said, stifling a yawn. "I could sleep standing up."

"Not in this wind, you couldn't," Jacques said, gazing out over the sea. "It reminds me of the *Côte Basque*. A little more savage, perhaps, but quite magnificent."

A man's voice called out as they drew close to the gates. "Who approaches?" it demanded, in the Gaelic tongue. "And what is your purpose here?"

Ewan peered up at the shadowed figure atop the gatehouse. "I would speak with the laird of Castle Cathan," he shouted. "Does Calum MacKellar still hold the seat?"

An elongated moment of silence ensued, then, "Who asks?"

Ewan lowered his gaze and shifted in the saddle.

Twelve years.

"I assume he's demanding a name," Jacques said.

Ewan gave a single nod. "Aye."

"So, why do you hesitate? Tell him who you are, Brother. And tell him *what* you are, in case he does not understand the significance of our garb."

Ewan doubted the latter to be true. Everyone in the clan, and others besides, knew of its long affiliation with the Templars. "My name is Ewan Tormod MacKellar," he called out. "I'm a Soldier of Christ and of the Temple of Solomon, and the second-born son of Laird Calum MacKellar. Open the gates."

This time, the resulting silence stretched out even longer.

"Do you think he has fainted from shock?" Hammett asked, squinting up into the gloom.

"Nay." Ewan settled back in his saddle. "'Tis merely the sound of a man struggling to make sense of what he heard."

"Wait there," called the voice from above, moments later.

"An interesting language," Gabriel observed. "I shall endeavour to learn it while I'm here."

"'Tis no' a bad idea, that." Ewan cleared his throat and tried to calm his stretched nerves. "I doubt anyone here will take too kindly to your *Sasunnach* babbling."

"I never babble," Gabriel said, frowning, "in English or any other language."

The indignant reply teased a smile from Ewan as he dismounted. He approached a small, grated portal in the gate, wondering whose face he would see when it opened.

The resulting wait only served to heighten his angst, and he sought out the customary comfort of his sword hilt. As he wrapped his fingers around it, his unsettled thoughts veered unexpectedly onto another road. "Eight days," he said, looking back at his cohorts. "It has been eight days since the edict. I cannae help but wonder what—"

From behind him came the sound of the small portal opening. Ewan drew breath and turned toward it, seeing… no one.

Puzzled, he moved closer. "Would it hurt you to show yourself?" he asked, squinting into emptiness.

The sudden flare of a torch through the small window startled Ewan and also, apparently, the person on the other side of the gate, since he heard an audible gasp. It was a response he'd come to expect from those who looked upon him for the first time.

"So, now that you've seen my face," he said, hardening his tone, "might I ask that you return the courtesy?"

"Who are you?" asked a female voice. "I was told you had news of my brother. Is that true?"

Brother? Ewan's instincts bristled. Something felt wrong. Out of place.

Gabriel asked Ewan's unspoken question. "Why is a woman challenging our presence here?"

Why indeed?

"I already gave my name," Ewan said, seeing only shadowy shapes beyond the torchlight. "And as for news of your brother, I'm no' certain who you mean. It might help if I knew to whom I am speaking."

Morag? Is that you?

A mumbled exchange of words could be heard beyond the door, followed by a soft cry. Then, "Please, good knight, repeat your name again." The woman sounded breathless. "I need to hear you say it, for my own sake."

Aye. It has to be her. Twelve years! No longer a child.

Ewan leaned in and put his mouth close to the small opening. "Is that you, my wee lass?" he asked. "Not so wee anymore, I'm thinking. You'll have seen, what… seventeen summers now? I've been away a good while, so I'm no' certain how well you'll remember me."

"Dear God, it cannae be," she said, her voice raspy. "Ewan? Is it you? Truly?"

"Aye, it truly is." His throat tightened. "Will you please open the—?"

Another cry cut off the rest of his words, followed by the clattering of bolts being pulled and lock bars lifted. At last, the castle gates swung open.

It seemed to Ewan, for a fleeting moment at least, that time paused. Unmoving, he looked upon the small group of people before him; three men, two of them armed, the third holding a flaming torch that battled against the elements.

And a lass at their head, pale-faced and breathing hard, arms at her side, hands fisted.

The gloom barely subdued the reddish glow of her hair, errant strands of it writhing in the wind, the rest draped over one shoulder in a loosely bound mass. The stubborn curve of her chin was the same as Ruaidri's and reminded Ewan of how wilful she had been, even as a child. Small, and of slender build, the lass nevertheless stood straight as a reed and stared at Ewan as if seeing a ghost.

He stepped forward.

"You've grown a bit since last I saw you, Morag," he said, "but you're still as bonny as I remember."

The utterance of her name seemed to awaken her from a trance. She blinked and tugged at her shawl as she approached, stopping less than a stride away. A slight frown settled on her brow as she studied Ewan's face, her gaze at last coming to rest on that damaged part of it. Ewan waited for the expected response, but she neither balked nor turned away. To his utter surprise, she touched her fingertips to his disfigured flesh, making him flinch.

Her frown deepened, and Ewan swallowed over what felt like a stone in his throat.

"And you have obviously suffered," she said, tears shining in her eyes as she met his gaze again. "But you're still alive, thank God and all His saints. We have wondered all these years, Ewan, and I have prayed for your return. Every night since you left, I have prayed for it. Ruaidri has, too. And… and you wear the white mantle, I see. Are you truly a knight of the Temple?"

Ewan inclined his head. "These past ten years."

"One of God's own warriors, then, like our Grandsire. I swear I can scarce believe my eyes." Uttering a soft groan, she threw herself forward and hugged him, nestling her head against his chest. "My beloved brother, home at last. We have missed you so much."

Ewan should have stepped back and put space between them. To touch a woman—any woman—was forbidden, unless to provide aid or protection. But, unable to reconcile heart and doctrine, he ignored the rule and returned the hug with genuine ardour. "I have missed you too, wee lass," he said, swallowing against what felt like a lie. "I dinnae travel alone, either, in case you have nae noticed."

She untangled herself and glanced past him. "I noticed, aye. Bid your friends enter, please, that we might close the gates again. I should imagine you have journeyed some distance and must be weary. Hungry too, no doubt."

"Both, I confess." Ewan summoned the others with a gesture and then turned back to his sister. "But it troubles me to find you here alone. Where's our father? And Ruaidri?"

"I'm no' precisely alone, Ewan," she replied, turning to the men who stood in silence at her back. "Duncan, we have guests. I trust you'll make preparations? Dinnae argue with me, please. Brody, cease gaping like a codfish and close the gates. Niall, you'll see to the horses."

Brody, whose mouth had been hanging open, looked sheepish. "Sorry," he said, continuing to stare at Ewan with unabashed fascination, "but is it true what you say? Are you really a Templar knight? And your friends as well?"

"Brody!" Morag snapped. "The gates. Now!"

"You always were a fiery wee thing," Ewan said, watching as the men dispersed without further comment. "A temperament to match that red hair. Tell me, what does *no' precisely alone* mean, precisely?"

A glimmer of tears appeared in Morag's eyes, and Ewan felt a sudden twinge of dread.

"What's wrong, lass?" he asked. "'Tis plain something is amiss. What of your mother? Where is she?"

Morag answered with a shake of her head and looked past him again at Gabriel and Jacques. Both men had dismounted and were leading their horses into the courtyard. Morag's brows raised at the sight of Hammett driving the loaded wagon, with yet another horse trailing behind. "It seems we each have much to tell the other," she said, "but will you first introduce your friends? Afore aught else, I would ken who we have under our roof, especially since I get the impression they mean to stay more than a day or two."

Ewan shifted his mind away from dark thoughts and waved his companions over. "How's your French?"

Morag blinked. "They're French?"

"Nay. Only the wee lad, there, who goes by the name of Hammett. Jacques Aznar, leading the grey horse, is Basque and Gabriel Fitzalan is a *Sasunnach*. But they're comfortable in French. English as well, if you'd rather use that."

Morag gasped and stared at Gabriel. "You brought a *Sasunnach* to Castle Cathan? Are you mad? He'll no' live to see the sunrise."

"Och, dinnae say that. Any man who threatens Gabriel would be making a grave mistake." Ewan sighed. "These men are nae threat to anyone here, Morag. They're Knights of the Temple. Warriors of Christ, loyal only to the Holy See and each other. Gabriel is as a brother to me. Jacques too. I'll no' tolerate a lack of respect to either one." He shifted his gaze and dropped into English. "Jacques, Gabriel, this is my wee sister, Morag who, for reasons I have yet to discover, seems to be in charge here."

Morag frowned at him and then turned her gaze back to Jacques and Gabriel.

"Welcome to Castle Cathan, good sirs," she said, also in English. "It would seem I stand in the presence of greatness, which in turn begs the question of why that might be. What, under God's great sky, would bring three Templar knights, a wee French laddie, and a wagon load of… whatever that is, to this remote corner of Scotland?"

"I'll tell you," Ewan replied, "right after you tell me what is going on here."

*

The arrival of three Templar knights at the gates of Castle Cathan would have created a bit of a murmur at the best of times. That one of the Templars happened to be Calum MacKellar's alienated second son turned the murmur into a barely controlled clamour. All at Castle Cathan, not that there were any more than a dozen, had herded into the great hall like sheep, eager to see the visitors for themselves.

From the laird's dais, Morag had announced her brother's return with a voice beset by emotion, and a chorus of greetings had echoed across the hall. Ewan picked out a few familiar faces in the crowd, while others he could not recollect. He wondered, too, at the small size of the gathering. Surely, there should be more folk than what he now looked upon.

Audible whispers of disapproval had emerged when Gabriel had been introduced, but Ewan wasted no time in quelling them. Jacques' introduction had been met with mild curiosity. As a Basque, he was a foreigner, but not an enemy. The same went for young Hammett.

Yet Ewan couldn't shrug off a gut-feeling that something was awry. The structural strength of Castle Cathan was as he remembered it, but the air within *felt* different somehow, as if the clan's spirit had been wounded and had not yet rallied.

Introductions complete, Ewan and the others had settled at the laird's table and listened to Morag's tale. As her account unfolded, he realized his gut had been correct.

Regret, he thought, had to be the bitterest of all emotions; a desolate sensation that gnawed at the conscience. Time did not negotiate. It had flown by and snatched away any chance to make amends. Chilled by more than the draught seeping through the shutters, Ewan stared at his sister without seeing her as he absorbed all she had said. The blood pounded in his ears as he struggled against an onslaught of memories, particularly those leading up to his departure and the last time he had seen his father.

He now knew that it had been the final time.

Laird Calum MacKellar had been gone not quite a year, felled by a merciless ague that had cut through Clan MacKellar like a scythe. He and many others of his clan had been taken, children and women among them, including Euna, Calum's wife.

Morag's mother.

"*Màthair* had been in poor health for a while," Morag said. "She gave birth to a stillborn son in the spring of last year. The birthing near killed her too, so she was already weak when the ague struck. She was the first to go."

"May Christ have mercy on you, lass, you have lost so much," Ewan said.

"Not just me, Ewan." Morag's eyes grew bright with fresh tears. "I dinnae think there's a family in the clan that has nae been affected in some way. That now includes yourself. Calum MacKellar was your sire, too."

Ewan's throat tightened. "Where does he rest?" he asked, already knowing the answer.

"At the *Eaglais Chruinn*, next to our grandsire," she replied. "You'll be going there, no doubt, and taking your friends?"

He nodded. "Tomorrow morning, first thing. Is Father Iain still there?"

"Aye. Never changes. I swear God doesnae want to take the man."

Food and drink had been placed before them although Ewan had yet to touch any of it. His appetite had disappeared, due mostly to self-recrimination. He had once vowed never to return to Castle Cathan. Aye, the vow had been spat out in anger, but did that make it any less valid? And if not for threat to the Templars, would he ever have returned home? No one had forced him to remain with the Order. He'd always been free to leave had he so wished. Yet he'd chosen to stay, shunning his past. And his family.

Cursing inwardly, Ewan pushed his unused plate aside and curled his hand into a fist. Morag placed her hand atop it, her pale, slender fingers bare of adornment.

"I'm sorry 'tis no' a happy homecoming for you, Ewan," she said. "But despite what you might be thinking, Da never once spoke ill of you after you left, nor would he allow anyone else to do so. He always hoped you'd return. You've always held a place in our hearts. I swear Ruaidri would be weeping with joy if he were here."

Morag's words, meant to placate, actually twisted like a blade in Ewan's gut. He silently cursed his stubborn pride and struggled to voice a question he was afraid to ask.

Ever perceptive, Jacques leaned in and asked it for him. "Where is your brother, *demoiselle*? Does he yet live?"

"Aye, he does," Morag replied, and Ewan bit back a sigh of relief. "At least, I pray he does. He took himself off five days ago to get wed."

Ewan's brows lifted. "To get wed?"

"Aye, to Elspeth MacAulay." She released a soft sigh. "Alastair MacAulay has been pushing for an alliance ever since Da died. Ruaidri has never officially met the lass but agreed to MacAulay's offer. Said it would keep the wolves from the gates. But I'm worried, Ewan. I cannae explain it, but something doesnae sit well with me. It's been five days. Ruaidri should be back by now."

"Alastair, you say?" Ewan asked, frowning. "Is he not the eldest son?"

Morag nodded. "Aye. Malcolm MacAulay died from the same ague that took our father. 'Tis Alastair who is laird now. Elspeth is his sister, of course. And there's Brochan, too. Elspeth's twin."

Gabriel spoke. "Did your brother take anyone with him?"

Morag shook her head. "Nay, he went alone. Alastair was supposed to meet him at the bothy atop the eastern pass and escort him the rest of the way."

Ewan grunted. "About a day's ride from here, aye?"

"To the bothy? Aye, thereabouts."

"And Dunraven is about a half-day's ride beyond that," Ewan said. "So, three days travelling, there and back."

"Which leaves two days for a wedding celebration," Jacques said, with a shrug. "Not unreasonable, surely."

"That's what Duncan reckons, but I cannae lose this feeling that something is wrong." Morag lowered her gaze and picked a speck of fluff off her skirt. "I dinnae trust Alastair MacAulay and said as much to Ruaidri. The man's eyes are set too close together for my liking."

Twelve years had passed, but Ewan recognized the reticence in his sister's demeanour and knew what it meant. He nudged her arm. "What are you not telling me, lass?"

"I've told you everything of note," she said, squaring her chin and meeting his gaze.

"Och, I think there might be a wee bit more yet," Ewan said. He didn't want to admit that he shared Morag's unease, that her story had already raised several questions in his mind. "Something else is weighing you down. Dinnae deny it."

Morag held her expression a moment longer, then her face crumpled. "Oh, Ewan," she said, a sob in her voice, "'tis because of me that Ruaidri is marrying the lass."

Ewan frowned. "What do you mean?"

"Alastair MacAulay offered for me first, but I refused him," she said, her voice breaking. "Alastair wasnae too happy, to say the least. He insisted the union go ahead. Said the alliance was important for the clan's survival."

Ewan grunted. "His clan or ours?"

Morag sniffed. "Both, I suppose. In any case, Ruaidri wasnae too happy with me, either." She dropped her gaze. "Things have nae been easy since Da died. I ken it's important to keep on good terms with neighbouring clans, but I... I just wasnae ready for marriage. Especially to Alastair MacAulay. In truth, I dinnae like the man at all."

Ewan sighed. "Did he make threats, lass?"

"Alastair?" She grimaced. "Not precisely."

"There's that word again." Ewan cocked his head. "Tell me what he said, precisely."

She shrugged. "He said the agreement was binding, and Ruaidri was obliged to hold to it. To break it wouldnae bode well for the clans' alliance. So, Ruaidri offered to wed Elspeth instead, but Alastair still wouldnae agree. He wanted my dowry, you see. Not that it was much, mind you. Some livestock and a couple o' horses, is all."

Ewan shot a quick glance at Gabriel and Jacques. "So, what changed Alastair's mind?"

"Ruaidri offered to pay a bride price for Elspeth. In the end, Alastair agreed to take half my dowry, though he wasnae too happy about it." She grimaced again. "So, you see, 'tis my fault Ruaidri has gone."

Ewan shook his head. "He's clan chief, Morag. He's doing what he must to protect his own, and that includes his wee sister. Dinnae fash. I'm sure he's fine. He'll likely show up on the morrow."

"I pray so." Morag touched Ewan's cheek. "But what a blessed night this is, anyway! 'Tis your turn now, dear brother. I would hear your own story. Where you went after leaving here, and how you came by this scar. Something tells me 'tis a need for sanctuary that has brought you back home. Am I right?"

"Aye, you are." Ewan smiled at her intuitiveness. "And I think we should tell you about that afore anything else. My story can wait."

Chapter Four

A solitary candle burned atop the carved granite altar, its golden flame casting a halo of light around the wooden crucifix that graced the back wall. The faint scent of incense hung in the air but failed to oust the musty odour that occupied the small, windowless space.

No mighty cathedral, this, yet the castle's small private chapel served the same purpose as any of the towering basilicas that scraped the skies of England and France. The stone beneath Ewan's knees was no less hard. No less cold.

He barely noticed the discomfort. He had whispered his prayers, submitted his penance, and asked for much needed guidance. Yet peace of mind continued to elude him.

Ewan's gaze came to rest upon a tattered piece of fabric hanging to the left of the altar, its faded colours barely visible in the frail light. At one time, the cross emblazoned upon its surface had been as red as the blood in Ewan's veins, and the backcloth as white as virgin snow.

It had been carried thousands of miles over land and sea; frozen by winter frost, soaked by sea-spray, and bleached by hot, desert sun. It had borne witness to battle, and had been spattered with both Christian and Saracen blood.

Now it rested in quiet seclusion within this small Highland chapel.

His grandfather's Templar banner had served its purpose.

The bitter undertone of that observation further tainted Ewan's thoughts. Had all the Templar banners in France been torn down? Cast aside? Trampled into the dirt? Had the Order, so widely acclaimed throughout Christendom, served its final purpose?

It was unthinkable. Surely the Pope would intervene. He had to. Ewan breathed in a lungful of stale air and endeavoured to steer his mind onto calmer waters. No easy task.

Behind him, a door creaked. Ewan glanced over his shoulder and nodded a silent greeting as Gabriel approached. The man dropped to one knee, crossed himself, and whispered a brief supplication before rising to his feet once more. "The tales it could tell," he said, seemingly following Ewan's gaze. "Do you have any memory of your grandfather?"

Ewan shook his head. "None," he said, grimacing as he stood. "The man died even before Ruaidri was born."

"Yet his story lives on."

"And in a grand fashion." Ewan gave a sober smile. "He is something of a legend in the MacKellar clan. I was raised listening to tales of his remarkable feats. According to some, he single-handedly saved Christendom itself."

Gabriel shrugged. "Time and repetition tend to blur the truth."

"Aye, they do." Ewan sighed. "Which makes me wonder what will be said about our order in years to come. Its reputation has already been sullied by lies and exaggerations."

"Which is why I write," Gabriel replied. "I endeavour to keep a truthful account of our daily lives so those yet to come may understand who we are. Who we *were*. And there are others who inscribe as I do, Ewan. Much has already been recorded. Our rules, our conquests, our battles fought and lost. Which reminds me why I came to find you. I fear Jacques is currently losing a battle in the great hall."

Ewan tensed. "With whom?"

"Your sister." A rare expression of amusement flitted across Gabriel's face. "She is arguing with him over our sleeping arrangements. I don't believe I have ever seen our Basque brother quite as... irked."

"I'm sorry, but nay. A hundred times nay. Sleep on the damn floor if you must, but it'll no' be *this* floor, sharing the space with all and sundry." Hands on hips, Morag stiffened her shoulders and glared up at Ewan, the top of her head not quite level with his chin. "I understand you adhere to certain disciplines, but as I explained to your friend, this is nae a monastery, nor anything like. And being a Templar knight doesnae change the fact that you are Calum MacKellar's son, brother to our chief, and for now, at least, the clan heir. Whether you like it or not, that entitles you. Your auld chamber is empty, so you and your friends should use it. Your wee squire will be fine down here, mind. I'll find a warm spot for him. Ruaidri would support me in this, you know he would."

Ewan threw a resigned glance at Jacques, who failed to suppress a disapproving growl as he cast a dark glare at Morag. She responded with an equally unflinching stare and a raised brow.

Not long after, the three knights laid their pallets down in Ewan's old chamber in readiness to retire for the night.

Ewan lay back, folded his hands behind his head, and stared up at the ceiling. Fatigue pricked at his eyes, but his overwrought mind refused to entertain much hope of sleep. Other than a subdued whisper of wind from beyond the shutters, the only sound was that of a quill scratching against parchment. It came from the corner, where Gabriel sat at a small table, writing by the light of a solitary candle.

"She is enough to make a saint pray for patience," Jacques muttered, as if voicing his thoughts out loud.

A smile tugged at Ewan's mouth. Obviously, his sister had undermined Jacques' disciplined composure. "She's a Highland lass, Jacques. Dinnae attempt a victory. Settle for a compromise. 'Tis always safer."

"In this case, she is correct, however," Jacques continued, as if still talking to himself. "This is not a monastery, nor is it even a Templar holding. Given our position here, we have no choice but to adapt."

Ewan threw his friend a bewildered glance. "'Tis nae what you implied a wee while ago."

"True. But I have since given it some thought." He cleared his throat and turned to face Ewan. "As your sister reminded me, this is a secular domain. Consequently, many of our rules cannot be realistically applied here. Until such time as we are able to return to our own, we must tolerate a measure of disharmony."

"Disharmony?" Ewan felt a mild flutter of resentment. "I'm no' sure what you mean. They have taken us in, Brother, without question. Dinnae lose sight of that."

Jacques grimaced. "A bad choice of words. That we must allow ourselves some leniency is probably a better way to describe it. Within limits, of course."

"Our rules and self-restraint will be tested, no doubt," Gabriel said. "But I wonder, Ewan, at your choice of words too. Jacques and I have indeed been given refuge, but you are family, entitled to a place beneath this roof."

Ewan grunted. "I'm no' certain my father would have thought so."

"Your sister implied otherwise." Gabriel's brow furrowed. "From what she said, I got the impression your father felt your absence keenly."

"He likely missed having someone to fight with," Ewan replied. "We did naught but argue all the time."

Gabriel's frown disappeared. "About what?"

More images, like ghosts, rose up in Ewan's mind. "Anything. Everything. The man was as stubborn as a damn donkey. I couldnae please him. No matter what I did, he'd always find fault. I reckon he never forgave me for killing my mother."

Jacques gave him a sharp look. "Did he actually accuse you of that?"

Ewan pondered, and found himself surprised by his conclusion. "I'd have to say nay, he didnae actually voice it. It was more a feeling I had."

"It's a pity you never got the chance to resolve your differences." Gabriel's remark held no malice, but the reflection stung like vinegar in an open wound nonetheless.

"Aye, but there's nae point dwelling on something I cannae change," Ewan replied. "Right now, I'm more concerned about my brother's whereabouts."

Jacques propped himself up on an elbow. "You think he's come to harm?"

"I'm no' sure what to think."

"Have you thought about the repercussions if your brother is not found alive?" Gabriel asked.

Ewan blew out a breath. "It doesnae bear thinking about."

"But you've considered your obligation."

"My obligation to what?"

"To your clan," Gabriel replied. "You're the heir, Brother. If Ruaidri is lost, they will look to you for leadership. Your loyalty must surely be to them, which will mean rescinding your Temple vows."

Chapter Five

Darkness had all but retreated, scattered by a feeble morning light that still crawled over land and sea. Despite his weariness Ewan had slept little. He felt as though he'd crossed the furthest threshold of fatigue and surpassed any need for sleep. On this, his first morning since returning to Castle Cathan, he stood on the gatehouse roof and saturated his lungs with brisk air that intoxicated his blood. The subsequent rush of exhilaration both inspired and refreshed him, but he suspected it would not last.

Indeed, his spirit sobered even as he gazed at the distant line of snow-capped mountains, the imposing granite wall dividing MacKellar and MacAulay holdings. These ancient, northern lands had a wild, majestic beauty, but they were merciless to those who dared to cross them unprepared. And they were not without their secrets.

Where are you, Ruaidri?

Anticipation sat upon Ewan's shoulders like some accursed imp, tormenting him with all manner of imagined scenarios and possibilities. He had not voiced his fears to Morag. Like her, and everyone else at Castle Cathan, all he could do was wait and pray for his brother's safe return.

And that was not all that stretched his nerves. That morning, he had a mission to undertake. An obligation, of sorts. One that he did not entirely relish.

A footfall drew his attention.

"They're about ready for you," Duncan said, moving to Ewan's side.

Ewan glanced down at the courtyard, where Gabriel, Jacques and Hammett waited. "My thanks." He turned his gaze back to the hills. "I confess, I'd forgotten how bonny it is here."

"'Tis a blessing for the eyes, right enough," Duncan replied. "Dinnae fash, Ewan. The laird'll be back today, mark my words. Likely not till later, mind. 'Tis a fair ride from the bothy to here, especially since he'll have his lady with him."

"I pray you're right," Ewan said, heading for the stairs. "Stay vigilant, Duncan. We should be back by midday."

He descended, nodded his readiness to the others, and prepared to mount his horse just as Morag appeared. "Tell me, Templar, do you remember the way?" she asked, wrinkling her nose.

Ewan's mouth quirked as he stuck his foot in the stirrup and swung into the saddle. "Aye, my lady, I believe I do."

"Father Iain will think his time has come when he sees these white mantles approaching." She tucked an errant strand of hair behind her ear. "He'll ask where Ruaidri is, so please be careful what you say. He wanted to officiate at the wedding, but Alastair insisted the ceremony take place at Dunraven. Oh, and if the white heather is still blooming, will you please pick a wee sprig to put on our Grandsire's grave? I'm sure you know why. Maybe on Da's too, if you like."

The surrounding pine forest, dark and sweetly scented, granted the knights and their squire a peaceful, cloistered trail. Jacques chatted quietly with young Hammett, their conversation unobtrusive. Gabriel, never one for speaking without cause, sat his saddle in easy silence. Ewan, meanwhile, toyed with Morag's words like a dog worrying a bone.

Alastair 's insistence that the wedding take place at Dunraven further heightened Ewan's suspicion that something was afoot. He hoped his angst was ill-founded, of course. For reasons that needed no explanation, Ewan wanted his brother to come home. But, until Gabriel's observation the night before, he hadn't considered the other, far-reaching consequences that would apply should Ruaidri not return. Those consequences tacked an addendum onto Ewan's heartfelt prayers.

Should it be called upon—Heaven forbid—Ewan's obligation to his clan was irrefutable, but not without some qualms. To surrender his Templar existence would not be easy. He'd found stability within the ranks of the Brotherhood, something he had previously lacked. Aye, his ability to abstain from the pleasures of the flesh had been a challenge, but one he had obstinately—and successfully—met.

He remembered a time when mortal indulgences had filled his days and his nights. He also remembered a time when those indulgences had almost killed him. Unwilling to visit that dark period in his life, Ewan straightened his spine and looked ahead to where the trail exited the forest.

A short while later, they reined in their horses and gazed down at their destination. It was, for Ewan, a bittersweet moment. The last time he'd visited this sacred place, only one tomb had occupied the quiet interior. Now there were two.

"Remarkable," Jacques murmured.

"Unexpected," Gabriel added, "though it is precisely as you described."

"'Tis known as *Lorg Coise Dhè*," Ewan said, his heart quickening. "Which means God's Footprint. And that…" he pointed to a building nestled beside the tarn, "is *Eaglais Chruinn,* or the Round Church. It took my grandfather ten years to build it. A labour of love and a testament to his beliefs."

"God's Footprint. I should like to hear the story behind that." Jacques' gaze wandered over the landscape. "Such beauty. It stirs the soul."

"Aye, 'tis a special place. A sacred place." Ewan pressed his heels to his horse's flanks. "Come. I'll introduce you to its holy guardian."

To Ewan, Father Iain had always seemed ancient. Despite his advanced years, however, the old man's faculties appeared to function well enough. His hearing, for one thing, judging by his sudden appearance at the church door as soon as the horses drew near. The priest, clad in pale, priestly robes, lingered a moment on the threshold before stepping out, staff in hand.

Even from a distance, the man's sense of disbelief was apparent. He fidgeted on his feet and crossed himself.

Then, after a brief pause, he descended the remaining steps and stood on the path, watching. As they drew near, the priest crossed himself once more and stepped forward to greet them, his expression one of incredulity.

"A vision I thought never to see again." Of a slight build, Father Iain looked as though he'd be blown away by the merest hint of a breeze. His dark, weather-worn flesh created a stark contrast to his halo of silver hair and his quick green eyes glinted with what looked like tears. He banged his staff on the ground. "Are you come to fetch me home, my lords?"

Ewan smiled to himself as he dismounted, gratified to see that the man had changed little in twelve years. "Nay, Father Iain. I dinnae think our Lord is quite ready for you yet. Do you not know me?"

The priest blinked, moved closer, and squinted up at Ewan. "Curse my eyes, I thought you were my old friend sent back to give me absolution." He reached up and touched Ewan's face with a hand that trembled with age rather than fear. "Battle scars, I presume?"

Ewan nodded. "Aye."

"Still, you look just like your grandsire. Och, and he'd be proud to see you wearing the mantle, Ewan. Beyond proud. You've been gone a wee while, aye? When did you get home?"

"Yester eve," Ewan replied, conceding that twelve years was indeed a wee while to a man of Father Iain's years. "'Tis good to see you, Father. You've no' changed at all. These are Brothers Jacques Aznar and Gabriel Fitzalan. They dinnae speak the *gàidhlig*."

Father Iain's brows rose as he peered at Jacques and Gabriel. "Then I shall continue our discourse in French, a language almost as beautiful."

"This is Father Iain Bànach," Ewan said, to his companions. "Templar priest and a friend of my grandfather."

Jacques inclined his head. "We've heard much about you, Father Iain."

"All good, I trust," the priest replied. "Welcome to *Lorg Coise Dhè*, my lords." He frowned as his gaze settled on Hammett and the cart. "And you too, laddie, though I pray this doesnae mean what I think it means."

Ewan's smile dissolved. "I'm afraid it does, Father."

"God protect us." Father Iain crossed himself. "Well, I'll no' hear of it out here. You'll come inside and tell me all."

*

Sunlight tumbled through a single arched window, capturing the image of the red cross that stained the glass. The blurred reflection fell across the carved effigies of two knights that lay side by side; a calculated consequence. The window's southern aspect harvested much of the sunlight on clear days.

The white heather, though a little tired in appearance, had still born some blooms. Ewan had gathered a couple of sprigs and bent to place one on each grave. Then he stood for a while in quiet contemplation. He sought peace. Nay, he sought answers. Maybe one would bring the other.

Like the great red deer that roamed the highland glens, he and his father had locked antlers many times. But over what? He couldn't remember anything of great worth they had squabbled about. They had all been petty things. Unnecessary things. Big storms in small puddles.

Perhaps the resentment he'd harboured for so many years lay buried beneath his grief. Or had it, without him even realizing it, dissipated like a morning mist? In any case, he no longer felt it. Other feelings surfaced instead, the bitterest of all being regret.

A footfall behind him pulled him from his musings.

"Your sire always said you'd come back," Father Iain said. "He never doubted it."

Ewan shifted on his feet. "But a wee bit late to make amends, Father. If I'm honest, I must ask myself if I'd be here at all if no' for Philippe's edict."

"Dinnae trouble yourself with such anxieties, Ewan. God has a plan for you, no doubt, and you must trust it. I still cannae believe it has come to this, though. History will condemn the king's action, mark my words. Let it be known that *Lorg Coise Dhè* will always be a refuge for any brethren who need it."

"'Tis already known by those highest in the order, Father." Ewan sighed and glanced over his shoulder at the empty church. "I suppose we're done here, for now."

"For now, aye. Your brothers await you outside."

"Then we'd best be off, or Morag will fret."

"I pray Ruaidri will be there to greet you, too." Father Iain grimaced and scratched a spot behind his ear. "He's a canny laird, much loved by his clan. 'Twould be another harsh blow should he be lost."

Ewan shook his head. "It doesnae bear thinking about."

Father Iain squeezed Ewan's shoulder. "All you can do is pray and keep the faith, lad."

"Does it still hurt?" Morag asked, later that afternoon, as she touched her fingertips to Ewan's scar.

"Nay, although I cannae bear the sun on it." He grimaced. "It did hurt a wee bit at first, though."

"A wee bit?" Morag huffed. "I cannae fathom the pain you must have suffered. And you said you were pinned to the ground. Who saved you?"

Ewan grunted. "I wish I knew. I remember commending my soul to the Lord's keeping, and then hearing a voice and seeing a figure before the world went dark. My mind playing tricks, I suspect."

Morag blinked. "Why do you say that?"

"Because it—he—spoke *gàidhlig.*"

"How strange. What did he say?"

"He said, 'Not today, Brother. Not today'." Ewan shrugged. "I remember naught after that. When next I opened my eyes, I was on board a Templar ship headed for Cyprus. No one I spoke to could tell me how I got there."

"This is the first I've heard of this story," Gabriel said. "A figure, you say? Did you see his face?"

"Not clearly. His silhouette blocked the sun."

"A guardian angel," Morag said.

"Or simply a brother who coincidentally spoke your language," Jacques said. "We were many that day."

Ewan grimaced. "Aye, and we lost most of them in that offensive."

"It was not our finest moment," Gabriel said. "Ruad was the last—"

The door to the laird's private chamber crashed open and Brody all but fell into the room. "Riders approaching!" he gasped. "Two of them, on the low road."

Morag shot to her feet. "Is it Ruaidri?"

"Um, nay." Brady hesitated, his expression nervous. "I… I believe one of them is Alastair MacAulay."

Ewan's scalp prickled. Fingers wrapped around his sword hilt, he rose to his feet.

"Alastair MacAulay? But why would he…?" Morag turned wide, fearful eyes toward Ewan. "Oh, God, nay. I cannae bear it. Something must have happened to Ruaidri."

"Now then, wee lass, dinnae jump to conclusions." Yet bile burned the back of Ewan's throat as he moved to her side. "Let's find out what brings them here."

"But it has to be something to do with Ruaidri," she said, grasping Ewan's arm. "It has to be."

Ewan didn't answer, for he could only agree and had no desire to do so.

Brody hopped from one foot to another. "Should I open the gates?"

"Let him announce himself first." Ewan glanced at Gabriel and Jacques. "He's no' aware I've returned, remember? We should prepare a wee welcome for the man. Get back to your post, Brady. Follow procedure but say naught about me being here."

Brady gave a single nod and then fled.

The impatient hammering of a fist against oak rattled around the courtyard as Ewan and the others stepped outside into the late afternoon dusk. Then the hammering stopped, replaced by a loud, harsh demand.

"Open the gates!"

Brody, already back at his post, leaned over the battlements, his verbal challenge inaudible to Ewan. It obviously raised Alastair MacAulay's hackles, however, since the furious reply was quite clear. And alarming.

"You ken fine well who I am, you wee shite. Open the damn gates. I demand to speak with Ruaidri MacKellar."

Ruaidri? Ewan frowned. Had he heard right? *Why would he be asking to speak to Ruaidri?*

Morag tugged on Ewan's mantle. "I… I dinnae understand," she said, dropping into Gaelic. "Why is he asking for Ruaidri?"

Ewan gave his head a slight shake, not quite willing to acknowledge the only possible answer

Jacques grunted. "He doesn't sound like a man bringing bad news."

"No," Gabriel said. "He sounds angry."

Ewan translated. "He's asking to speak to Ruaidri."

"Your brother?" Jacques frowned. "But he'd have no cause to do that unless…"

Ewan finished the sentence in his head. *Unless Ruaidri never arrived at Dunraven.* His gaze shifted to the distant snow-capped mountains. *Six days. God help us.*

Duncan, panting, stumbled to Ewan's side. "What's going on?"

"Let's find out." Ewan gripped his sword tighter and moved forward. "Open the gate, Duncan."

It opened with a groan, and Duncan staggered backwards as two horsemen charged into the courtyard like marauders. The aggressive entry was short-lived, both lathered beasts tugged to a sudden, sliding halt on the cobbles.

"Obviously, not the welcome they expected," Jacques murmured.

No, it wasn't, judging by the expressions of shock on the men's faces. Ewan studied the visitors. One of them, seated astride a hefty black horse, he didn't recognize. The other, however, seated atop a skittish roan, aroused a clear memory. With his untamed mop of tawny hair, square jaw and close-set eyes, there could be no mistaking the eldest son of Malcolm MacAulay. The resemblance to his late sire bordered on uncanny.

"Who, by Odin's hairy balls, are you?" Alastair MacAulay asked, trying to settle his agitated mount. "And what is your business here?"

Ewan gave a sober smile. "Those are nae your questions to ask, MacAulay."

A brief flash of surprise swept across the man's face, followed by a scowl. "Who are these men, Morag?"

"Dinnae answer him, lass," Ewan said. "You're forgetting your manners, MacAulay. At least have the courtesy to dismount if you wish to parley."

Lips pulled back in a snarl, MacAulay reached for his sword. "Ye can wipe my arse with your bonny white mantle, Templar. I'll no' move from this saddle till I have the answers I seek."

"Then you'll be sitting up there a good while." Ewan threw back his cloak, exposing the hilt of his sword. "You're the intruder here, not I. Dismount, hand over your weapons, and we'll talk. Either out here in the cold or inside by the fire. I dinnae care which."

The man opened his mouth as if to answer, but closed it again, eyes narrowing as he regarded Ewan. "I know you," he said, leaning forward and jabbing a finger in Ewan's direction, "though you were naught but a whelp the last time I saw you. You didnae have that devilish mess on your face, either." He straightened again. "Ewan MacKellar, the absent son. And a Templar knight, as I live and breathe."

"Alastair, why are you here?" Morag stepped forward, wringing her hands. "Ruaidri left six days ago. Did he no' arrive at Dunraven?"

The man seemed oblivious to Morag's question. "As I live and breathe," he muttered again, apparently lost in thought as he shifted his gaze to Jacques and Gabriel. "Templar knights at Castle Cathan. Why would that be?"

"Have you gone deaf, MacAulay?" Ewan asked, his tone tempered like steel. "Answer the lass."

Alastair MacAulay threw him a scornful look. "Nay, I havenae gone deaf, MacKellar." He dismounted and gestured for his cohort to do likewise. "'Twill be dark in an hour, so we'll need shelter for the night. We'll talk, aye, but not out here."

The man's arrogance had Ewan reaching for patience. He squared his stance and gave Alastair a tight smile. "Your weapons," he said, glancing from one man to the other, "or we go no further."

Nostrils flaring, Alastair hesitated. "I dinnae see why—"

"And I dinnae care to explain." Ewan half-drew his sword and nodded toward Hammett. "You can give them to the young squire there. You'll get them back when you leave."

Alastair spat out a curse and unfastened his sword-belt, gesturing for his companion to do likewise. "I dinnae care for your demeanour, Templar."

Ewan merely renewed his smile and watched as the men handed over their swords. "There," he said, "that wasnae too painful, was it? And you are correct, Laird MacAulay.

I am Ewan MacKellar, second son of Calum MacKellar and a knight of the Temple. Welcome to Castle Cathan."

*

Ewan's worst fears had been confirmed.

Alastair nodded toward his companion. "Tasgall and I waited at the bothy for two days," he said, "but Ruaidri never showed. It was cold enough to freeze the arse off the Devil, so we headed back to Dunraven to thaw out. We left again yesterday, and here we are."

Despite the fire glowing in the hearth, Ewan felt chilled to his core. They sat in Ruaidri's private chamber off the great hall, away from prying eyes and ears. Ewan's gaze drifted to the shuttered window, his mind's eye seeing beyond it, knowing another night sat in readiness to make its dark claim upon the land.

Knowing that Ruaidri was out there, somewhere.

Six days. Nigh on seven. May Christ have mercy.

"Why did you return to Dunraven?" Ewan asked. "Why did you no' come straight here?"

Alastair sniffed. "Like I said, we were frozen, and Dunraven was closer. We also needed food and so did the horses." He gave a half-shrug. "Besides, we've kept to our side of the agreement. 'Tis your brother who has failed to keep his."

A thoughtless remark, one that had Ewan biting his tongue. Morag made a sound that tore into his heart. Seated beside her, he drew her close.

"Hush, lass," he murmured. "We'll search for him."

"May God forgive me," she said, clutching at Ewan's shirt. "I knew something would go wrong. I just knew it. And just like I told you, 'tis all my fault."

"Dinnae say that."

"But 'tis true." Morag's resigned, flat tone worried Ewan more than if she'd had hysterics. "If I'd married Alastair, Ruaidri would still be here."

Alastair snorted. "I cannae argue with that, Morag MacKellar. You should have taken my offer."

Ewan felt Morag flinch. "I suggest you curb your tongue, MacAulay," he said, gritting his teeth. "Or I'll be showing you and your lapdog the way out."

"And I'll be happy to assist you," Jacques said, drawing a surprised glance from Ewan.

Alastair's expression darkened as he glared at Jacques. "I dinnae like to be threatened, Templar. 'Specially by a foreigner."

"Neither do I," Tasgall growled, eyes narrowed.

Jacques raised a brow. "I do not make threats, *Messieurs*," he replied. "Any action I take shall be executed swiftly and without warning."

Alastair sputtered and began to rise, but Ewan waved him back. "Dinnae be a fool, MacAulay. Sit your arse down and mind your tongue!" His gazed drifted to the shuttered window again. "Ruaidri is out there somewhere, and I mean to find him and bring him home. I'll be leaving at first light."

"Aye, and we'll be leaving too." Alastair scowled at Jacques and then nodded toward Tasgall. "We'll help with the search for your brother, of course."

Tasgall grunted his agreement.

Ewan took a moment to scrutinize Alastair's companion. At most, he looked to be around thirty summers; a little older than Alastair. Of average height, he had a powerful build and a wild appearance, with unkempt rat-brown hair that hung past his shoulders, and a thick, braided beard. A warrior, without doubt. One who, at that moment, appeared to be somewhat ill at ease. As if sensing the scrutiny, he met Ewan's gaze and held it for a moment, eyes narrowing before looking away.

"As will I, Brother," Gabriel said, gaining Ewan's attention, who nodded his thanks and looked to Jacques.

"It goes without saying, my friend," the man said, his expression grave.

Morag lifted her head. "I want to come too."

"Nay, wee lass, and there'll be no argument," Ewan replied, his tone firm but gentle. "'Twill be a hard ride, and we might be gone for a few days." *Besides, I dinnae want you there when – if – we find Ruaidri. It likely willnae be a pleasant sight.*

He waited, expecting some kind of resistance. But Morag merely heaved a soft sigh and rested her head against his chest again.

Touched by the bleakness of his sister's spirit, Ewan closed his eyes against a sudden and unexpected sting of tears. Not from regret this time, but grief, its ache oppressive and bone deep. Father and brother. One dead, the other likely to be. It seemed as if his entire family had been chosen for hardship. The foundations of his faith shuddered beneath the burden of it.

A hand squeezed his shoulder. "Thank God you're here, Ewan,"

Ewan opened his eyes and gave a bitter laugh. "Dinnae tell me I'm being tested, Jacques."

"I don't need to." Jacques glanced at Morag. "And not only you. All you can do is pray and keep the faith."

Ewan frowned, remembering that Father Iain had said the same thing.

Alastair cleared his throat and scratched his chin. "I'm curious about what brought you back here, MacKellar. 'Tis no ordinary homecoming, is it? Not when you arrive wearing that Templar garb, and with two other knights besides. And what happened to your face, by the way?"

*

"He is not a pleasant man," Jacques said, later that night, "and his concern for your brother's wellbeing, while voiced, seemed to lack sincerity. He was more interested in learning the reasons for our exile than in your brother's disappearance. Despite what has occurred, it's as well, I think, that your sister avoided marriage with him."

Ewan's thoughts about Alastair MacAulay had been flowing along a similar vein. He shifted on his pallet and folded his hands behind his head. "I cannae say I disagree, Jacques, although I suspect the man's bluster is bigger than his balls."

"Do you believe his account?" Gabriel asked. "That your brother never arrived? It occurred to me that with Ruaidri out of the way, Morag might be more easily persuaded to marry Alastair."

"Who might thereby challenge the lordship of your clan," Jacques finished.

Ewan grunted. Similar suspicions had whispered in his ear even as Alastair MacAulay had ridden through the castle gates earlier that day.

"Alastair MacAulay is no saint," he said. "He seems to be much like his sire, from what I recall of the man. Loud, arrogant, and no' afraid of a fight. But to kill Ruaidri in cold blood?" He grimaced. "I doubt the auld laird would have done any such thing, and I cannae accuse Alastair of it. For now, at least, I'm prepared to believe that some misfortune befell Ruaidri on his way to the rendezvous."

"I have given it some thought," Jacques said, after a pause. "And with your approval, Ewan, I believe I should stay behind. It might be prudent to have a clear mind and a steady hand here. Not to mention an extra sword."

It was a fair point.

"Aye," Ewan replied. "Now you mention it, I'll feel better knowing I dinnae have to worry about Morag. Just the four of us then, and I pray we'll solve this puzzle. A man cannae just disappear without a trace."

Can he?

Chapter Six

Daylight, like Ewan's hope, was in short supply. They left Castle Cathan at the crack of dawn, heading out beneath bleak, winter skies. The day would be short, the ride long. Consequently, they set a punishing pace during the first part of the journey, hoping to arrive at the mountain pass with a couple of hours of daylight to spare.

The road through the glen followed an easy, undulating route alongside the burn. Part of it also wound through thick forest, where wandering tree roots might sabotage the trail and wolves undoubtedly roamed. But the risk of mishap, especially to a horseman as experienced as Ruaidri, would have been slight. This was his land, and he knew it intimately. Even so, Ewan kept his eyes busy, but saw nothing that gave him pause.

Far greater dangers, he knew, lay ahead. Traversing the mountain pass was never without risk, and that risk increased tenfold during harsh weather. At this time of year, the combination of ice, snow and low clouds made for a formidable trinity. One wrong step, one slip of a hoof on icy bedrock, could mean disaster. Fear of what might have become of his brother sickened Ewan's stomach.

They arrived at the foot of the pass with some daylight to spare.

"We'll lead the horses from here," Ewan said, his remark directed at Gabriel, who gave a nod. "The track is steep and narrow."

He squinted up at their serpentine route, not liking what he saw. A layer of clouds blanketed the tops of the mountains, rising and falling as the wind moved it along. The landscape looked bleak and unwelcoming. His gaze scoured the misted slopes, seeking any sign of a fallen man or horse.

"You saw nothing untoward on your way here?" he asked of Alastair. "Nothing that gave you pause?"

"You asked me that last night, Templar, and my answer has nae changed. Nay, I saw nothing at all." Alastair kicked a leg over his saddle and slid to the ground. "The clouds were down, it was pissing rain, and I wasnae looking at anything but the path."

"What of you?" Ewan levelled his gaze at Alastair's surly henchman. "Do you recall seeing anything that seemed—?"

"Nay, he'd have told me if he had." Alastair gestured ahead. "Take the lead, Tasgall. And keep your eyes skinned."

The man, seated astride a large black horse with a slash of white on its face, threw a sour glance at Ewan and slid from the saddle.

"Can the man no' speak for himself?" Ewan muttered.

"Apparently not," Gabriel replied, gazing up at the mountains. "And I fear things do not bode well for your brother, Ewan. 'Tis a hostile domain, and desolate."

The prophetic warning was hardly necessary. The likelihood of finding Ruaidri alive after so long had to be nigh on hopeless. "Aye," Ewan replied, bitter anticipation gnawing at his gut. "I fear we face a recovery rather than a rescue."

A chill wind circled around them as they climbed, bringing tears to Ewan's eyes and a tingle to his gloved fingers. The lonely cry of an eagle occasionally pierced the winter air, and from somewhere in the undergrowth, the distinctive clatter of a red grouse gave a territorial warning to others of his kind. Otherwise, the men travelled the trail in sombre silence.

Ewan's eyes ached from squinting right and left, looking for any sign of his brother, but the rugged terrain gave nothing away. At least, not at first glance. The faded outcrops of heather and wilted stalks of bracken could easily obscure the body of a man. If they found nothing close to the trail, what then? Where might they begin to look?

As it happened, Ewan didn't need his eyes. About halfway through the climb, an acrid stench permeated the wind, and his nostrils flared. To a warrior who had witnessed the carnage of battle, the odour was undeniable. Unmistakable. And horribly familiar.

"Ewan," Gabriel said, and it was all he needed to say.

"Aye, I smell it," Ewan replied, gut clenching as he breathed in death's sickening bouquet. *Christ have mercy.*

At that moment, Tasgall halted his horse and raised a hand, his attention apparently fixed on a point below him and to his right. He glanced back, his gaze locking with Ewan's as he pointed into a narrow gully that ran away from the path like a giant gouge in the hillside.

"There's something down there," he called, his voice tossed by the wind. "Looks like the remains of a horse."

Ewan's gut tightened further.

At that particular spot, the path widened and angled back on itself, like a bent elbow. Underfoot, a mix of exposed bedrock and loose shale made the steep incline even more precarious. Alastair moved to Tasgall's side and peered over the edge. He grimaced, gave Ewan a dark, fleeting glance, and snapped a command at his henchman. "Move ahead, Tasgall. Let the Templars approach."

Ewan stepped forward and peered into the gully. It was little more than a large fissure, in truth—a natural catchment for falling rocks and debris. And atop the rocks lay the grisly remains of a horse. Had he only seen flesh and bone, Ewan might still have grasped at a measure of hope. He might have speculated the remains to be those of a loose horse, perhaps driven onto the mountain by wolves before tumbling to its death.

But this horse had belonged to someone. It had been tacked and ridden, evident from the saddle, which still sat askew on its back, and the bit that rested between the gaping, exposed teeth. The horse also had a black mane and tail.

"He took Goliath. His bay gelding."

Yet, despite all the damning evidence, a single question pushed to the front of Ewan's brain. *If this is Ruaidri's horse, where's Ruaidri?*

"'Tis nae wonder I didnae see the thing yesterday." Alastair sniffed. "I didnae notice that odour, either. Is it your brother's horse?"

Ewan eyed the steep slope at his feet. "I cannae be sure," he said, at the end of a sigh. He dropped his horse's reins and pulled his sword. "I need to go down there."

Using his weapon as a makeshift staff, he half-slid, and half-clambered down the precarious slope. At the bottom, he sheathed his blade, nostrils flaring anew at the stench. Wolves and likely other creatures had certainly feasted on the remains. Some of the bones had been scattered or dragged away.

Despite his non-committal response to Alastair, Ewan had no doubt this was Ruaidri's horse. Ruaidri's fate remained uncertain but was not difficult to surmise. Had he survived the fall and lain injured, he would not have lasted long in such harsh conditions.

God forgive him, but Ewan found himself hoping his brother's death had been quick. That he had not suffered or at least suffered little. He crossed himself as he glanced about, disturbed to see no sign of Ruaidri. Maybe he'd survived the fall and managed to crawl away, only to die somewhere nearby. Any blood trail, of course, would have been washed away by the rain.

Then something further along the rockfall caught his attention. It looked like fabric of some sort. A remnant of clothing, perhaps? Heart racing, Ewan clambered over to where it lay and lifted it, somewhat taken aback by its heaviness. It was a man's cloak, he realized, its unusual weight due to being saturated with snowmelt and rain.

It also had a pungent, cloying odour.

Ewan's gaze fell to the drops escaping the cloak's hem. They tumbled with rhythmic precision, each one an opaque splatter of red upon the rocks. He held his breath and spread the cloak wide, gut clenching at the sight of a large, ominous stain that darkened much of the lining. The rain had diluted it somewhat, but there could be no mistaking its origin. Or what it meant.

Then a glint of metal drew his gaze to the rocks at his feet. He bent and eased the object from its granite niche, settling it in the palm of his hand. The sight of it made his own blood run cold. His vision blurred as memories surfaced; memories of his father, fastening his cloak with an ancient Norse pin made of twisted silver. A pin that had been shaped into an open-ended circle, with two intricately-carved dragon heads facing each other. A pin that would have passed to the first-born son upon his father's death.

Death.

The place stank of it.

"I'm so sorry, Ruaidri," Ewan whispered, closing his fingers around the familiar piece of jewellery. "Forgive me."

*

Firelight chased the shadows into the corners, and the burning peat lifted much of the chill from the air. It also threw out a thin spiral of smoke that curled upwards to escape through a hole in the bothy's roof. Most of it, anyway. Enough remained to sting the eyes and grate on the throat.

Sitting cross-legged, Ewan pulled a whetstone from the pouch on his belt and set about sharpening his blade. He needed to do something other than pray.

"The wolves likely scattered his bones." Alastair made a sucking noise as if trying to dislodge a morsel trapped in his teeth. "Which is why you found no trace. It's been a sennight, too, so there'd be little left to find, I fear."

Ewan frowned, but said nothing.

"From Templar knight to clan laird," Alastair continued. "'Tis odd how things come about."

Ewan remained silent and his brow remained furrowed. Could the man not take a hint? He had no desire to make conversation, least of all with Alastair Macaulay.

"Your sister isnae going to take the news of your brother's death too well," Alastair went on. "'Tis a blessing she has you to step into his shoes. Of course, it also means you'll be obliged to fulfil any remaining commitments."

At that, Ewan lifted his head. "Do you have a point to make, MacAulay? If so, make it and be done. If not, shut your mouth or share your redundant observations with your lapdog. I'm in nae mood for idle talk."

Seated beside Alastair, Tasgall bared his teeth and released a dog-like snarl. "Dinnae underestimate me, MacKellar. I'm nae slouch with a blade."

Ewan straightened and raised a brow. "Is that a challenge, *skamelar*? If so, I gladly accept. I'm in a fine mood for—"

"Brother." Gabriel placed a hand on Ewan's arm. "There's been enough blood spilled on this mountain already."

"I agree," Alastair said, evenly. He leaned back and propped himself up on an elbow. "Ruaidri's death is a tragedy, aye, but it willnae stop the sun from rising on the morrow. You're the laird of your clan now, Templar, whether you like it or no'. And you've assumed the obligations that go with that title."

Ewan suppressed a sigh and bent his head to his blade once more. "I'm aware of that."

"Which means you'll be needing an heir," Alastair said. "Which, in turn, means you'll be needing a wife."

Ewan grunted. "Worry about your own marital bed, MacAulay. I understand your last attempt at securing a bride wasnae very successful."

Alastair snorted. "I dinnae worry about filling my bed, Templar. I'm no' the one sworn to celibacy. What kind of a daft vow is that anyway? A man's cock isnae just for pissin'."

Ewan drew a controlled breath and lifted his head once more, fixing Alastair with a narrow-eyed glare. "Disrespect the Order or my brother again, and I swear I'll shove this blade into your mouth and out the back of your head. That'll be *after* I've hacked off your cock." He switched his gaze to Tasgall. "And while I'm at it, I'll put your mongrel out of his misery as well."

At that, Tasgall leaned forward and gave a low, menacing growl.

Gabriel neither moved nor spoke, a telling response from the English knight. One, Ewan knew, that spoke of suppressed, simmering anger. Alastair was on dangerous ground, if he did but know it.

Perhaps he did, for he huffed and waved a nonchalant hand. "Och, dinnae take on. 'Tis merely that there are other things to consider. Things that cannae be ignored, nor should they be delayed overlong. Longshanks might be dead," he spat into the fire, "may he burn forever in Hell, but his accursed son yet lives. Your own problems aside, dinnae forget that Scotland's hard-earned freedom is a fragile thing. Clans shouldnae be fighting among themselves. They should be allied, their families bonded through marriage. United, they're stronger. 'Tis all I'm saying."

"And this is neither the time nor the place to say it," Ewan replied. "My brother's bones havenae long been scattered through these mountains. And his clan have yet to be told that they've lost…" He swallowed against an unexpected surge of grief. "That they've lost their laird. So, for now, MacAulay, you'll curb your tongue."

"For now, then, I will." Alastair stood, arched his back in a stretch, and wandered over to the door. "And I am sorry about your brother, Templar, but pay heed. The agreement 'tween our families, as far as I'm concerned, still stands and should be honoured, either by you or your sister. I'm going for a piss."

Chapter Seven

Ewan and Gabriel returned to Castle Cathan at dusk the next day. The entire way home, Ewan had thought about what he would say. How to break the news to his sister. He knew she'd be waiting. Hopeful. Fearful. Sadly, her hopes were about to be destroyed, her worst fears confirmed.

Sure enough, they'd hardly had time to steer their horses through the castle gates before Morag flew across the courtyard to greet them, her step faltering as she drew near.

"Where is he? Did you find him?" Chest heaving, she looked past them as if expecting to see Ruaidri. When Duncan closed the gates, she turned to Ewan, her eyes wide, her expression full of expectation and fear.

"We found his horse, Morag," Ewan said, dismounting. "Dead on the rocks below the path."

"Goliath?" She hugged herself and let out a soft cry. "What about Ruaidri?"

"I found only this." Ewan held out the brooch. "And his cloak. You're shivering, lass. Come on inside, where it's warm."

As if in a trance, Morag took the brooch and examined it, stumbling as she fell into step beside Ewan. He bit back a sigh and tucked her free hand into his arm.

Duncan also fell into step beside them. "Ewan?" he murmured, the unspoken part of his question quite clear. Ewan shook his head in answer and the man let out a soft groan and crossed himself. "God have mercy," he said, his voice faltering. "God have mercy."

Others had already begun to gather on the steps, their expressions bleak, their voices silent. They stepped aside as Ewan and Morag entered.

"You may give them the news, Duncan," Ewan said. "Tell them I'll speak to them in a wee while. For now, I need some time alone with my sister."

He shepherded Morag into Ruaidri's private chamber, where she tugged her hand free of his arm. "Where's Ruaidri, Ewan?" She trembled visibly as she clutched the silver cloak pin to her breast.

At that moment, from somewhere outside, came the distant howl of a wolf. Wondering if he'd imagined the beast's ominous timing, Ewan cast a glance at shuttered window. The sound of a second howl brushed a chill across his nape.

"I told you, wee lass," he said. "We found his horse, dead in a gully. Fallen from the mountain path."

Her lip quivered. "Aye, I heard that. But where's our brother?"

Ewan knew she sought a different answer to that given earlier, that her mind refused to accept the terrible truth.

"I found no trace of him other than his cloak." Ewan gestured to Morag's clenched fist. "And that silver pin."

"Then—" A flicker of hope flared in her eyes as she looked past him, her sight obviously turned inward. "Then he might still be alive. Injured. Waiting for us to find him."

"Morag—"

"Waiting for us to find him and bring him home." Her gaze met Ewan's again. "You have to go back, Ewan. You have to find him."

Christ help me. "There's no chance of him being found alive, lass. Not after this long."

Her chest heaved. "But how can you say that? You cannae be certain."

"Aye, I can. Harsh weather aside, Ruaidri's cloak was drenched in blood. And..." He released a sigh. "Wolves have been at the horse. Some of its bones have been scattered. From what I saw, I suspect the same fate befell our brother."

Morag hiccupped on a sob and shook her head. "But…
you cannae just leave him out there all alone! Please,
Ewan."

Ewan groaned and cupped her cheek, catching a tear
with his thumb. "His remains could be anywhere, Morag,
but his soul is in God's care now. He'll never be alone
again."

"Are…" She swallowed. "Are you certain he no longer
lives?"

"I'm certain, wee lass. I'd no' be here if I thought there
was any chance he'd still be alive. I'd be out there, looking
for him."

"Aye, of… of course you would." She drew a shaky
breath and looked down at the brooch, still cradled in her
palm. "Then I pray he didnae suffer too much."

"I have prayed for the same."

Still regarding the brooch, she fell silent for a few
moments, though Ewan could almost hear the whispers of
unspoken thoughts in her head.

"I told you so," she said at last, meeting Ewan's gaze
once more. "Before he even left, I had a bad feeling. I
pleaded with him not to go, but he wouldnae listen. He
promised me… he promised me he'd be back soon."

"And I'm sure he meant it. But something obviously went wrong."

"'Tis all my fault."

"Dinnae say that."

"But it is." Her face crumpled. "Oh, Ewan, I cannae bear it. I'll miss him so much."

Ewan sighed and took her in his arms, rocking her gently as she wept.

As will I. Nay, as have *I. And now it's too late to change that, may God forgive me.*

Sniffling, she peered up at him. "Do you think Alastair MacAulay had anything to do with this?"

"I saw no proof of it."

"'Tis not what I asked."

He grimaced. "To say I dinnae have suspicions would be a lie, but I'm no' sure they're justified. I dinnae like the man much, which is likely clouding my judgement."

"Well, guilty or no', there'll be no alliance 'tween our clans now."

"'Tis not what Alastair said. He reckons the agreement should still stand."

"I dinnae see how." She shuddered. "Please dinnae make me marry the man, Ewan. I cannae even imagine—"

"I'll not let that happen, wee lass, have no fear. You need never worry about Alastair MacAulay. He and his hound are away back to Dunraven, and I doubt we'll be seeing either of them again for a good while. Right now, we have more important things to think about. We need to honour and mourn our brother, for one."

"I still cannae grasp that he's gone." Morag's eyes filled with fresh tears as she regarded the silver pin once more. "I thank God for sending you back to us, Ewan. I dread to think what would have become of us otherwise."

Ewan bit back a sigh. It did seem as though his return home had been orchestrated, somehow. And something told him the challenges he faced had only just begun.

Chapter Eight

From her quiet corner in the great hall at Dunraven, Cristie Ferguson watched the commotion currently taking place at the head table. Alastair, her half-brother, had just hurled a string of vile curses at the little serving maid who'd splashed wine on the table while filling her master's goblet. Something of an exaggerated show of annoyance, considering the minor offence.

The maid, her face redder than a smacked arse, fled from the table in tears as an uncomfortable hush descended on the room. Elspeth, seated beside Alastair, scowled at him and muttered her obvious disapproval. Lip curled, Alastair sloughed off the reprimand with a flick of his hand and turned to speak to his henchman, Tasgall.

Such scenes had become common since the laird of Dunraven had returned from Castle Cathan two weeks earlier. Like a bear with a thorn in its paw, Alastair had been in a continuously vile mood, snapping and growling at everyone. He'd never been the most congenial of men, but these days people went out of their way to avoid him, Cristie included. Then again, she'd never purposely sought out her half-brother's company, nor would she. There existed no fondness between them.

She released a small sigh. It should have been a happy time at Dunraven. A time of celebration. Elspeth should have been married by now and living in her new home. With her new husband.

Cristie wondered, again, about the unfortunate young man who had died in the mountains. Ruaidri MacKellar. The laird of a neighbouring clan, who'd agreed to marry Elspeth, and who was on his way to do exactly that when he'd met his demise. They'd found his horse, or what little remained of it, in a crevasse. Of the missing laird they'd found no sign other than a bloodied cloak and a silver pin.

Wolves had likely dispatched the remains, Alastair said.

"Mind if I sit with you, lass?" The voice startled her, as did the appearance of her other half-brother, Brochan. Despite being Elspeth's twin, he shared little physical resemblance to her. Elspeth, with her curly chestnut locks and fair complexion, favoured her sire's bloodline. Brochan, in contrast, emulated his late mother's colouring, with sleek hair as black as soot, and skin that never lost its golden glow even in winter. "Alastair's still in a shite mood," he continued, settling himself at her side, "and best left to himself, if you ask me."

"Nay, of course I dinnae mind." A rare occurrence indeed, for one of her noble siblings to seek out her company. Somewhat unnerved but determined not to show it, Cristie folded her hands atop the table to stop their fidgeting. "Though I can understand him being upset, Brochan. A man has died, and horribly, may God rest his soul."

Brochan grunted. "Aye, though I get the feeling Alastair's anger is less about Ruaidri MacKellar and more about Elspeth right now."

She frowned. "Why would he be angry at Elspeth? He should be sympathizing with her. She's just lost her betrothed."

"A man she'd never met," Brochan pointed out. "She's genuinely sorry about MacKellar's death, mind, but in truth, she was never keen on the marriage. It was Alastair that pressed for it."

"I wasnae aware of that." Cristie regarded Elspeth with the usual sense of quiet admiration. Secretly, she longed to be more like her older half-sister. More self-assured. More graceful. Less afraid of speaking her mind. Perhaps not as stubborn, however, nor quite as quick to anger. Cristie would never be as beautiful, of course. She had not been bestowed with quite the same comeliness. "I thought she wanted it."

"Nay, nor does she want the next one. She's dug her heels deep in the ground this time, too, refusing to budge. 'Tis mostly why Alastair is in such a dark mood. They argue about it all the time."

Cristie's brows lifted. "The next one?"

Brochan gave her a bemused glance. "Did you no' hear about the Templars at Castle Cathan?"

"Um, nay."

"God's teeth, lass, where have you been hiding?"

"I've no' been hiding anywhere." Cristie clenched her hands tighter. "I just dinnae pay attention to gossip."

"'Tis nae gossip, Cristie. There are Templars at Castle Cathan." Brochan gave her a playful nudge. "You should be more forthcoming. You're like a wee, shy mouse, lingering in dark corners, coming out to nibble on a bit of food now and then before scurrying back into your hole. Folks here forget you even exist most of the time."

The latter remark, though made lightly, had a sting to it. "Which doesnae bother me at all, Brochan." She raised her chin a notch and feigned nonchalance. "I'm quite happy being by myself."

"The expression on your face says otherwise," he replied, gently. "But, to bring you up to date, a few weeks ago, the French king ordered all the Templar knights in France to be arrested. Some managed to escape, and three of them turned up at Castle Cathan, one of them being Ruaidri MacKellar's younger brother, Ewan, who's been absent for twelve years. He'll be the laird now, of course. And Alastair wants Elspeth to marry the man."

Cristie pondered for a moment. "Why?"

Brochan gave her a puzzled glance. "Same reason as before, silly lass. He wants a blood alliance."

She shook her head. "Nay, I mean, why have the Templars been arrested?"

"Ah." Brochan's expression turned grim. "They've been accused of blasphemy and heresy, among other things, though the knights at Castle Cathan say the charges are false."

Cristie absorbed and pondered further. The renowned Order of the Temple, in her mind at least, possessed something of a mystical status. A holy army that surely even a king should not deign to challenge. For Cristie, the image of a Templar knight was that of a chaste and fearless warrior, sword in hand, fighting battles in the arid heat of the Holy Land. It seemed odd to think of such men exiled to the chilly highlands of Scotland.

"Well, I have to say, 'tis a wee bit soon to be discussing a new marriage alliance." She glanced at Alastair again, who was still muttering something to Tasgall. "Poor Ruaidri MacKellar has nae been dead even a month. His family surely need time to mourn."

Brochan grunted. "I agree, but Alastair's like a dog with a bone for some reason. He willnae let it go. He's wasting his time with Elspeth, though. She's as stubborn as an Irish donkey and isnae about to give in. She'll no' marry a battle-scarred monk, she says."

Cristie's eyes widened. "A battle-scarred monk?'

"Ewan MacKellar's face has been scarred by fire, apparently." Brochan shrugged. "As for being a monk, I dinnae see how he can sustain his Templar vows anymore, now that he's laird."

"'Twould be difficult," Cristie said, cocking her head. "Can Alastair no' try asking for the MacKellar lass's hand again?"

"Morag is her name, and I believe she's made it very clear she'd never marry our dear brother, no matter what." Brochan chuckled. "For all his bluster, Alastair is nae match for two stubborn Highland lasses. He may as well bang his head against yon wall."

"Well, that does explain his mood." Cristie rose to her feet, thinking she couldn't really blame Morag MacKellar for refusing Alastair's proposal. "If you'll excuse me, Brochan, I'm going for a wee walk before I scurry back into my mouse hole."

He grimaced. "Och, I meant no offence, lass. But I wasnae jesting about being more forthcoming. We share the same sire, after all." A twinkle came to his eye. "In truth, I'd say Alastair is actually the bastard in this family, but dinnae tell him I said that."

Cristie laughed. "I willnae."

"And dinnae wander too far from Dunraven on your walk. The wolves are bold right now. They've been attacking the livestock. Fergus has been setting traps and putting out poisoned meat."

Brochan's unexpected concern brought a grateful smile to Cristie's face. "Thank you, but I never go very far. Around the castle walls, is all. Or perhaps along the shore of the loch."

Turning to leave, Cristie cast another glance toward the head table and froze as her gaze collided with Alastair's.

This was no random glance on his part, however. It felt more like a scrutiny, as if he'd been watching her for a prolonged moment. As if to confirm Cristie's gut feeling, his eyes narrowed a little and his mouth curved into a slow smile. Then he raised his goblet as if making a toast, the smile staying with him as he turned away.

Cristie closed her slack jaw, puzzled by Alastair's behaviour. Perhaps she should have returned his smile and acknowledged his perusal, but the encounter had taken her by surprise. First Brochan. Now Alastair. She asked herself why, all of a sudden, her brothers were taking notice of her. Especially in Alastair's case. The man had never paid her any mind. Then again, maybe he'd simply seen her chatting to Brochan, and it had drawn his attention.

Yet, she felt there had been more to it. Alastair's expression had been one of attainment, as if he'd just solved an unsolvable riddle. The brief exchange had been unusual and, for some unfathomable reason, unsettling.

"Are you all right, lass?" Brochan asked. He followed her gaze to the head table, where Alastair was now saying something to Tasgall. "Is something wrong?"

"Nay. My mind wandered for a moment, is all." Cristie tugged her wool shawl tight around her shoulders and gave him a quick smile. "Good eve, Brochan."

A chill breeze awaited her outside. It clouded her breath and chased the stink of peat-smoke from her hair. For a moment, she considered going to fetch her cloak, but shook off the idea. If she set a good pace, she'd stay warm enough.

She nodded her thanks to the gatekeeper and exited through the castle's postern gate. Then, she picked up her feet, headed along the path that skirted around the loch, and soon became lost in thought.

For the first time since moving into Dunraven, and despite Alastair's questionable attention, Cristie felt the inherent stirrings of kinship. As Brochan had pointed out, she shared the same sire as the noble family. Her mother, Fiona Ferguson, had been a weaver of the fine woollen cloth that kept the MacAulay clan clothed and warm. A bonny woman, it seemed she had, at one time, caught the roving eye of Malcolm MacAulay, the previous laird.

Whether her mother had been ravished or seduced, Cristie didn't know for sure, though she tended to believe the latter. Cristie had never heard a bad word spoken about the laird, who had openly acknowledged Cristie's heritage. Too, as long as Malcolm MacAulay lived, and even after his death, Fiona Ferguson's small cottage had always been kept in good repair and there had always been food on the table.

It seemed, then, that the laird had retained some fondness for the lass whose virtue he had claimed, though he'd shown little interest in his baseborn daughter over the years. Only after her mother's demise, three months earlier, had Cristie learned of the auld laird's wishes. That Fiona's child—*their* child—should not be left alone and unprotected, but allowed to live at Dunraven.

Not so much a child anymore. This was Cristie's seventeenth winter this side of Heaven, the day of her birth not easily forgotten since she shared it with that of the Christ child. From whence came her name. She had also learned her mother's trade, and found much pleasure in working her loom, which now sat by the window in her small chamber.

The hoot of a nearby owl intruded into her thoughts, and her step faltered as awareness returned. She let out a soft gasp, unaware, till then, of how far she'd walked and how dark it had become. Ahead lay a wooded area, the path disappearing into eerie blackness. The owl hooted again, and a mild thrust of panic hastened Cristie's heart.

Mindful of Brochan's warning, she turned, meaning to scoot back to Dunraven before night descended in full. The unexpected sight of large, dark figure moving toward her forced a stifled scream into her throat. The figure halted and held up a hand.

"Dinnae be afeared, Cristie," a familiar voice said. "'Tis I, Tasgall."

"Tasgall!" Cristie's hand flew to her chest as she let out a sigh of pure relief. "By all the saints of Alba, you scared me near to death."

Tasgall approached, his bearded countenance wearing what might have passed for a smile, but in the twilight looked more like a snarl. The man's appearance alone intimidated most folks at Dunraven, and his gruff manner only added to his daunting demeanour. Yet, oddly, Cristie had never feared the man, nor felt any kind of apprehension in his presence.

"You've been gone a wee while, so thought I'd make sure you'd no' come to harm." He gave her a reproving look. "You should know better than to be out here after dark. I warrant you dinnae have a blade with you, either."

Cristie wrinkled her nose. "Nay."

"Daft lass."

"I was daydreaming and lost track of time," she said in defence as warmth flared in her cheeks. "And I wasnae aware you were watching out for me, Tasgall."

"I wasnae, but perhaps I should from now on," he said, his tone teasing. "Alastair was asking for you, and Brochan said you'd gone for a walk. When you didnae return, I thought I'd better come looking."

"I see. Well, thank you." Frowning, she tugged her shawl tighter. "What does Alastair want with me?"

"I havenae a clue. 'Tis not just you, either. Brochan and Elspeth have been summoned also. I'm sure it's naught to worry about."

Unbidden, and somewhat brazenly, he tucked Cristie's hand into the crook of his elbow. "In case you stumble," he said, by way of explanation.

Cristie smiled but said nothing, though she silently admitted to feeling reassured to have Tasgall at her side. He was, without doubt, Alastair's best and most fearless warrior.

*

Judging by the glaze in his eyes and the crimson flush on his neck, Alastair had obviously had a drink or two. He stood, feet apart, hands behind his back, and studied the three faces before him. Tasgall, as always, lingered nearby, leaning against the wall, a casual hand resting on his sword hilt.

They had gathered in the solar, where a lazy peat fire smouldered in the blackened hearth and light from several tapers chased shadows into the corners.

'Well?" Elspeth raised her brows and regarded her elder brother. "What is this about, Alastair?"

He sniffed and rocked on his heels. "A marriage."

She gave him a wary look. "A marriage?"

"Aye. 'Tween the MacAulays and the MacKellars."

"God's bollocks." She huffed and folded her arms. "Here we go again. Get it through your daft skull. You'll have to roast my feet over a fire before I agree to marry Ewan MacKellar."

"Dinnae tempt me," Alastair growled, fixing her with a dark glare. "I might be persuaded to pluck out that wicked tongue o' yours, as well. But, as it happens, I've done Ewan MacKellar a favour and found him a more amenable bride."

Elspeth gave a humourless laugh. "And who might that be?"

An odd little chill brushed over Cristie's scalp. She held her breath, awaiting Alastair's answer. He didn't give it. A movement to her side drew her attention. She glanced over at Tasgall, who had straightened his spine and was regarding Alastair with a puzzled frown.

"My motivation for this alliance has changed a wee bit," Alastair continued, ignoring Elspeth's question, "and that's because I have reason to believe the MacKellar clan has recently acquired some additional wealth. A good deal of wealth, in fact."

He fell silent and regarded his small audience as if waiting for someone to speak.

"The Templars," Brochan said, after a few moments. "Is that what you mean? You think they brought some kind of... of treasure with them?"

"I'm certain of it." A telling gleam lit Alastair's eyes. "The so-called 'poor soldiers of Christ' are the wealthiest military order in Christendom. Do you really think Ewan MacKellar and his cohorts would leave France empty handed? Nay, never. You cannae convince me they didnae have any time to stash some of their coin on the ship. I found out they arrived at Castle Cathan with a half-dozen horses and an ox pulling a wagon. What I need to find out is what was on that wagon and where it went. No one I spoke to seems to ken, or else they dinnae care to speak of it. The latter, I suspect."

"Even if you're right, what does that have to do with us?" Brochan asked. "'Tis nae business of ours what the Templars brought with them."

"Who is this bride you mentioned?" Elspeth demanded.

Again, Alastair ignored her. "I disagree, Brochan. I mean to find out what, exactly, those knights brought with them. And I reckon the only way to do that is to insist the marriage agreement is fulfilled, thereby allying ourselves with the MacKellar clan on an intimate level."

Elspeth gasped. "You expect a lass to marry Ewan MacKellar and become your *spy*?"

"Aye, I do," Alastair said, his lip curling "'Tis traitorous to be hiding wealth that might be used for Scotland's cause."

Elspeth blew out a breath. "How much coin have you given to Scotland's cause? This addlepated obsession of yours has naught to do with Scotland. It has everything to do with you!"

"The Templars have naught to do with our political conflicts, Alastair," Brochan said, his tone composed. "Why should they volunteer support to Scotland, financially or otherwise?"

Alastair scoffed. "Because they've been given safe haven here."

Brochan shook his head. "Nay, I cannae agree with your logic. Besides, Ewan MacKellar is no foreigner to these shores. He's a Highlander, born and bred."

Alastair scowled. "All the more reason for him to offer support for his homeland. And dinnae forget, he's harbouring a *Sasunnach*. An enemy of Scotland. I dinnae much trust that Basque knight, either."

Brochan shook his head again. "The *Sasunnach* has no allegiance to the English king. He's sworn to his Order and to the Pope. I cannae speak for the Basque's integrity, but I doubt he's a threat, either."

Alastair waved a dismissive hand. "I dinnae care what you think. I mean to find out what was on that wagon."

"Which begs me to ask again, who is this bride you speak of?" Elspeth put her hands on her hips. "And what makes you think Ewan MacKellar will agree to wed some lass who isnae MacAulay blood?"

"But she is MacAulay blood," Alastair said, his gaze sliding over to Cristie. "And he'll agree to the union. I'll make sure of that."

The air stilled as all eyes turned toward her. Cristie stood as if made of stone, unable to move or speak. She had misheard, surely. Or misunderstood. *Me? Wed Ewan MacKellar?* Alastair had to be jesting. Besides, her MacAulay blood had no political value. She was base-born. The daughter of a weaver. No laird in the land would ever consider her a suitable bride.

"Nay!" The challenge shattered the fragile silence. Hand atop his sword hilt, Tasgall stepped forward, his gaze darting between Alastair and Cristie. "Laird, you said—"

"Step back, Tasgall, and hold your tongue," Alastair snarled at his henchman. "I'll no' tell you again."

Tasgall's nostrils flared and the grip on his sword tightened visibly. For a moment, he held his ground. Then, with a sullen glance at Cristie, he retook his place by the wall.

"Well, I'll no' be holding *my* tongue." Mouth twisted into a sneer, Elspeth glared at Alastair. "You've truly lost your mind, brother. What, under God's great sky, makes you think Ewan MacKellar will even consider marrying a bas—?" She faltered and gave Cristie a contrite smile. "I meant to say, Cristie might carry our blood, but she doesnae carry our name."

Alastair rocked back on his heels. "Ewan MacKellar doesnae know that."

"What do you mean?" Cristie asked, at last finding the wherewithal to speak. "Elspeth is right. He'll no' marry me."

"I believe he will." A gleam came to Alastair's eyes. "If he thinks you're Elspeth."

Silence descended once more, broken a moment later by a burst of mocking laughter—from Brochan. "Christ almighty, Alastair," he said. "Listen to what you're saying! You cannae give the man a false bride."

"Why not?" Alastair shrugged. "I need someone to get close to Ewan MacKellar, to find out what those Templars managed to smuggle out of France. A lass—a *wife*—can get intimately close. Think of it as a mission, Cristie. An assignment, if you please."

"I cannae believe what I'm hearing." Elspeth tapped a forefinger to her temple. "Have you lost your mind?"

"I'll no' do it." Cristie folded her arms across her chest as if to muffle the frantic clatter of her heart. Alastair had obviously over imbibed. Or maybe the wine he'd drunk had been sour. "You cannae make me."

A corner of Alastair's mouth lifted. "Och, I think I can, lass, but I'd rather you agreed without forcing me to take more… drastic measures."

"Meaning what?" Brochan asked. "Are you threatening her?"

"Nay, of course not." Alastair gave Cristie a sober smile. "Well, maybe a wee bit. But I trust it willnae come to that."

Cristie swallowed. "I cannae marry a man falsely, Alastair. You ask too much of me."

"'Nay, she cannae. 'Tis madness." Elspeth shook her head. "The repercussions dinnae bear thinking about. To Cristie. To you. To the clan."

"Elspeth is right, Alastair. You have to think about this." Again, Brochan kept his tone calm. "Even if you discover the existence of this supposed wealth, what do you intend to do? Ask Ewan MacKellar to simply hand it over? He'll laugh at you."

"Let me worry about that." Alastair waved a dismissive hand. "I've said all I'm going to say for now. I wish to speak with Cristie alone, so the rest of you begone. And you'll say naught of this to anyone, is that clear?"

"As if I would." Elspeth gave a bitter laugh. "I'm ashamed just thinking about it. Dinnae do this, Cristie. You'll regret it more than anything our daft brother might threaten you with. Mark my words."

"Our father would never have done such a thing, Alastair," Brochan said, giving Cristie a concerned glance.

Alastair grunted. "Our father isnae here." He glanced over at his henchman. "You too, Tasgall. Out. And close the door behind you."

The man frowned. "But, laird, there are—"

"Out, I said! I'll speak to you later."

Cristie waited till the door closed. "I'll no' do this, Alastair." She clenched her fists. "You cannae make me, no matter what you say."

Alastair heaved a sigh and settled into one of the two throne-like chairs by the brazier. "Sit," he commanded, gesturing to an adjacent chair.

Cristie stared at him in defiance for a moment, but her courage soon crumbled beneath his hard, unwavering stare. "I'll no' marry Ewan MacKellar," she muttered, sliding into the chair.

A corner of his mouth lifted. "Aye, you will."

Cristie shook her head and attempted a different argument. "What if he doesnae want a wife?"

"We have an agreement. He's obliged to hold to it."

"But you made the agreement with Ruaidri MacKellar. Not—"

"It was an agreement 'tween clan chiefs." Alastair sniffed. "Ewan MacKellar must honour it. He *will* honour it."

"But there is no honour in what you ask of me." Cristie gripped the chair's arms. "To wed a man falsely? To lie with him? I cannae do that. 'Twould be a carnal sin."

"So saith a wee bastard," he muttered, callously. "You'd no' be here if your mother hadnae lain with my father."

"You cannae compare that to this," she cried. "My mother didnae deceive your father."

"He was your father too." Alastair leaned forward, pinning her with a dark gaze that surely emulated the Devil himself. "Do this, and you'll want for naught for the rest of your life, no matter the outcome. I'll make certain of it. Just like our father did for your mother."

"But I'm the daughter of a weaver. I ken little about clan affairs." Tears of desperation pricked at the back of

Cristie's eyes. "What if Ewan MacKellar finds out the truth about me? Which he surely will. I'll hang for it!"

"I'll no' let that happen. As for clan affairs, I doubt you'll have much to do with them. Bear in mind, no one at Castle Cathan has ever seen Elspeth, and few beyond Dunraven even know about your existence." Alastair sighed and sat back. "If you work quickly, you'll no' be there very long. Just find out where the Templars have hidden their spoils, and leave the rest to me."

A whisper of fear told her to accept. Her conscience warned against it. "And… if I refuse?"

"You do so at your peril."

"Meaning what?"

"You're here at our father's behest, Cristie." His arrogant smile lasted but a heartbeat. "And, like I said, our father isnae here anymore."

His meaning was quite clear, yet still she dared to resist. "You cannae be sure they even have any spoils. This might all be for naught."

He grunted. "They're hiding something. I'm sure of it."

"But what you ask of me…" She shook her head. "Please, Alastair. There must be another way."

A tic arose in Alastair's jaw and his knuckles paled as his grip tightened on the chair arms. "Dinnae disappoint me, lass. 'Twould no' be wise."

'You're like a wee, shy mouse, lingering in dark corners...'

And Alastair was like a serpent. Coiled and ready to strike at the wee mouse should it dare to attempt an escape. The whispers of fear grew louder.

"If... if I should discover what they brought with them, what then?" Bile burned the back of her throat. "How... how do I let you know?"

His taut expression slackened a little. "Tasgall will pay you a visit every fortnight or so. I'll think of some ruse. If and when you have news, you can pass it on to him."

She tried one final, feeble attempt at reason. "But, as Brochan said, Ewan MacKellar isnae about to hand anything over. At least, not without a fight."

"And, as I told him, I'll worry about that." One russet brow arched, Alastair leaned forward. "So, what's it to be, lass? Aye or nay?"

*

Fingers woven into a prayer-knot beneath her chin, Cristie knelt beside her bed and stared up at the dark recesses of her ceiling, where the light from her small candle could not reach. A sennight had passed since her meeting with Alastair, since the struggle with her conscience had begun. Her mind still refused to be quiet, yet Alastair's quietly spoken threats subdued the voices of reason and honesty.

"I dare nae refuse him," she whispered. "I'm afeared of what he'll do. God, please, help me."

But her prayers provided sparse comfort. Her apprehension persisted, writhing mercilessly in her gut. Fearful of being cast out, or worse, she had made her choice. She had agreed to give false testimony before God. To mislead a man into a fraudulent marriage—a man she knew by name only. Surrender to him, not as an innocent young wife, but as a deceiver.

Ewan Tormod MacKellar.

She knew little of him. He was, or had been, a Templar knight. Therefore, a devout man. Yet also a warrior, his face supposedly scarred in battle, though she cared little about his appearance. Rather, she cared more about his demeanour. Was he kindly, or brutish? Either way, he surely did not merit such wicked deceit.

"Nay, I cannae do this," Cristie whispered, for the hundredth time that week. "I cannae—"

But what hellish choice do I have?

Her time was up. They were due to leave at dawn. She squeezed her eyes shut.

A sudden rap at the door startled her. Wincing, Cristie struggled to her feet, turning to face the door as it swung open.

Elspeth stood on the threshold, her face steeped in shadow.

Cristie bristled at the blatant lack of respect. Such displays from her half-sibling had been common of late. Cristie understood why, of course, but her stretched nerves were at the point of snapping. "'Tis courteous to wait for permission to enter," she said, raising her chin, "and I didnae give it."

"Dinnae speak to me of courtesy," Elspeth replied, a chill in her voice. "And I dinnae need to enter. I can say what I have to say from here."

"Well, I've nae wish to hear it." Cristie folded her arms. "You've made your feelings plain enough these past few days."

"Because what you're doing is wrong," Elspeth countered, "and you'll live to regret it, believe me."

"As you've told me several times." Cristie shrugged. "And I havenae once denied it. Maybe if you'd agreed to marry the man, I'd no' be in this—"

"Dinnae dare place any blame for this madness on my shoulders," Elspeth snarled, the shadows on her face serving to accentuate her displeasure. Cristie opened her mouth to rebut, but paused. Weary of arguing—weary of *everything* in her life at that moment—she heaved a doleful sigh.

"I dinnae blame you for any of it, Elspeth," she said, her throat tightening. "Please, just… just leave me alone."

Elspeth didn't move. "I dinnae doubt Alastair's threatened you," she said, after a moment, her voice softer, "and I realize there's little to be done about it, since you're at his mercy. He'll no' listen to me or Brochan, either. To tell you true, I also get the feeling there's more to this than he's saying."

Cristie frowned. "What do you mean?"

Elspeth shrugged. "I dinnae ken. All I can do is pray his cursed scheme does less harm than good to you, as well as the poor man you're deceiving. And, with that in mind, I brought you this." She held out a hand. "You might need it."

Cristie stepped forward and took the small, leather pouch from the girl's grasp. "What is it?"

"The solution to a possible problem."

"What problem?"

"If you…" Elspeth heaved a soft sigh. "If you should find yourself carrying Ewan MacKellar's child, make a tisane from this and drink it. 'Tis very potent, so a small pinch is all you'll need, steeped in a cup of hot water." She crossed herself. "And may God forgive me. May He forgive you too, Cristie."

Cristie looked down at the small, nondescript pouch resting in her palm, her blood chilling as understanding seeped into her brain.

"Och, nay, Elspeth," she said, lifting her head. "I could never do such a—"

But the threshold stood empty. Elspeth had gone.

Cristie's gaze shifted to where the saddle bags sat, packed in readiness for her journey on the morrow. Tears clouding her vision, she wandered over, opened one of the bags, and tucked the small pouch safely inside.

Chapter Nine

A chill wind, sharp enough to sting the ears and inflame the cheeks, blew in from the sea. Worse, a fine drizzle hurtled in with it, clinging to hair and clothing like spiderwebs. Ewan cast his gaze over the three weather-beaten visitors before him, his attention lingering a little longer on the young woman seated astride a dappled pony.

Alastair MacAulay's arrival had been announced at the onset of dinner, just as Ewan had taken his seat in the great hall. As usual, the man was accompanied by his boorish henchman, whose face seemed to be moulded into a permanent scowl. But this time they'd brought a lass as well. And Ewan knew, without being told, who she was.

"Given what happened to your brother, I didnae think you'd be too keen on coming to Dunraven, so I've brought the lass to you." Alastair MacAulay, without prompting, dismounted and gestured toward his charge. "My sister, Elspeth Kirstie MacAulay, pledged to the laird of the MacKellar clan. She comes from fine MacAulay stock." He sniffed and eyed Ewan up and down. "I guarantee she'll make you a good wife once you toss that Templar garb aside."

Duncan, who stood by the gate, gave an exaggerated cough. Ewan ignored him. Instead, prompted by Alastair's bold announcement, he studied the lass who had been promised to his brother.

Her face, what little Ewan could see of it, appeared pale to the point of ghostly. A pair of wide, dark eyes gazed out from folds of her hood, the finer details of her features further obscured by the gloom of late evening. Her bare hands, small and equally pale, grasped the reins, knuckles tight, implying nervousness. Her slumped shoulders spoke plainly of misery and fatigue.

The lass returned Ewan's gaze, unflinching at first, but lowering her eyes moments later. Whether the response was prompted by his scarred features or simple modesty, Ewan couldn't tell. Nor did he really care. The audacity of the situation had aroused his ire to the point of making his sword-hand twitch.

Standing at Ewan's side, Morag gave a quiet snort. Ewan threw her a brief, warning glance and then shifted his attention back to his uninvited, unexpected, and unwanted visitors. Decorum demanded he greet them; especially the lass, whom he'd never met. But obstinacy and a good measure of resentment pushed any kind of cordial greeting back down his throat.

"I've havenae agreed to marry anyone, MacAulay," Ewan said, grappling with an urge to toss them out on their wet arses. "You should have taken the time to discuss this with me before bringing the lass all this way. It would have saved time and embarrassment."

"There's naught to discuss," Alastair replied, appearing nonplussed. "A dray horse, a half-dozen cattle, and a dozen sheep. 'Tis the price already paid for Elspeth's hand. So, the agreement still stands as far as I'm concerned. And since we *have* come all this way, a warm fire and a goblet of spiced wine wouldnae go amiss about now. In case you havenae noticed, the weather is shite, and my wee sister is weary and half-frozen."

Ewan eyed the lass once more and surrendered to chivalry. "Come in, then, and warm yourselves." He nodded toward the stables. "Hammett and Niall will see to your horses. I'll wait for you inside."

Ewan turned on his heel, grasping Morag's elbow just as she opened her mouth. "Hold your tongue, lass," he muttered, dragging her along with him. "Just let it be."

"You dinnae ken what I was about to say," she said, tugging her elbow free and scowling up at him.

"Was it a pleasantry of some sort?"

The scowl disappeared as her mouth twisted. "Not precisely."

"I thought as much." Blinking wind-driven tears from his eyes, Ewan entered the keep, unfastened his mantle, and shook the drops from it. "Dinnae provoke the man, Morag. 'Tis bad enough that he's here."

"Aye, when barely a month has passed since we lost Ruaidri." She slid her cloak from her shoulders too, and gave it a vigorous shake, sending drops flying. "I cannae fathom why he's in such a hurry to marry off the lass."

Ewan grunted. "No doubt he has his mad reasons."

"Will you honour the agreement?" she asked, without inference or undertone.

"The agreement was made with Ruaidri, not me."

"That doesnae answer the question."

"I'm still a Templar, Morag." He gave her a sober glance. "Does that answer the question?"

"I dinnae see how you can be both, Ewan, marriage alliance or no'," Morag said, following him into the hall.

"The clan needs a laird. A man they can trust. Our father is gone. Ruaidri is gone. To you, then, falls the obligation."

He didn't respond to Morag's observation, but it had merit, of course. Ewan knew where his obligations now lay. Indeed, he had assumed the role of laird in his head—but not yet in his heart. To give up the mantle was not easy. To rescind the vows that had transformed his life and given him purpose felt like a betrayal. Thus far, he'd clung obstinately to his doctrine, unchallenged by those who looked to him for leadership. But it couldn't last. He knew everyone, including Jacques and Gabriel, were simply giving him time to grieve the loss of his brother. Time to adjust.

Six weeks had passed since the Templars had been condemned by the French king. So far, there had been no news from that country. The fate of those arrested had yet to be learned, but it would likely not bode well. And nearly a month had passed since Ewan had stood on a mountainside and watched blood drip like red rain from his brother's saturated cloak.

Consequently, Ewan's purpose, whether he liked it or not, had changed.

"You have the look of a burdened man," Gabriel said as they retook their seats at the table. "Is everything all right?"

"Everything is fine," Ewan replied, thinking the exact opposite as he reached for the bread. "It seems MacAulay has taken it upon himself to bring me a bride, but since I have nae need of one, he's wasted his time. I've offered them shelter for the night, but they'll be on their way on the morrow."

A ripple of surprise spread through those present as Alastair, Tasgall, and the lass entered the hall.

"Ruaidri's bride?" Jacques asked, watching as they approached.

"Ewan's bride now." Morag said. "Alastair reckons the agreement still stands."

"And does it?" Gabriel leaned forward. "Is it binding?"

"Nay." Ewan frowned into his goblet and took a gulp of wine. "I dinnae want a wife."

"MacKellar!" Alastair's voice rang out as he drew near. "Your bride is cold and hungry and needs food and rest. Some clan hospitality would be welcome here."

The remark, obviously calculated, hit its intended target. The low hum of conversation ceased as more than a dozen pairs of questioning eyes turned toward Ewan.

"Damn his bones," Ewan muttered, gritting his teeth as he rose to his feet. Then, "I'm nae certain of whom you speak, MacAulay," he replied, his voice now carrying clear and strong, "but if it's your wee sister you're referring to, we'll make sure she's made comfortable. Leave your wet cloaks by the fire to dry." He gestured to a nearby table. "Then be seated, please, and help yourselves."

The lass, standing between Alastair and Tasgall, looked down as if embarrassed. Alastair assumed a smug smile and glanced around the room as he shrugged off his wet cloak. Despite Ewan's refute, the seed of a possible upcoming marriage had been planted. The damage done. A soft hum of conversation began again, little more than a purr of shared whispers.

Ewan hardened his jaw and retook his seat.

"The lass is quite bonny, actually," Morag mumbled from behind her goblet. "Looks naught like Alastair, fortunately. It makes me a wee bit sad to see her, Ewan."

Ewan threw his sister a puzzled glance. "Why?"

"Because I was worried she might be homely, but I think Ruaidri would have approved." She heaved a sigh. "'Tis of no consequence now, though, since she'll never be our brother's bride."

"Dinnae upset yourself," Ewan said, his gaze settling on the lass who had also shrugged off her cloak and now sat between Alastair and Tasgall. He quietly agreed with Morag. Though no great beauty, the lass was not at all unpleasant to look upon.

Of slight build, she nevertheless had a womanly shape, her slender curves evident beneath her blue kirtle and white shift. Her near-black hair hung over one shoulder in a thick, plaited rope, and a flush of colour now sat upon her previously pale face. A heart-shaped face, beset with large eyes of an indefinable hue and graced with an unremarkable nose and solemn mouth.

"She looks young," he murmured.

"She's seventeen summers, same as me," Morag said. "She's Brochan's twin."

"Aye, I do have some recollection of them." Ewan frowned. "Father took Ruaidri and me on a hunting trip to Dunraven one time, and I have a vague memory of folks there fussing over two wee bairns."

"Chosen by God," Morag muttered.

Ewan looked at her. "What is?"

"That's what her name means," Morag replied. "Elspeth. Chosen by God."

"Are you suggesting that is somehow relevant?"

"Nay." She shrugged and tore off a morsel of bread. "Just saying."

*

"'Tis an honour to meet you, Laird MacKellar."

Blue. Elspeth MacAulay's eyes were blue. But dark, like indigo, not bright, like the summer sky. Candlelight reflected in their depths. That, and perhaps a glint of fear, its spark evident just before the lass lowered her gaze. Ewan wondered if she feared him or the way he looked. Maybe both.

Not that it really mattered, in truth. The lass had been promised to Ruaidri, not him. Ewan had no intention of wedding Elspeth MacAulay.

"Likewise, my lady. Sit, please." His response caused the lass to regard him once more. A timid, fleeting glance, accompanied by the hint of a smile as she took her seat.

"She's a wee bit shy." Goblet in hand, Alastair dropped into a chair and released a soft belch. "But she'll warm your bed, MacKellar, right enough. It was a fine meal, by the way. My thanks."

The lass's cheeks flared, as did Ewan's ire, and he tamped down a desire to rebuke his uncouth guest. "Naught has been discussed, Alastair."

"Then let us discuss it." Alastair lounged back and crossed his feet at the ankles. At his behest, they had retired to the laird's private chamber at the end of the evening meal.

"I would prefer to do so without the lady present," Ewan replied.

"Why? This concerns her." Alastair took a gulp of wine. "I would prefer the ceremony be performed as soon as possible. I dinnae like being away from Dunraven for too long. You have a priest here, I trust?"

Ewan firmed both jaw and resolve. "There will be no ceremony, MacAulay."

Alastair gave a mild grunt. "Maybe I should point out that the MacKellar clan is vulnerable," he said, "allied with no one of import since your grandmother died. Your father didnae even send out his sons to foster. A bizarre lapse of tradition, and most unwise. I spent my boyhood with the MacLean's, who are my grandmother's kin. Because of that, I have the ear of some powerful Highland chiefs. What of you? Who would you call upon for help if obliged to do so? The Templars?" He scoffed. "I think not. You were away when the ague hit. It cut down both our clans, but yours suffered more than mine. You need this alliance more than I do, MacKellar, you cannae deny it. More than that, you need heirs. Some strong sons. And Elspeth, here, will give you those."

Despite Ewan's resolve, much of what Alastair said had a ring of truth to it. Still, he could not – would not – be pushed into a marriage he didn't want. Especially so soon after Ruaidri's death.

"My brother has been dead not even a month," Ewan said. "'Tis a little early to be handing over his promised bride to the new laird."

"Bollocks." Alastair sniffed. "Ruaidri's death has left your clan vulnerable. You're the only remaining heir. 'Tis as well you returned when you did. God's will, perhaps. 'Tis time to take off that mantle and—"

"Enough!" Ewan's lip twisted. "I'm neither prepared nor willing to take a wife, especially the one meant for my brother." He shifted his gaze to the lass, who sat in grave silence. "Forgive me, my lady. My refusal of your hand is entirely a result of circumstance. I dinnae mean to offend."

She shook her head. "I'm nae offended in the least," she said, casting a sideways glance at Alastair. "You've been more than gracious, Laird MacKellar. And I'm truly sorry about the loss of your brother. It was tragic."

"My thanks." Ewan replied, impressed with her gentle reply. Unlike her brother, the lass at least possessed a modicum of grace.

Alastair grunted, downed the contents of his goblet, and then raked a narrow-eyed gaze over Ewan. "I'm curious, MacKellar. Why are you still wearing that Templar garb? You cannae be laird and Templar both. Perhaps, then, 'tis nae so much Ruaidri's death which influences your decision, but a misplaced allegiance."

The remark, if Alastair did but know it, struck an invisible target on Ewan's conscience. Still, he maintained a benign expression. "I ken where my allegiance lies, Alastair, and I dinnae need a wife to prove it." He rose to his feet. "That being so, I see no point in continuing with this. The discussion is over."

Alastair's facial pallor darkened till it matched the dregs in his goblet. He pushed himself upright. "Refusing the lass will be a mistake," he muttered, through gritted teeth. "I suggest you think more on it before morning."

Ewan strode over to the door and opened it. "I will, undoubtedly," he replied, "but dinnae expect my answer to change. I bid you good night, both, and trust you'll sleep well."

Chapter Ten

Ewan's heart and mind refused to reconcile. Consequently, sleep eluded him.

For ten years he'd adhered steadfastly to his Templar vows. Admittedly, his zealous Highland blood had pushed him to recklessness at times. In contrast, his inherent obstinacy had bolstered his determination to observe the Templar rule. With little deviation, he'd been devout, chaste, and obedient. His courage had never been questioned, nor had his skill with sword and lance. A monk with a warrior's heart.

It had not always been so.

There had been a time when he'd paid homage to his goblet and found solace in less righteous company. Women had taken his silver in exchange for carnal pleasure. Ewan had earned that silver with a blunt sword, challenging men to bouts of bruising, but generally benign, combat. He'd almost always bested his opponent. Having little care for his own life made him brazen. And fearless.

Then, one dank autumn evening, Ewan's ability with the sword caught the attention of Gilbert de Mauleon, a seasoned Templar knight and regional Master. The man had dragged Ewan off the streets of Paris, sobered him up, and introduced him to the order of warrior monks. It changed his life. Nay, it *saved* his life.

He squirmed beneath his blankets and wondered what had become of his old master. Had the man managed to elude arrest?

And with that thought came another.

Does the Order of the Temple even have a future anymore?

The question had him tossing and turning even more. With his sight turned inward, he gazed up at the shadowed ceiling. "I'm no' sure where my loyalties lie," he whispered, and then frowned. "Nay, that isnae true. I ken exactly where they lie. I'm just afraid of—"

What? What am I afraid of? Surrendering my allegiance to the Temple? Or accepting my responsibility as laird?

Morag's observation came back to him. *"I dinnae see how you can be both, Ewan, marriage alliance or no'."*

She was right, of course. And in truth, Ewan's decision had been made for him. He simply needed to commit to it, which was proving to be easier said than done.

Frustrated, he left his bed, dressed warmly, and made his way outside. The ugly weather had cleared, giving way to starlit skies and a bright, full moon. Ewan paused atop the steps and breathed deep, cleansing his lungs with the crisp night air as he fastened his sword belt.

He then took another deep breath and gazed up at the stars. It was indeed a fine night. A bonny night. One that, under different circumstances, might have lifted his burdened spirit.

A sharp northwest breeze, not quite vigorous enough to be called a wind, skipped over the castle walls. To Ewan's puzzlement, it carried with it the faint sound of voices—a shared conversation between male and female. Curious, he cocked his head to listen, seeking the direction of the sound, frowning when he found it.

The gatehouse?

Ewan uttered a curse, heaved a disappointed sigh, and set out across the courtyard. Niall, the watchman, had never been one to shirk his duty, or even take it lightly. Yet, without doubt, there was a female on the gatehouse roof. A serious breach of the rules.

Such disobedience was unacceptable at any time, but seemed especially irreverent now, so soon after Ruaidri's demise. It could not—would not—go unpunished. The lass, too, whoever she was, would answer for her indiscretion.

Wishing to keep an element of surprise, Ewan kept his footfalls soft as he climbed the dark, spiral staircase. The sight that greeted him atop the roof stopped him dead.

What, by all things sacred, is she doing here?

"There are hundreds of islands out there, lass," Niall was saying, as he gazed out over the water with his back to Ewan. "Maybe even thousands. Some of them are little more than rocks, mind, so you couldnae live on them. Over there is Ireland. Down that way is the Isle of Mann. And to the south, of course…" he spat over the wall, "England."

Some movement must have drawn the lass's eye. Ewan's white mantle, maybe, lifted by the breeze. In any case, she caught sight of him and parted with a sharp gasp.

"Shite!" Niall, sword half-drawn, spun around, guilt washing over his face as he realized who stood before him. "I mean, sorry, Laird. You startled me."

"Only because you were no' paying attention." Ewan's gaze flicked briefly to the MacAulay lass, who looked like she'd been caught in an illicit act. "What are you at, Niall?"

The man fidgeted. "Er… 'tis simply explained, Laird."

"Then explain it."

"'Tis not his fault, Laird MacKellar." The MacAulay lass stepped forward, her face pale in the moonlight. "I asked if I might look at the sea, and he kindly agreed."

Niall grimaced. "It was only to be for a wee while, Laird. I didnae have the heart to refuse."

"I didnae mean to cause trouble," the lass went on. "'Tis just that I've never—"

Ewan held up a hand, which silenced her, and glared at Niall. "You're on duty, lad. You're aware of the rules."

The man gave a resigned sigh. "Aye, I ken. Forgive me, Laird. I take full responsibility for the lapse."

The lass shook her head. "Nay, please! 'Tis entirely my fault, not his."

Ewan raked his gaze over her. "Do you often wander about at night unescorted, my lady?"

"Um, nay, not usually." She gave him a hesitant smile. "I couldnae sleep and came out for some air. When I saw how bright the moon was, I thought I might climb up here to take a wee glimpse at the sea. I'd never seen it till today, you understand. I didnae have much time to look at it when we arrived, and since we'll be leaving in the morning, I'll no' have time then, either." She glanced at Niall. "I never meant for your watchman to get into trouble. I'm sorry, truly."

Ewan studied the lass. Moonlight cast a silver gilt over her dark hair, strands of which twirled freely in the breeze. They, in turn, created moving shadows across her face. It was a strange, alluring effect that served to accentuate the mystery of who she was. He knew naught but her name, after all, although his first impression had not changed. She seemed pleasant enough. Perhaps, though, not as shy as Alastair had indicated.

The idea of fostering a rapport with her felt like a betrayal of sorts. At the same time, Ewan admitted intrigue, curious to know more about the woman who should have been Ruaidri's bride. His throat tightened at the thought, though he kept his expression benign.

"I appreciate the explanation, my lady," he said. "Nevertheless, you shouldnae be up here."

Perhaps he imagined the touch of colour rising in her cheeks. "I understand, of course," she replied. "I'll leave right away."

"I'll escort you down." Ewan nodded at Niall. "As you were, lad. I'll speak with you later."

Niall had the wherewithal to look chagrined. "Aye, Laird."

Ewan gestured to the stairwell. "I'll go first," he said. "'Tis beyond dark in there and I didnae bring a flame. I'll be your shield, should you stumble."

"Thank you," she replied. "I'll try not to trip over my feet. And thank you too, sir, for your kindness." This last to Niall, who granted her an easy smile that dissolved beneath Ewan's stern glance.

They descended in silence and without mishap, finally stepping out into the moonlit courtyard.

"Thank you again, Laird MacKellar." The lass raised her hood and looked up at him. "Please, dinnae be too hard on your watchman. I apologize, again, for any trouble I've caused. There's no need to bother yourself further. I'm sure I'll be fine now."

"'Tis nae bother." Ewan regarded her, wondering why he didn't quite feel ready to let her go just yet. "I must confess, my lady, I find it odd that you've never seen the sea till today. Have you been locked away in Dunraven all your life?"

She looked momentarily unsettled. "Nay, I...um..." Frowning, she glanced down. "'Tis more accurate to say that I've never been to the coast. I have seen the sea before, actually, but 'twas from afar and on a misty day, so I couldnae tell where the waves ended and the sky began. I've smelled and tasted it on the air many times, too, but till today, I've never seen it up close."

Ewan had no reason to doubt her explanation. It seemed innocent enough. "Are you tired, lass?"

The question appeared to puzzle her. "Tired? Nay… well, maybe a wee bit."

"Only, I wondered…"

She blinked. "What?"

Ewan nodded toward the western side of the castle. "If you'd like to see the sea up close, there's a wee postern gate back there that leads out to the cliffs. 'Tis an unobstructed view. I'll be happy to escort you, if you wish."

Uncertainty showed in her expression as she glanced to where he'd indicated. "I'm nae sure I should, really."

"Why? There's naught to fear."

She fidgeted on her feet. "I fear only that I've inconvenienced you enough already, Laird MacKellar."

"Not quite." He leaned in and lowered his voice. "Dinnae fash. I'll be sure to tell you the moment I find you tiresome."

The brief look of shock on her face made his mouth twitch, something she apparently noticed a moment later.

"You're teasing me," she said, smiling.

Ewan smiled back, tussling with a forbidden urge to offer his arm to the lass. He hadn't touched a woman in ten years. Well, other than Morag, of course. And even that benign contact, strictly speaking, went against the code. He'd made allowances, though, given the sad circumstances of recent weeks.

He reasoned with himself. This was merely an exercise in graciousness. The lass—his guest—wanted to see the sea. So, he'd show it to her. Then he'd dispatch her back to her chamber, where she could prepare to return whence she came.

"Aye, I'm teasing you," he said, presenting his elbow. "Come."

For a fleeting moment, he saw something undefinable flare in her eyes. He sloughed off an odd impression that it had been the same glimmer of fear as when they'd first been introduced. But the lass's smile didn't waver as she'd placed her hand in the protective crook of his arm.

Likely a trick of the light, then, or the flicker of a shadow.

Keeping his longer stride in check, he led her to the postern gate, a small portal set flush in the castle wall, where it backed onto the coast. Built from thick oak and reinforced with metal studs, the hefty door could only be opened from within. Ewan pulled back the iron bolts, lifted the latch, and tugged the door open. Beyond, a wide, grassy shelf edged the rugged cliffs that overlooked the shore.

"After you, lass." Ewan released her and stepped to the side. "Mind your step."

She moved past him into the clutches of the breeze. It snatched at her hood and threw it back, giving freedom once again to the errant strands of hair that danced and twirled around her face. Ewan pulled the door closed behind them, and watched her.

"Oh!" The lass's exclamation, softly expressed, yet so full of wonder, spoke of her delight.

From this unobscured viewpoint it seemed as though the world lay at their feet, the burnished sea stretching out to the dark horizon. Moonlight had strewn a wide path across the waves, turning them to polished silver. Urged on by the breeze, the waves tumbled onto the rocky shore and exploded into shards of frosted foam.

"'Tis a fine sight always." Ewan gazed out across sparkling expanse. "But especially on a night such as this."

"'Tis beyond splendid," the lass murmured, as if to herself. "The power of it stirs the soul."

"Aye, it does." Drawn by her quiet enthusiasm, Ewan moved to her side. "And its power should never be underestimated."

"I should very much like to see it in a storm." She took a tentative step forward. "Do the waves ever reach all the way up here?"

"The spray does at times, aye. Dinnae move too close to the edge, lass. A strong gust of wind will topple a wee thing like yourself."

"Is there a path somewhere, down to the shore?"

"Aye."

"Where is it?"

"Over yonder, where the shelf cuts in," Ewan replied. "But there'll be no clambering down the cliffs in the dark."

A sigh escaped her. "I suppose it wouldnae be wise."

Ewan grunted. "Maybe Alastair will allow you to go there before you leave."

The lass gave him a dubious look—one that said Alastair would never allow such a thing. "Aye, maybe."

She turned and continued her contemplation, but Ewan sensed a decline in her enthusiasm and, for some reason, it bothered him. It seemed the lass possessed a natural curiosity. One that had been newly awakened, he suspected, by her escape from whatever sheltered world she had inhabited thus far. It would be a pity not to indulge it a little. The words spilled out before he could stop them.

"I'll take you there myself, if you wish. Once the sun is up."

The offer obviously surprised her, for she snapped her head around to look at him, a slight frown on her brow. "That's very kind of you, Laird MacKellar," she said after a moment, turning her gaze back to the moonlit waves, "but I doubt we'll have the time."

Maybe it was the beauty of the night, shared with a bonny young lass who, for some unfathomable reason, intrigued him. Maybe it was nothing more than simple kindness on his part. Or maybe it was sheer, lunar madness that drove him to speak again.

"If it is what you want, I'll ensure we have time, my lady."

The remark garnered the same instant reaction as before, only this time, she appeared startled.

"Thank…" Her fingers went to her throat as she cleared it. "Thank you, Laird."

She sounded more apprehensive than appreciative. At first, Ewan didn't quite know what to make of it. Then it occurred to him. Maybe he was not the only one with misgivings about this revised marriage alliance. His thoughts had been presumptuous. And his behaviour contradictory.

The lass had been pledged to Ruaidri, the respected laird of her neighbouring clan. Now, however, she faced the possibility of a union with a battle-scarred Templar knight. A man who hadn't even tried to hide his disapproval and resentment from the moment she'd arrived. Indeed, he'd all but publicly denied her only hours before. Yet, here he was, exchanging pleasantries with her beneath the full moon, and promising to take her on a dawn excursion to the seashore.

"What am I doing?" he murmured, glancing skyward.

"Laird?"

Grimacing, he drew breath. "I must beg your forgiveness, my lady. I've treated you unfairly. Truth is, recent events have left me uncertain about many things, including the marriage agreement that brought you here. You were promised to my brother, after all. A man who has not yet been dead a month, may God rest his soul. Agreeing to take his place as your husband so soon after his demise feels like..."

"A betrayal?" she finished, a softness coming to her eyes. "I do understand, believe me. And I dinnae blame you at all for having reservations. I confess, I have a few myself."

He felt certain he didn't need to ask what they were. "I'm nae as frightening as I look, lass," he said, his subsequent smile meant to reassure.

To his surprise, she appeared mildly affronted. "If the scarring on your face troubles me, Laird MacKellar, 'tis merely because it implies you have suffered unspeakable pain. Otherwise, I dinnae find you frightening in the least, but I confess to having some concerns about the marriage agreement."

The first part of her declaration, voiced with profound sincerity, touched Ewan's heart. The latter part should have also agreed with him, for it served to support his own misgivings. So why, then, did he feel a pinch of disappointment?

"Might I ken what they are?"

"Simply that I…" Her eyes searched his face as her mind obviously searched for words. "I fear there are too many obstacles between us."

Ewan raised a brow. "Go on."

"You're a Templar knight. A monk." She brushed a loose strand of hair from her face. "To marry will mean surrendering your vows."

He dipped his head. "Aye, it will."

"And 'tis plain you are reluctant to do so.

"Also true. I confess I'll nae surrender them with ease. But, as laird, I have little choice, married or no'."

"Perhaps, but I cannae help but wonder if it might be better for us to wait."

"Yet your brother doesnae wish to wait, for some reason."

She wrinkled her nose. "Alastair is…"

"A stubborn arse?"

A smile curved her mouth. "I dinnae think I'd have said it quite that way, but aye, he can be. And I happen to agree with you—'tis a wee bit soon for all this, considering Ruaidri has nae been long gone."

For some reason, Ewan felt compelled to challenge her remark. "Yet, on the other hand," he said, "the sun will rise on the morrow, and every day after that till God decides otherwise. Life, in some fashion, will go on."

She blinked. "What are you saying?"

A good question. What am I saying? That I'm willing to spend the rest of my life with this lass? Eventually, I must take a wife. If not her, then who? And when?

"I'm nae sure." He shrugged. "Maybe I'm saying there's little point in waiting. If the agreement still stands, perhaps we should honour it."

Wide-eyed, she stared at him in silence for a few moments, and then lowered her gaze. "If that is what you've decided, then so be it."

"I have nae decided anything." Frowning, Ewan tipped her chin up, dismayed to see tears in her eyes. "For sure, I'll no' wed a lass who doesnae wish to be wed, if that be the case."

It was a question, although he had not formed it as one. In the short amount of time they'd spent together, Ewan had felt his stubborn resolve weakening. Quite simply, he liked the lass. She had a nice manner, and seemed possessed of an infectious enthusiasm for life—something that appealed to him. And the way she'd risen to Niall's defence had impressed him.

Nor was he blind to the allure of her femininity, although he would not allow his mind to dwell on her physical attributes. Lust, unbridled, had a way of steering men onto sinful paths, as he knew to his detriment.

He was still a knight of the Temple. Until such time as he surrendered his mantle and pledged his troth, any thoughts of an intimate nature would be tempered. God knows, he'd had years of practice. Chastity, at first, had proven to be a torment, one alleviated by ardent prayer, plus a fervent commitment to hours of physical training. Eventually, over time, Ewan's carnal desire had been controlled if not restrained. That was not to say, of course, that it would not be reignited in the marriage bed.

Unless he found himself with a reluctant bride.

Certainly, something about the lass nudged at his instincts. She gave him a vague impression of furtiveness, as if she knew some great secret but was not willing to share it. Perhaps it was nothing more than the shyness

Alastair had mentioned. In any case, she seemed to possess a measure of uncertainty. Not unlike his own.

"You're very kind, Laird MacKellar," she said. "Dinnae pay me any mind. I'm just a wee bit tired, is all."

Could that be it? Mere fatigue? Her response, though credible, still left him wondering. He decided not to pursue it. At least, not then and there.

"Understandable," he replied, tucking her hand into his arm again. "Allow me to escort you back inside, then, so you can rest. We have to walk around to the main gate, where I suppose we'll find out if Niall is paying attention or not."

"Please dinnae be hard on him," she said, as they set off. "Truly, it was not his fault."

"It was entirely his fault," Ewan replied. "But dinnae fash. I'll have words with him, but I'll no' bother with a lashing this time."

"A *lashing*?" He felt her scrutiny. "You would lash a man for such a thing?"

"Aye." Ewan's mouth twitched. "If no' for your pleading, lass, I'd be giving him a half-dozen strokes."

Her laughter escaped a few moments later, a sweet sound that made him catch his breath. "You're teasing me again, Laird MacKellar."

"Ewan," he said. "My name is Ewan."

"Ewan," she repeated, as if tasting the word.

"May I call you Elspeth?"

Her fingers twitched against his arm. "Aye, if you wish."

"Chosen by God."

"Pardon?"

"'Tis the meaning of your name. Chosen by God." He smiled. "Or so my sister informs me."

"Ah, I see." The lass appeared to ponder for a moment. "Alastair hoped to marry her."

"Aye, I ken."

"If she'd agreed," she murmured, "I likely wouldnae be here now."

Ewan grimaced. "While that is likely true, I'd prefer you didnae mention it to Morag. I fear she blames herself for Ruaidri's death."

She released a sharp gasp. "Curse my tongue! It was a careless observation. I didnae mean any harm."

"A fair observation too, but I would rather it be left unsaid."

"Of course. May God forgive me. I seem to be causing naught but trouble tonight." A sigh shuddered from her. "I'm sorry, Laird."

"Dinnae fash, lass." He leaned in. "And my name is Ewan."

Chapter Eleven

Cristie pulled her blanket up to her chin, curled into a ball, and buried her face in her pillow. She had been wrong to pray for Ewan MacKellar to be a kindly laird, a man who would do her no harm. Instead, she should have asked God for a brute. A mean-tempered, sanctimonious, battle-hardened knight, who held women in contempt.

It might have been easier, then, to think about betraying him.

But from what she'd seen so far, Ewan MacKellar was, indeed, a chivalrous man. Stubborn, she suspected, and certainly pious. But fair in his treatment of others, true to his beliefs, and gentle with women. He also valued integrity. It would not be wise, she mused, to deceive such a man.

"Any lass would be fortunate to be your wife," she whispered. "For sure, you dinnae deserve the likes of me. Please tell Alastair you havenae changed your mind. Tell him you dinnae want to marry me. Tell us we have to leave. Send us back to Dunraven this morning. Please, Laird MacKellar."

Please, Ewan.

But Ewan MacKellar's original aversion to the marriage alliance might have changed, thanks to Cristie's stupidity. Damn her curiosity. She should have stayed in her chamber instead of venturing out to look at some moonlit vista. Then again, she never thought for a moment she'd come face to face with the laird himself. Not at such an unsociable hour. And certainly not atop the gatehouse.

And why, by Odin's great beard, had she then agreed to go with him to the clifftop? To stand beside him, so close that, despite the breeze, she could feel the warmth emanating from his flesh, and smell his vague, masculine scent. Had the promise of a bonny ocean view tempted her, or had it been something else? Something less tangible but more intriguing.

Maybe she should have feigned distaste at the sight of his scarred face. Pretended she'd found his appearance offensive, rather than seeing a careless tumble of russet-coloured hair framing a noble brow, strong jaw, and a fine, full mouth.

She hadn't imagined his assessment of her, either—at first critical, even resentful, and then curious. Nothing that gave her cause to ponder. But then she thought she saw something else stir in the depths of his dark eyes.

Interest.

Any doubt of that perception disappeared when he offered to accompany her to the beach at sunrise. Her implication that there'd be no time for such an excursion had only made things worse. He'd gone even further, suggesting he'd make time. After that, he'd hinted that the marriage agreement might not be a bad thing after all.

Then, dear God, he'd called her by name—her *false* name—and invited her to address him with equal familiarity. At that moment, sickened by her deceit, she had almost confessed the truth of it.

But, more than Ewan MacKellar, she feared Alastair. Feared what he might do if she defied him. It seemed with every passing day the man became a little more reckless, like someone with naught to lose. Yet she failed to see how he could ever win. She also failed to see how she could ever begin to get away with a betrayal of such magnitude.

After returning from the cliff-top, Cristie had thanked the laird, professed fatigue, and returned to her bed. Not that she had any hope of sleeping, but hiding beneath the coverlet, for now, felt like the safest place to be. For sure, she had no intention of accompanying Ewan MacKellar to the shore.

However, evident from the muted sounds of clatter and chatter beyond her door, folks were stirring, preparing for the day. Cristie knew it wouldn't be long before she'd be obliged to resurface. She could only pray that Laird MacKellar had come to his previous senses, realizing the madness of moonlight had undoubtedly affected his mind. Indeed, since returning to her bed, she had prayed so hard, her head ached.

A knock came to the door, and Cristie held her breath. Maybe, if she feigned sleep, whoever it was might leave. But the knock came again, a little louder this time and accompanied by a muffled, female voice.

"My lady?"

Cristie squeezed her eyes shut. *Go away.*

The door opened a crack, evident from the soft creak, accompanied by yet another polite rap.

"My lady, forgive the disturbance, but your brother, Laird MacAulay, is insisting on speaking with you. I've been instructed to help you dress."

Cristie's stomach tightened. What was the urgency? Inwardly, she voiced yet another quick prayer, hoping that Ewan MacKellar had insisted they depart without further delay.

"Very well." Cristie rubbed her eyes and sat up. "Please, come in."

*

Cristie had been directed to the solar, where she found Alastair lounging in a chair by the hearth. Tasgall stood near the door, his job quite clear—to ensure privacy. He gave Cristie a brief, humourless smile as she entered. Undoubtedly, this meeting had been arranged with Laird MacKellar's knowledge and permission.

Cristie's throat went dry.

The sun had barely risen, yet already Alastair's eyes had a glaze to them. As usual, he had one hand wrapped around the stem of a goblet. He regarded Cristie with a satisfied expression and nodded to an adjacent chair.

She took it, arranged her skirts, and met Alastair's gaze.

"Well done, lass," he said, a corner of his mouth lifting. "I'm nae sure quite how you did it, but well done,"

Behind her, Tasgall cleared his throat.

"I dinnae ken what you mean, Alastair." Cristie swallowed. "I've done nothing."

"'Tis not what I heard." He leaned forward. "A moonlight tryst? Perfect."

God help me! What has been said? Cristie knotted her fingers in her lap and shook her head. "It was no tryst. I didnae intend to meet with Laird MacKellar at all, in fact. It was purely by chance."

"Nevertheless, meet him you did, and impressed him, by all accounts. A short while ago, he informed me that he's reconsidered and, assuming you're agreeable to it, will go ahead with the marriage. He's summoning a priest from somewhere, and the ceremony will take place tomorrow morning. It'll be a small gathering." Alastair sniffed and took a swig from his goblet. "MacKellar says he doesnae feel comfortable having a big celebration so soon after the death of his brother, which is understandable."

Oh, nay! Cristie felt the familiar prickle of tears. "But I'm no' agreeable to it, Alastair. I have never been agreeable to it."

His lip curled. "Dinnae start, Cristie. This has already been discussed."

"Aye, but having met the man last night, I can tell you that Laird MacKellar isnae a fool. I cannae possibly pretend to be someone else! He'll see through me. He'll see through my lies. I'm certain of it."

"Then dinnae lie." Alastair glanced at the door and gritted his teeth. "And keep your damn voice down."

"Dinnae lie?" Bewildered, Cristie shook her head. "What are you saying?"

"I'm saying dinnae lie." He leaned forward. "MacKellar has never met Elspeth. No one here has. So, for the most part, you can just be yourself, and no one will suspect a thing. 'Tis only your name that needs to be false."

Dear God. Cristie shook her head again. "You ask much of me, Alastair."

She didn't dare mention that she now harboured some genuine esteem for Ewan MacKellar. That deceiving him felt even more loathsome than before.

"The sooner you find out what was on that wagon, and what became of it, the sooner you can return to Dunraven. Tasgall will return in a fortnight or so to see what you've learned, and depending on his report, you can leave the rest to me."

Cristie sighed. *Whatever that means.*

Tasgall cleared his throat again, which drew a glance from Cristie. The man lifted a brow and gave her a tight smile. Was it meant to reassure? If so, it failed.

It seemed Ewan MacKellar had agreed to set aside his Templar trappings, surrender his holy vows, and pledge himself to her. For the rest of his life.

And it would all be for naught.

Cristie dared to look to the future and saw nothing but anguish.

Chapter Twelve

Friday, November 11th, 1307

Earlier that morning, Ewan had closed the lid on his trunk and condemned his Templar robes to darkness. In removing them for good, he'd expected to feel more regret that he actually felt. It was Jacques who had helped alleviate the strain of progression from Templar knight to clan chief.

"At heart, you will always be a knight of the Temple, Ewan," he'd said. "The basis of our faith and courage is not something to be lost, but something to be kept always. Your grandfather's legacy lives on, as will yours, through your sons."

Soon after, the small group had gathered in the small chapel to witness the marriage. Candleflames flickered atop the altar, and the heady aroma of incense hung in the air. Father Iain's voice echoed softly off the walls as he conducted the holy service.

The lass who would, God willing, carry Ewan's sons, gazed up at him, her flawless skin burnished by the glow of candlelight. Her eyes, fringed with a wealth of thick lashes, shone like deep pools of indigo. Her abundance of black hair had been neatly braided and woven with dried sprigs of lavender and heather.

She wore a woollen robe of deep blue. It sat loosely on her, Ewan noticed, as if she'd recently lost weight. A white girdle, embroidered with silver and blue flowers, cradled her hips, and her right hand clasped a sprig of white heather, brought from *Lorg Coise Dhè* by Father Iain.

"You look very bonny, Elspeth," Ewan had told her, before the ceremony began. He'd been rewarded with a shy smile.

Now, Father Iain paused, waiting for her to repeat the vow he had just spoken.

"I…" Her lip trembled. "I, El…Elspeth Kirstie MacAulay, take thee, Ewan Tormod MacKellar, to be my wedded husband…"

She was undoubtedly nervous. When at last Ewan slid the ring onto her finger, a tear slid down her cheek, though she countered it with another smile.

Once the final blessing had been done, Ewan took his new wife's hand and led her into the great hall for a quiet celebration. The idea of a fully-fledged wedding feast, with all its revelry and bawdiness, had not sat easy on Ewan's conscience. It was yet too soon after Ruaidri's death.

Still, food and drink were plentiful, and the pall that had sat over Castle Cathan in recent weeks eased somewhat as the feast progressed. His bride, however, said little and ate even less. Ewan noticed her eyeing her wedding ring, her brow furrowed.

The small, twisted circle of gold had belonged to his mother, though it hadn't been used as a wedding band.

"I'll get you your own as soon as I can, lass," he said. "This has all been a wee bit rushed."

The frown vanished as she clenched her fingers. "There's nae need," she said. "This one is fine."

"Still, I think it might be nicer for you to have your own." Ewan leaned in. "We'll no' stay here much longer, Elspeth. 'Tis yet early, and the day is fine, so I thought I might make good on my promise from the other night and take you down to the shore. If you'd like, that is. I reckon there'll be a bonny sunset this eve."

She nodded. "Um, aye, that would be nice. The sun at Dunraven goes down behind the mountains, so we dinnae actually see it set."

"Maybe you'd like to eat something first. You've hardly touched your food."

"I cannae eat. I… I'm a wee bit nervous, is all."

"I understand," Ewan replied. "I'm a wee bit nervous myself."

Her eyes widened. "You are?"

"Aye." He lowered his voice. "I'm nae sure if you're aware, lass, but I've never been married before either."

"Oh." A blush spread across her cheeks as she dropped her gaze to her plate.

Ewan chuckled. "Dinnae fash. I'm sure, between us, we'll figure out what this marriage thing is all about. We have the rest of our lives, so we can take our—"

A man's raised voice caught Ewan's attention. He turned to see Jacques, sword half drawn, on his feet and face-to-face with Alastair MacAulay.

The surrounding buzz of chatter faded as Ewan rose. "What's going on?" he demanded.

"This *man…*" Jacques all but spat out the word, "owes your sister an apology."

Alastair's lip lifted in a sneer. "And this *foreigner* needs to learn his place."

"And both of you will stop this now, please!" Morag, standing behind Jacques, threw Ewan a desperate glance. "'Tis my brother's wedding day!"

Ewan lifted a brow. "What did he say to you, Morag?"

Morag shook her head. "It doesnae matter, Ewan."

"It was but a jest." Alastair hiccupped and staggered backwards. "Tell your cohort to sit his sanctimonious arse down."

"I'll tell you what he said." Jacques' lip furled also. "He implied your sister, in refusing to wed him, had missed an opportunity to... *know* him better. And then he *fondled* himself. It was a crude, insulting gesture, and he will apologise for it."

"Aye, he most certainly will." Ewan narrowed his eyes. "Apologise, MacAulay. 'Twould be a pity to have to throw you out of your sister's wedding."

A movement to Ewan's side caught his attention, and he glanced over to see Tasgall making his way to the dais.

Aye, and here comes Alastair's hound. Now we might have a problem, because I ken for certain Jacques willnae back down.

"Alastair, please! I dinnae want any trouble."

Ewan turned and blinked at the sight of his wife, on her feet, her gaze levelled at Alastair.

Alastair scowled at her and opened his mouth as if to reply, but instead, held up a hand, halting Tasgall's approach.

"I apologize for my rudeness, my lady," he said, dipping his head at Morag. He then threw a sneer at Jacques. "There. Are you satisfied?"

Jacques mumbled something unintelligible, sheathed his sword, and sat down. Morag rolled her eyes at Ewan as she took her seat as well.

Ewan managed to suppress a smile. Not that he found Alastair's insult amusing in the least. Jacques' response to it, however, had amused him. The Basque had developed an obvious fondness for Morag, a protectiveness that had shown itself from the start.

Ewan heaved a breath and held out a hand to his bride. "Come on, lass," he said. "Let's leave them to it."

She gave him a dubious look. "Are you no' worried there'll be trouble?"

He shook his head. "I'm no' worried in the least. I dinnae believe your brother is daft enough to push Jacques too far." *Or brave enough.*

"My brother is drunk," she murmured, placing her hand in Ewan's. "Knowing him, he'll be away to sleep it off soon."

"His usual routine?"

She sighed and picked up the sprig of white heather. "Aye, I'm afraid so."

Ewan ignored the soft jeers and whistles as they left the hall, though he sensed his wife's discomfort. "They dinnae mean any harm," he said, his hand tightening around hers as he guided her into the hallway. "Wait here. I'll send a maid to fetch your cloak. You might want to change your wee slippers as well."

"Nay, I'll go." She tugged her hand free, lifted her skirts, and started for the stairs. "'Tis nae bother."

*

"May Christ forgive me."

Cristie perched her arse on the edge of her bed and pressed her right hand to her heart as if to quell its wretched clatter. At the same time, she frowned at the ring on her left hand. The band of gold that had belonged to Ewan's mother felt heavy on her finger. The weight of guilt, no doubt. Then again, a ring of her own, gifted from Ewan, would be even more of a burden on her conscience.

The ring was not the only hand-me-down, either. Cristie's blue robe had belonged to Alastair's mother, who had obviously been somewhat more curvaceous, judging by its loose fit. Preferable, though, to wearing one of

Elspeth's cast-offs as a wedding gown. That would have been sordid beyond words. Cristie shuddered at the thought.

And what of the night to come? Did she dare refuse Ewan MacKellar his husbandly rights? She could surely come up with some excuse. She prayed he'd be lenient. After all, he'd shown her nothing but kindness so far.

But for how long?

Her throat tightened at the thought of having to use the small bundle Elspeth had given her.

She steered her mind elsewhere and sniffed the sprig of heather Ewan had given her. She'd heard of the legendary white flowers, but had never seen them till today. The priest had brought the sprig with him. Cristie wondered from where and resolved to ask Ewan.

Maybe, if she asked, he'd tell her where the Templar treasure was, too. And then she could leave. *But what...?* She closed her eyes. *What if Alastair is wrong? What if there is no treasure? Or what if Ewan refuses to speak of it? What then?*

"Stop," she whispered, setting the sprig of heather aside. Using both hands, she rubbed her temples, trying to stem the chaotic whirl of thoughts in her head. How long had she been sitting there? Ewan would be wondering as to her whereabouts.

She changed her shoes, shrugged on her cloak, and scurried down the stairs, praying for strength and wishing she were a thousand miles away from Castle Cathan.

"Ah, here she is." Ewan stood with the priest who had overseen the ceremony. Cristie's befuddled brain took a moment to remember the man's name.

She inclined her head. "Father Iain."

"My lady." The priest gave her a smile. "I understand you're going to watch the sunset. I should think it'll be a bonny one tonight. Speaking of which, if you'll both excuse me, I must be getting home."

"Gabriel will escort you, Father," Ewan said.

"Aye, he told me. He's likely waiting for me already." He bobbed his head. "Blessings to you both, and may God keep you."

Ewan lifted the man's hand to his lips. "God keep you too, Father Iain."

Cristie offered a smile, and watched the little man scurry off down the hallway.

Ewan held out a hand. "Ready?"

"Aye," she replied. The warm flesh of his palm felt callused against her fingers, his grip strong, yet gentle. The sensation all but stole the breath from her lungs. And damn her disobedient heart! *Why does it skip whenever he touches me?* "Does Father Iain live far?"

"Nay. An hour's ride, maybe. But he's older than the hills, so I feel better having Gabriel go with him."

"Is that where the white heather grows? I should like to see it."

"It grows not far from where he lives."

"You've known him long?"

"All my life." They stepped outside, where the sun already sat low in the sky. "He was a friend of my grandfather's."

"Who was a Templar, aye?"

"Aye, for a time."

Cristie paused, arranging her thoughts. "I can imagine it must have been a shock to have to leave France as you did. Have you had any news?"

His grip tightened slightly. "None yet."

"You must have left in a hurry."

"Aye. We had little warning."

They came to the postern gate and Cristie waited while Ewan tugged it open.

"So, you just left everything behind?" She stepped out onto the clifftop, her question forgotten as she took in the view. "Oh, Ewan. 'Tis magnificent."

The sun, at this time of year, did not stay above the horizon for long, and the shortest days were yet to come. Already, the western skies had taken on a fiery glow as the northern night approached.

"This way." Ewan led her toward the section of cliff he'd mentioned the previous night.

Cristie clasped her hood tight at her throat, her eyes watering as the sharp breeze buffeted her face. Ewan led her down the path—a sandy trail that hugged the cliff face as it sloped down to a small, crescent beach.

At the bottom, Cristie laughed with delight as her shoes sank into the sand. "'Tis nearly as white as snow." She bent to touch it. "And so soft! The shoreline around Loch Raven is mostly pebbles and mud."

"Ruaidri and I used to play down here as children," Ewan said. "Morag, too. We'd build castles and forts in the sand. Ruaidri always had to be the laird. Said it was his right, being the elder son."

The wistfulness in his voice drew Cristie's attention. She straightened to look at him and placed a hand on his arm. "Maybe we should no' have come, Ewan."

His expression softened. "Nay, lass, I wanted you to see it. Besides, I dinnae mind speaking of Ruaidri. My memories of him are valuable to me. Especially now."

"I'm sure you must miss him."

He grimaced. "I have *missed* him because I didnae come home. 'Tis a regret I must learn to live with."

"I'm sorry."

"So am I." Smiling, he reached for her hand again. "Enough melancholy. 'Tis a day for celebrating, since it seems I've found myself a bonny wee bride. Let's walk down by the water."

Even as Ewan's fingers curled around hers, Cristie felt a cold jolt of reality. For a brief moment, as Ewan had spoken of Ruaidri, she had forgotten about her false identity. She had simply been Cristie Ferguson—an ordinary lass on a windswept beach, listening to a man share fond memories of his dead brother, and admitting his regrets. She'd been utterly absorbed by the sentiment of it, her empathy genuine.

It frightened her to think that she could feel so at ease with Ewan MacKellar, that being with him could feel so natural.

Because Cristie Ferguson could never be with him.

Never.

Chapter Thirteen

Earlier that day, Ewan had fished a shell out of a tidal pool and given it to his new bride. She'd accepted it with unabashed delight, smiling as she'd turned it this way and that. True, it was a fine specimen—a large spiral, fully intact, its ridged surface mottled with leopard-like spots. Its rosy aperture, as smooth as glass, matched the colour of the evening sky. Ewan had oft seen similar shells in the warmer climes of the world but couldn't recall ever seeing such a thing on a Highland beach.

Now, the lass's hand visibly trembled as she placed the seashell atop the bedside table, next to her sprig of white heather.

"If you put the aperture to your ear," Ewan said, unbuckling his sword belt, "you'll be able to hear the sea."

She turned to him, her expression dubious. "The sea?"

"Try it."

She did so, smiling as her eyes widened. "How... how can this be?"

"I dinnae ken, in truth." Encouraged by her response, he returned her smile. "But I'm glad it pleases you, Elspeth."

Like a candle being extinguished, the lass's smile vanished and her expression sobered, as if she'd just remember where she was, and why.

While on the beach—for the most part at least—she'd appeared to be at ease. They'd walked and talked, stopping here and there to explore the rock pools, admire the sunset, and watch the waves. Ewan had been infected by the lass's enthusiasm for her surroundings. His life as a Templar also fascinated her, judging by the questions she'd asked. For the most part, he'd humoured her curiosity, though doctrine forced him to deflect some of her enquiries.

Her intelligence was unquestionable, yet Ewan had the impression she lacked education. *Somewhat irregular for a noble lass.* She readily admitted she couldn't write, although she expressed a desire to learn.

When asked about her own childhood, she'd shied away and changed the subject. Ewan had let it go. His own upbringing had also been somewhat irregular. Unlike most sons, neither he nor Ruaidri had been fostered out, but trained in the ways of knighthood by their father.

As the glory of the sunset blazed across the sky, Ewan had dared to raise his bride's hand to his lips. He'd heard her breath catch and felt her hand stiffen.

After, he'd threaded his fingers through hers and led her back to the castle, where they'd gone straight to Ewan's chamber—their chamber. While they'd been gone, it had been made ready for them.

The light from several candles cast a soft glow over the space. A bowl of fragrant dried herbs sat on the bedside table, their subtle scents suffusing the air. A tray of bread, cheese, and fruit had been placed on another table by the window. Beside it, a flagon of wine and two goblets. The canopied bed had been spread with fresh furs, its linen sheets doubtless warmed with hot-stones.

It was an intimate welcome.

And the lass had become as skittish as a hare.

She replaced the shell on the bedside table, hesitating a moment before turning to face Ewan once more. An image arose in his mind—that of a mouse caught in a trap.

But then, Ewan was not without some trepidation of his own. None of his experiences compared to this. Oh, he knew how to pleasure a lass. It was not something a man forgot, even when that man had abstained for many years. But he'd readily admit to a lack of experience in the art of wooing and seduction. Certainly, he had never lain with an innocent. The women he'd bedded had all been willing, oft times their services paid for. Nor would he ever force a lass to surrender to him, especially not his wife.

"Are you hungry, lass?" he asked, gesturing to the food tray. "You didnae eat much today."

"Not terribly, in truth. Later, maybe."

"Right." He cleared his throat, strode over to a chest in the corner, and removed a parcel from it, its linen-wrapping neatly tied with a blue ribbon. "Sit with me then," he said, settling himself on the edge of the bed and patting the spot beside him. "I have something for you."

She fidgeted and tied her fingers in knots at her waist. "Ewan, I think you should ken—"

"I'll never make you do anything you dinnae wish to do, lass." He patted the spot beside him again. "Please, just sit with me."

With some hesitation, she did as bid, dropping her gaze to her lap. Ewan's heart quickened as he breathed in her scent, its sweet bouquet already familiar to him. He took a moment to examine her. A rosy hue coloured her cheeks— put there, likely, by the sea breeze. The same breeze had also dishevelled her hair, pulling several strands free from her braids. Her downcast eyes allowed him to better see her thick fringe of dark lashes, with their tantalizing curl.

She was, he thought, a picture of innocence and beauty. And she was his. He felt a sudden flare of protectiveness, the strength of which surprised him.

"I wanted to give you some wedding gifts, but I confess I wasnae quite sure what you might like." He handed her the parcel. "So, I hope you like these."

"Thank you." For a moment she appeared bewildered, as if the concept of receiving a gift was foreign to her. "But… I have nothing to give you."

"No matter." He gestured to the parcel. "Go ahead. Open it."

With the parcel resting on her lap, she loosened the ribbon and unfolded the wrapping to expose what lay within. Her soft gasp drew a half-smile from Ewan. Then, to his gratification, she laughed—a short, sweet, sound of delight.

"Oh, 'tis so *bonny*!" She brought the comb closer to better examine it, stroking its polished surface with a fingertip. "I dinnae believe I have ever seen the like. What is it made of?"

"Tortoiseshell," he replied. "Do you like it?"

"Very much." Eyes bright, she flashed him a smile. "Thank you. And what is this?"

Setting the comb aside, she lifted a silk shawl from the wrapping and held it up. Like a banner, it unfurled, revealing swirling patterns of sapphire blue and emerald green.

"I thought the blue would match your eyes," Ewan said, and then frowned as the silence stretched out. The lass simply sat there, gazing at the shawl, saying nothing. Ewan shifted. "It doesnae please you?"

To his dismay, she shook her head.

"Ah." He shifted again. "Is it the colours you dinnae care for?"

"You misunderstand, Ewan. 'Tis simply that I cannae find the words." She snuggled the shawl against her cheek. "'Tis beautiful. So soft! And the colours are glorious."

Ewan felt a warmth in his groin and fought off an urge to touch her. "I'm glad you like it."

"I love it. I love *them*. You brought them with you? From France?"

He wondered, vaguely, if that mattered. "Nay, I acquired them here."

"Oh." Her brows lifted. "I didnae ken such things could be found hereabouts."

Unable to resist, Ewan reached over and lifted a sprig of lavender from her hair, allowing his knuckles to graze her cheek. "I'm afraid the wind stole much of your garland."

The response was instant, akin to a curtain being pulled, or a door closing. Body tense—and clutching her gifts—the lass slid from the bed. "Um, I should put these somewhere safe."

Ewan bit back a sigh. "Elspeth."

"Aye?"

"There's naught to fear."

"Do you mind if I put them back in this chest? For now, anyway."

"What is it you're afraid of, lass?" He heard the lid of the chest open and then close. "The act of love is a fine thing when shared 'tween husband and wife. A natural thing."

A sigh drifted to his ear. Then she came and stood before him. "I'm no' exactly afraid, Ewan. 'Tis just…"

He rose, took her hands in his, and studied her. Contrary to her denial, fear lingered in her eyes. "'Tis just what?"

Her chest rose and fell as she looked down at their joined hands. "I have something to ask of you, and I pray you will try and understand why I ask it." She met his gaze. "I fear, though, it might be... too much for you to allow."

Frowning, he inclined his head. "Ask it then, and we'll see."

"I ask that... that you grant me some time. Before you... before *we* consummate our union."

His brow cleared. "Is that all? Aye, of course. We can eat, if you like. Have some wine before—"

"Nay, I..." She shook her head. "I mean, some extended time, Ewan. A sennight, perhaps, or even a wee bit longer. I would prefer to know you better before I give myself to you. You're still a stranger to me."

It took Ewan a moment to grasp what she'd said, and several more to respond. The unorthodox request more than warranted a denial. The lass was of age, and he had his rights. Yet, upon consideration, he had little choice but to acquiesce, since the alternative would give him no pleasure. But he would not concede without a stipulation of his own.

"I'll no' pretend to be happy about it," he replied, "but I'm a man used to restraint, and shall continue to practice it for now. As I told you this morning, we have the rest of our lives to figure out this marriage. That said, I would ask something of you in return."

She blinked. "What is it?"

"Dinnae shy away from me anymore, Elspeth. I might be a stranger, but I'm still your husband. Let me at least show you affection without reprove. From now on, I would see trust in your eyes rather than fear. You have no cause to fear me."

Her lip trembled. "Aye, of course. Thank you, Ewan."

Ewan nodded an acknowledgement and bit back a sigh.

Lasses. They were more complicated than he remembered. He glanced at his sword, where it rested against the wall. Seemed like he'd be busy in the practice yard for the next few days, working off some unspent urges.

His gaze then drifted to the bed. Being a monk had not made him a saint.

He released her hands. "Turn around, lass."

The familiar wariness arose in her eyes. "What—?"

"Trust me. Turn around."

She did so, saying nothing as Ewan loosened the laces on her gown, though the rise and fall of her chest implied that her angst remained

After this, he doubted he'd see such fear again. It was a test for her. And it was a trial for him. The soft nape of her neck beckoned, begging to be kissed. The scent of her tantalized, causing him to harden. "There," he murmured, dropping his hands. "When you're ready to retire, you should have nae trouble removing it."

Jaw set, he turned, grabbed a pillow and a couple of furs from the bed, and spread them on the floor beneath the window. He felt her bewilderment, but said nothing.

"What are you doing?" she asked, her voice little more than a whisper,

Ewan scratched his jaw. "Preparing my bed."

"But... you cannae sleep on the floor!"

"You cannae expect me to lie beside you, Elspeth. 'Tis asking too much."

"Then I will sleep on the floor!"

"Nay, you'll sleep in the bed. I'll be fine. The furs are comfortable enough." The guilty expression on the lass's face actually amused him, and he surrendered to a genuine smile. "But right now, I'm starving. Will you eat with me?"

Later, much later, Ewan lay on his furs and listened to the gentle rhythm of his wife's breathing as she slept. The enigma of her left him seeking answers. She possessed obvious passion, yet appeared to be shackled by uncertainty and fear. He wondered at the source. An event in her childhood, perhaps, which she found difficult to speak of.

The lass wanted time, and he would give it to her. Partly because, besides the fear he'd seen in her eyes, he'd noticed something else. Something that made him believe their union would, eventually, be all he hoped for.

Chapter Fourteen

"**She's** descended from a mare that belonged to my grandmother," Ewan said, his arms folded atop the gate. "Once this cursed rain stops, we'll go for a ride, and you can try her out. She's been well schooled and is a gentle wee thing. She'll give you nae trouble."

As if to agree, the white mare nickered softly.

"I have her elder sister." Morag pointed. "That bonny wee piebald down there. Her name is Aggie. You'll have to think of a name for this one."

Cristie, standing beside Ewan, stroked the mare's nose. "She's beautiful. I hardly ken what to say." Not a lie. She really did *not* know what to say. Any display of gratitude would be merely an act, and she wanted to weep for the dishonesty of it. Such a gift could never really be hers.

Morag shrugged. "Say, 'Thank you, Ewan, for this gift.'"

Cristie couldn't help but laugh. "Thank you, Ewan, for this *beautiful* gift."

"You're welcome, *mo chridhe*," he said, his smile brief.

Her treacherous heart quickened, as it did each time Ewan used a term of endearment with her.

"A gift of necessity," Morag said, "since your charming brother took your wee horse back with him."

Cristie grimaced. "It wasnae my horse, in truth."

"Still, I cannae fathom why the silly arse would be so mean as to—"

"Morag." Ewan gave her a pointed look.

She shrugged. "Sorry. Nay, I'm not sorry. Alastair *is* an arse. 'Tis a blessing you dinnae seem to have any of his traits, Elspeth. 'Tis cold out here, so I'm going in. I promised Jacques I'd beat him at chess again."

"Aye, we'll come too," Ewan said. "Unless you want to stay a while longer?" This last to Cristie.

"Nay." She shivered, a reaction to Morag's observation more than anything else. One day, they would all know the truth about her. They would understand that they had all been wrong. That she was as bad as Alastair, if not worse. "I'm a wee bit cold as well."

Ewan gave her a concerned look and slid his hand into hers. "Come."

Cristie's heart quickened again. His voice, his touch, simply being near him—all these things set her pulse rattling.

Nine days had gone by since the wedding, but it felt longer. With each passing day—and night—it became more and more difficult for Cristie to maintain her false identity and to keep Ewan at arm's length. Not that he'd shown any sign of impatience or frustration. To the contrary. He had courted her magnificently.

But that had actually made things worse

The burden on Cristie's conscience, and on her heart, had become a misery. She could neither deny nor arrest her growing attraction to Ewan, and had not thought to feel as strongly for him as she did. One thing she knew for certain, this fallacy could not continue.

She'd already considered running away. Absconding in the depths of night, and making her way back to Dunraven. The thought of such a venture terrified her, but she increasingly had little choice. Except, maybe, to confess all, and throw herself on Ewan's mercy.

But that would mean betraying her kin. And her clan.

She wondered when Tasgall might show up. Soon, she hoped, then she could beg him to take her home. Alastair's mad scheme had all been for naught. None of her enquiries led her to believe that any kind of wealth or Templar treasure had been hidden away at Castle Cathan. She had even explored the place for herself, to no avail. She had seen an empty wagon in the stable, unsure of whether it had been the one supposedly brought back by Ewan. If so, it had likely carried food, armour and weapons. Nothing more.

Ewan's hand tightened on hers. "Where are you, lass?"

She blinked and drew breath. "Sorry," she said, lifting her skirts as they climbed the steps to the keep. "I drifted away there for a moment."

"Are you ill? You've been pale of late."

"Nay, I'm fine."

"Homesick?"

The question almost made her laugh. "Maybe a little."

Ewan grunted and looked up at the dreary sky. "If the weather improves, we can arrange to visit Dunraven if you like."

Cristie's gut clenched. "Aye, that might be nice."

If I asked him for the moon, I suspect he'd find a way to capture it for me. He doesnae deserve this treachery. God help me.

Despite her denials of ill health, Ewan fussed over her that afternoon, tucking a blanket around her as they sat in his private chamber. On dreary days such as this, when the weather confined them indoors, he would tell her stories of the places he had seen. And she would listen, enthralled by conjured images of lands faraway; France, Spain, Egypt, and the Holy Land.

He described them well, making it easy for her to imagine the scenery and the people. That afternoon, he told her of the mirages in the desert. False images of palm trees and watering holes that beckoned the weary and the thirsty. And an illusion of a great sea, spread out over the sand, shimmering in the sun.

"But there is no water there," he said. "At midday, the sand is so hot you cannae walk on it without shoes."

"You never talk about the conflict," Cristie said. "Is it too painful?"

He gave her a sharp look. "Why would you want to hear about that?"

"I dinnae want to hear about it, precisely. But you were a Templar, there to fight for God. And obviously you did. So, I wonder why you never speak of it."

Ewan drew a slow breath and looked away. "You wouldnae recognize me, lass," he said, at last.

Cristie frowned. "What do you mean?"

"Battle does something to a man." He levelled his gaze at her. "'Tis as if an unknown being steps into his body and uses it. He cannae stop it. To resist it is to die. So, he gives it freedom. He allows it to maim and kill without mercy. But in the bloody aftermath of battle, he is forced to face the truth."

"The truth?"

"That the unknown being is him." He crossed himself. "The merciless killer is him. The truth of it can be difficult to bear. I know of some men who have found it impossible."

Cristie gripped the arm of her chair. "Oh, but Ewan, you cannae—"

A sharp rap came to the door.

Ewan heaved a sigh. "Come."

Morag popped her head around the door, looking decidedly sour-faced. "You have a visitor, Elspeth."

*

"Clothes?" Face flushed, Ewan regarded Tasgall with a look of disbelief. "You came all this way to bring my wife some *clothes*?"

"She didnae bring many with her from Dunraven." Tasgall set a bag down at Cristie's feet. "Alastair though she might need them, and—"

Ewan scoffed. "He thinks me incapable of providing for her? And you will address me as 'laird'."

They stood in a quiet corner at the back of the great hall. The shock of seeing Tasgall at Castle Cathan still had Cristie's head reeling. It seemed a prayer had been answered. Not that she would leave Ewan without feeling a good measure of heartache.

She placed a hand on his arm. "I'm sure Alastair didnae mean it that way, Ewan."

Tasgall cleared his throat. "If you'll just hear me out, Laird MacKellar. A few of these items belonged to Lady MacAulay, Elspeth's mother, may God rest her soul. Alastair felt Elspeth might like them."

Cristie tamped down an urge to vomit. Tasgall's explanation sounded ridiculous. Utterly implausible. Apparently, Ewan thought so too.

"Bollocks," he said. "You're lying, Tasgall. Dinnae take me for a fool. Just tell why you're here. What does Alastair want this time?"

Certain she was about to faint, Cristie tucked a hand into Ewan's elbow for support. He gave her a swift glance as his arm tightened around her fingers. Tasgall regarded her too, his brow furrowed.

"You're right, Laird MacKellar," he said, after a moment. "The clothes were naught more than a ruse. I'm here to enquire, on Laird MacAulay's behalf, about Elspeth."

Cristie felt Ewan's arm muscles twitch. "Explain."

"Laird MacAulay is worried about his sister," Tasgall said. "He knew she wasnae too keen on the marriage, so he sent me to make sure she is well and happy. 'Tis as simple as that. He'd have come himself, but he's a wee bit under the weather right now."

Cristie didn't think the second explanation to be any more plausible than the first. Then again, Alastair had a penchant for erratic behaviour, which possibly added credence to Tasgall's unlikely tale.

Ewan gave Cristie another glance and then turned a skeptical gaze to Tasgall. "And if I told you I beat the lass every night, what would you do?"

Tasgall tensed, visibly. "Surely, you dinnae... If that were so, I'd be obliged to tell Laird MacAulay."

"And what could *he* do? She's my wife, which means she is no longer his responsibility."

"I should imagine he'd pay you a visit anyway, but 'tis of nae consequence, since I dinnae see any evidence that she's been harmed." He looked at Cristie. "Have you?"

Cristie gasped. "Of course not. You can tell Alastair that I'm—"

"You can tell your *laird* that his sister is perfectly fine," Ewan said. "Though in truth, I find it hard to believe that he cares about her as much as you're implying. He didnae even bid her farewell after the wedding. Just left without a word."

Tasgall scowled. "He was nae feeling too good that day."

"I wonder why," Ewan muttered. "You may rest here a while, sirrah, but I want you gone by morning. And in case I dinnae speak to you again, be sure to tell your laird that any future concerns about my wife will be voiced by him personally. Not delivered by his lap dog."

Tasgall's hand dropped to where his sword hilt would have been had his weapon not already been confiscated. "I'll be sure to tell him, Laird MacKellar," he replied, hostility dripping from his words.

"Um, do you mind if I speak with Tasgall for a few minutes, Ewan?" Cristie asked. "I just have some questions about… about Brochan and some others at Dunraven. People I miss."

"Aye, I do mind." Ewan grimaced and rubbed the back of his neck. "But go ahead and ask your questions. I'll be in my chamber."

Cristie barely waited till Ewan had left the hall. She glanced about, thankful to see no one nearby. "Thank God you're here, Tasgall."

He frowned. "Why? What's happened? Have you found anything?"

"I just need to get out of here. Can we leave tonight?"

"But have you found anything?"

"Nay. But I cannae do this anymore."

"You have to wait a wee while longer." Tasgall shrugged. "Another ten days or so, Alastair said."

Cristie gasped. "Another ten…? Nay, please, I cannae. I want to go home, Tasgall."

"Alastair also said—"

"I dinnae give a shite what Alastair also said." Cristie gritted her teeth. "You have to take me back with you."

Tasgall shook his head. "You'd be seen leaving, lass. I cannae risk it."

"Well, you have to risk it at some point, so why not tonight? I can sneak out of the postern gate and meet you around the front."

"Alastair will no' be pleased, Cristie."

"Elspeth!" she hissed, glancing about. "And I dinnae care if Alastair is angry. I just cannae stay here anymore. I'll wait till Ewan is asleep and then I'll sneak downstairs to find you. Take a pallet by the door here, so I dinnae have to come all the way in."

Frowning, he raked his gaze over her. "You've no' been badly treated?"

"Nay." *I have never been treated so well.* She bit down against a sudden rise of tears. "I have to go, Tasgall. I'll see you later, all right?"

A growl sounded in his throat. "All right."

*

Cristie bent her head, pulled her braid over her shoulder, and closed her eyes. This would be the last time she'd feel Ewan's fingers brushing across her neck. The last time she'd hear his soft, focused breathing as he undid the laces on her robe.

It had become something of a night-time ritual. Intimate, yet innocent. He seemed to be taking longer tonight. She felt him pause, and his hands moved upwards till they rested on her shoulders. This, he had not done before. She held her breath.

The silence implied he had done the same.

His fingertips pressed gently into her flesh as his thumbs drew small circles at the base of her neck. Cristie pulled in a short breath as a delicious shiver slid down her spine. She should move away. Twist out of his grasp. Tonight, of all nights, she needed to be strong, and his touch weakened her.

Stop. Please. Stop.

His kiss brushed across the nape of her neck, soft and secretive, like a whisper.

And then he stepped away.

Cristie waited, hoping he'd touch her again and praying he wouldn't. She didn't dare turn around. Not immediately. For he might see the blur of tears in her eyes and misunderstand their meaning.

So, she blinked several times, lifted her head, and filled her lungs. Somewhat settled, she turned to see him arranging his furs and pillow on the floor, as he did every night. Every morning, he moved them back onto the bed.

"How is everyone at Dunraven?" he asked, rising to his feet and regarding her as if nothing had just happened. "Did Tasgall answer your questions?"

She nodded. "Aye, he did. Everyone is fine, thank you. Well, except for Alastair, of course, who is apparently under the weather."

"Hmm." A muscle ticked in his jaw. "I'm sorry if I was a wee bit harsh earlier. I'm afraid I dinnae like Tasgall much."

Cristie smiled. "Aye, I can tell. He's never done me any harm, though. And he's very loyal to Alastair."

Ewan's eyes narrowed slightly as he regarded her. "Did you choose a name yet?"

"A name?"

"For the wee mare."

"Ah." She shrugged off her robe, kicked off her slippers, and clambered up onto the bed in her shift. "Nay, not yet. I'll try and think of one before I go to sleep."

Later, Cristie lay awake, staring into darkness, listening to Ewan's breathing. Before too long, his gentle snores told her he'd fallen asleep. Yet still she waited, needing to be sure. Assured at last, she left her bed, slid her feet into her shoes, and gathered up her cloak.

The chamber door gave a slight creak as it opened. Cristie cursed inwardly, holding her breath as she waited to see if Ewan had been disturbed. But his quiet snores continued. After closing the door behind her with a little more care, she scurried down the candlelit stairs.

It felt like the dead of night, the hallways shadowed and silent. Sounds of slumber drifted out of the hall from those who slept within. Cristie tiptoed to the doorway and squinted into the gloom.

The glow of the fire and an hour-candle cast enough light to at least make out some detail. Cristie looked left and right, seeking Tasgall's pallet, which should have been by the door. Finding it proved to be easy, since there was only one pallet anywhere near the door. But it was empty.

Tasgall, it seemed, had gone.

Shivering, Cristie went and sat on the stairs, trying to see a way forward. She had choices, none of them easy. She could continue with the deception and continue to refuse to consummate the marriage. She could leave, sneak out of the postern gate, and make her way to Dunraven on foot. Or she could tell Ewan the truth. Throw herself on his mercy, and pray she wouldn't be hung for her treachery.

"Please God," she whispered. "Help me. Tell me what I must do."

Lost in the depths of despair, she didn't hear Ewan's approach. Only when he sat down beside her did she startle. "Ewan!"

"Has he gone?"

She almost feigned ignorance but decided against it. "Aye."

"Good." Frowning, he lifted her hand and brought it to his lips. "You're shivering, lass. Come back to bed afore you catch cold."

No reprimand. No questions. Just concern for her.

In that instant, Cristie knew she loved Ewan MacKellar. And in loving him, she also made a choice. She would confess. She would tell Ewan who she was and why she was there. It would destroy what they had, of course. Then again, what they had was not real anyway. Still, it would be hard to let him go. It would break her heart.

Tomorrow, she thought. I'll tell him tomorrow.

"Mirage." she said, seeing her reflection in his eyes.

A false reflection. An illusion.

He raised a brow. "Mirage?"

"'Tis the name I've chosen for the mare." She gave him a false smile. "Mirage."

Chapter Fifteen

Ewan paused on the threshold of the great hall and absorbed the scene within.

At first, everything appeared to be more or less the same, reminiscent of his first night back at Castle Cathan almost six weeks earlier. Shutters, locked in place with iron bars, kept both cold and daylight at bay, the latter replaced by the warm flicker of rushlight and tallow candles. Smoke from these climbed upwards, joining with the smoke from the fire before seeking escape through the louvre above the central hearth. A thick melange of human, animal, and culinary odours flavoured the air, some less pleasing than others.

The mood on this night, however, felt different. A little less sombre. The hum of conversation was the liveliest it had been since Ewan's return. Perhaps the spirit of Clan MacKellar, so long burdened by uncertainty and grief, had begun to rally.

The clan needs a laird, Ewan. A man they can trust. Our father is gone. Ruaidri is gone. To you, then, falls the obligation.

If words were weapons, Ewan thought, obligation would be the blade that cut a man off at the knees.

His gaze drifted to the head table, where his wife sat beside Morag and Jacques, the three of them engaged in conversation. Morag and Jacques' mutual attraction continued to amuse him, especially since both of them seemed intent on denying it.

Then again, perhaps the Basque knight knew exactly how the land lay. Ewan had oft thought there was more to Jacques Aznar than met the eye. The man had hidden depths, and a wile to match that of a fox. He also had the trust and respect of those at the highest level within the Brotherhood and the Holy Church. To underestimate him would be foolish.

And as for female temptation from a fiery-haired Scottish lass, Jacques was unlikely to surrender his vows, despite his obvious fondness for Morag.

Vows.

Ewan leaned against the wall, folded his arms, and suppressed a sigh as he watched his wife. Thus far, his wife in name only. Twelve days had passed since their marriage vows had been spoken, and the union had yet to be consummated.

He'd been patient, quite willing to court the lass. In truth, he'd enjoyed it. It had allowed him to better assume his role as husband and laird. And, despite their lack of intimacy, or perhaps because of it, his passion for his wee bride continued to grow.

Tasgall's recent visit had unsettled her. She'd disappeared in the night, and Ewan feared she'd intended to return to Dunraven with Alastair's shifty henchman. He hadn't voiced his suspicions to her. It was enough that she'd stayed. The reason for Tasgall's visit, however, continued to puzzle him.

Ewan shifted his thoughts back to his wife. He'd grown fond of the lass. More than fond, perhaps. Her curious nature continued to delight him. She lacked neither intelligence nor piety. Of course, he'd always been well aware of her womanly attributes, the gentle swell of her breasts and the graceful curve of her hips.

But he also admired the delicate shape of her hands and wondered what they would they feel like on his body. He liked the way her lips pouted whenever she pondered something, and he wondered what it would be like to kiss them. Then there was the soft blush that often arose on her cheeks when they conversed.

And her eyes continued to intrigue him with their blue depths. They still held secrets, but no more fear. Recently, he'd seen desire in them as well. He felt sure he'd soon be able to take his place in their bed. The mere thought of making love to her caused a tightening low in his belly.

Perhaps she sensed his gaze upon her, for at that moment she looked his way and smiled. Ewan returned the smile and stepped away from the wall, intent on joining her and the others at the head table.

He took but two steps.

"Laird," Duncan called, from the doorway, "You have a visitor."

Ewan turned and regarded the man—a priest—who stood beside Duncan.

"Do you ken who I am, Ewan MacKellar?" the man asked. "True enough, you've no' laid eyes on me for at least a dozen summers."

Ewan narrowed his eyes as he fished a memory from the depths of his mind. Aye, he knew the man, even though time had mapped its journey on his furrowed face. Of decent height, he possessed a straight posture that belied his age. His plain brown robe, belted with rope, fell to his ankles. A plain wooden cross, dangling from a thin leather thong, hung around his neck.

His hair, once thick as sheep's wool and the colour of coal, had turned as white as a shroud and circled his balding head like a halo. His blue eyes, however, twinkled as they always had, and showed no sign of shock at the sight of Ewan's scars.

Grinning, Ewan stepped forward and grasped the man's outstretched hand. "Father Joseph," he said. "It pleases me greatly to see you again. You're still spreading God's word around the Highlands?"

"And beyond," the priest replied. "I returned from Ireland nigh on a month ago. Been there almost two years. 'Tis a grand place with fine people, but the land of my birth always draws me back. I heard you'd also returned, and of the tragedy that greeted you. A shame about Ruaidri, may he rest in peace." He crossed himself. "To be more accurate, I only heard, at first, that we had knights of the Temple in our midst, and I wondered if they'd sought sanctuary from the persecution in France. I didnae ken you were one of them till I enquired further. Och, but your sire would have been proud, lad. As would your grandsire."

The priest's words summoned up a familiar pang of regret. "What news from France, Father? We've yet to hear anything of it."

The priest grimaced. "Widespread arrests and imprisonment are all I've heard about, Ewan, which is likely as much as you. But it doesnae bode well, I'm afraid."

"Nay, Father, it doesnae." Ewan sighed. "And I'm nae longer with the Order. If you dinnae already ken, I'm now clan laird and married to the wee lass seated beside Morag over there."

"Married?" Frowning, the priest followed Ewan's gaze. "Who is she, Ewan?"

"Elspeth MacAulay. Alastair's sister. You're aware auld Malcolm died?"

"Aye, I heard he'd passed." The priest's frown deepened. "Elspeth MacAulay, you say? Brochan's twin?"

"Aye."

Are you referring to the lass with the dark hair?"

"Aye."

"The one in the grey robe?"

"Aye, the very same." Ewan wondered if the years had turned the priest a bit daft. "Come. I'll introduce you."

Father Joseph touched Ewan's arm as if to stop him. "I've already met Elspeth MacAulay, lad. It was some time ago, but I remember her well enough."

"Even better." Ewan smiled. "'Twill be nice for her to see a familiar face."

The priest clicked his tongue. "Och, somehow I dinnae think she'll be very glad to see mine."

"Why not?" Ewan looked over at the table again to see his wife watching them. "I dinnae understand, Father. Is there a problem?"

"Aye, it would seem there is." Father Joseph grimaced and rubbed the back of his neck. "And I'm no' quite sure how to tell you about it."

A chill settled between Ewan's shoulder blades. "Tell me about what?"

"I'm thinking you should sit first, Ewan. Or, better yet, maybe we should go somewhere a wee bit more priv—"

"Nay, Father." Ewan ran a hand through his hair and glanced again at the head table. "You'll say what you have to say right here. I assume it has to do with my wife?"

"Aye, I'm afraid it does." Father Joseph grimaced again. "And I fear you're no' going to like it very much."

Ewan's hand drifted to his sword hilt. "Tell me."

"Well…" The priest drew breath and met Ewan's gaze. "I dinnae ken who you've married, Ewan, but that lass sitting over there isnae Elspeth MacAulay."

The man might as well have stuck a blade in Ewan's heart. Stupefied, he could but stare at the priest for a moment. "You jest," he said on an exhale.

Father Joseph shook his head. "May God strike me dead if I do."

An icy wave of disbelief filtered through Ewan's brain as he turned his gaze back to his wife. She appeared to be listening to Morag, but even as he watched, her eyes once again met his and her smile faded.

"Nay, Father Joseph, you surely are mistaken." Bile scorched the back of Ewan's throat. "The… the lass has likely changed since you last saw her. You said yourself, it's been a while, aye?"

"It has indeed, but such a transformation isnae possible," Father Joseph replied. "The lass seated over there looks nothing like Elspeth MacAulay. Brochan is dark-haired, but Elspeth MacAulay has hair a similar colour to your own. I'd never make such a claim 'less I was certain of it, Ewan. If you still dinnae believe me, confront her with it. See if she denies it."

"Confront her," Ewan repeated, still staring at his wife, who stared back. Had she paled? Or was it a trick of the light? Morag, perhaps sensing the scrutiny, also looked their way. Recognition turned her questioning expression into a smile, and she waved them over.

"Come," the priest said, urging Ewan forward. "It would seem a sin of great proportions has been committed. Let's find out what this imposter is doing here."

Imposter? Ewan's pulse throbbed in his throat as they approached the table.

"Father Joseph!" Still smiling, Morag rose to her feet as the men drew near. "I confess it took me a wee moment to realize who stood at my brother's side. 'Tis pleasing to see you again." Her expression sobered. "Much has happened since your last visit, I'm afraid. Judging by the look on your face, I'm thinking Ewan must have told you some of it already."

Father Joseph didn't answer, nor did he give any indication he'd even heard Morag's greeting. His sombre gaze stayed on Ewan's wife, who remained seated, her chest rising and falling as she met the priest's scrutiny. Fear evident in her eyes, her knuckles whitened as she grasped the chair arm.

Ewan felt another thrust of pain beneath his ribs. He bit down and tightened his grip on his sword hilt. *Christ have mercy. What kind of evil is this?*

Jacques' scraped his chair back and rose to his feet. "Is something wrong, Ewan?"

Ewan drew a hard breath. "I'm told there is," he said, staring at the woman who he believed to be his wife. "But I pray to God I've been misinformed."

"What do you mean? Misinformed about what?" Morag tipped her head and regarded Ewan with a frown before glancing down at her sister-in-law. "What is this about?"

"Step aside, Morag." Ewan moved forward. "I wish to speak to my wife. On your feet, Elspeth."

All colour drained from the lass's face as she rose. She appeared shaken, and reached for the table, using it as support. Her obvious discomfort only served to heighten Ewan's growing fear. In a practiced stroke, he unsheathed his sword, the tell-tale hiss of the blade's withdrawal enough to draw attention. Around him, the clamour of conversation receded like a tide, and the room fell silent.

Ewan narrowed his eyes at his wife. "This priest here tells me you're no' who you claim to be," he said, pointing his sword at Father Joseph. "Tell me he's lying, and I swear I'll cut him down where he stands."

Father Joseph's mouth fell open. "What? Och, nay, Ewan Mackellar, you'll lower your blade this instant. I dinnae lie. I ken Elspeth MacAulay by sight and, as God is my witness, this woman isnae Elspeth MacAulay!"

A collective gasp rippled through the hall, and Morag let out a soft cry. "Nay, Father Joseph, what are you saying? You're surely mistaken. I cannae believe—"

"Be silent, all of you! Let's give my..." Ewan drew a harsh breath. "Let's give this lass a chance to defend herself." He pinned her with his gaze. "Well? I'm waiting. Speak, for Christ's sake. Deny the priest's accusations. Declare him to be a liar."

A hand settled on Ewan's shoulder, startling him. "Easy, Brother." Gabriel's calm voice drifted into his ear. "Lower your sword."

Ewan growled and shrugged Gabriel's hand away. "Why do you hesitate, lass? Why do you no' defend yourself? Answer me."

"Because I... I cannae," she replied, her lips trembling.

Ewan heard her response, and yet still he reached, hoping. Praying. "Aye, you can, Elspeth. Deny it. Deny *him*. Tell me he lies."

"She cannae deny it," Father Joseph said. "Can you, lass?"

"Nay, I… I cannae." A feverish glaze shone in her eyes. "I'm so sorry, Ewan. The priest speaks the truth."

Another collective gasp, more pronounced, swept through the room as Ewan's blood turned to ice. "Christ, help me," he whispered. "What treachery is this?"

"I was going to tell you the truth, I swear it." The lass clasped her hands, prayer-like, beneath her chin. "May God forgive me, I'm so sorry."

Body and soul torn apart, Ewan stood as if made of stone, his wretched mind struggling to reconcile the devastating truth. In a single, perverted moment of time, his wife had become a complete stranger. Someone he knew nothing about. Everything she'd said, all they'd shared, had been a complete lie.

All of it.

Worse, he'd been gullible—nay, *stupid*—enough to believe her. He'd trusted her. Courted her. *Desired* her. Most devastating of all, he'd surrendered his holy vows for her, and had all but surrendered his heart. Meanwhile, every passing day—and every night, damn her to Hell—she had mocked him. Made a fool out of him.

The initial, mind-numbing impact of shock waned, replaced by a choking noose of fury and shame. The lass who called herself Elspeth continued to gaze up at him, pale-faced, her expression taut and anxious. Ewan's heartbeat thundered in his ears as he moved his blade away from the priest and pointed it at her heart. A surge of rage swept through him like wildfire. It took all he had not to strike her down.

"May the Devil take you," he murmured, his throat so tight he could scarcely draw breath. "Who are you, then, you lying bitch?"

The lass flinched and let out a cry.

"We'll get to the truth of it, Brother." Jacques moved between them, placed his hand atop Ewan's where it rested on the hilt, and pushed the blade down. "But not here. Not like this. Stay your weapon."

But Ewan couldn't tear his gaze away from the lass who had deceived him. How could he have been so blind, so easily fooled? Her eyes remained locked with his, spilling tears that tumbled down her cheeks. False tears, no doubt.

"I'm sorry to the depths of my soul, Ewan," she said, her ragged voice barely more than a whisper. "I was going to tell you the truth tonight. I swear before God, I regret deceiving you."

Before God?

The vow jerked Ewan from his paralysis, and his mouth lifted in a sneer. "Bring her," he snarled, slamming his sword into its scabbard. Then he turned on his heel and left the hall, the silence of his clan ringing in his ears.

*

The laird's chamber seemed to be void of air. Teeth chattering, Cristie stood in the middle of the floor and fought wave after wave of giddiness, each one threatening to topple her.

"Slow your breathing," Gabriel muttered as he moved to stand beside her, "and the vertigo will pass."

She tried to do as he said, willing her broken heart to lessen its dreadful clatter. Her life lay in worthless ruins. What a fool she had been. She would never be the same. Never. No amount of Templar treasure could justify the harm she had done to Ewan. A good man. A man she had come to love. *Nothing* could justify it. At that moment, she would have given her life to turn back time and put things right.

God help me.

Five pairs of eyes were trained on her: Gabriel, Jacques, Morag, the priest... and Ewan, of course. Animosity thickened the air, the worst of it coming from Ewan. Despite sensing his hostility, she dared to meet his gaze. Her remorse, after all, was genuine, although she knew he'd never believe it. The warmth of affection she'd seen in his eyes had gone, replaced by something cold and unreadable. She shivered. "Ewan, I—"

"Be silent," he snarled. "You'll speak only when spoken to. Is that clear?"

Cristie gave a hesitant nod.

"First," he said, "I'll have your name. Your *real* name."

"C-Cristie," she said, knotting her fingers together. "My real name is Cristie Ferguson."

Ewan gave a bitter laugh. "Named for our Lord," he muttered, shaking his head. "May He forgive you for what you've done, lass."

"He might, but I never will," Morag said, her voice strained. "I cannae fathom the depth of this... this deceit. Or the reason for it."

"Aye, she had us all fooled, for sure," Ewan said, his voice softening but his expression still grim. "I cannae quite grasp the enormity of it."

Fresh tears welled in Cristie's eyes. She felt Ewan's pain more acutely than her own, and ached to tell him, over and over, how sorry she was. How much she regretted betraying him. How much she loved him.

"So, *Cristie Ferguson*, what is your real purpose here?" he asked. "I've nae doubt it's at Alastair MacAulay's behest, but why would you pretend to be his sister?"

To hear her real name on Ewan's lips for the first time, spoken with such contempt, almost pushed her to her knees. "I'm Alastair's half-sister," she replied. "Malcolm MacAulay sired me, but I… I am base-born."

Morag snorted. "Och, well, there you go. A bastard. Just like all the Macaulay clan."

Ewan frowned. "Enough, Morag. Let her finish her sordid wee tale."

Cristie blinked and rubbed her temple. "When… when your brother didnae show up, Alastair was angry. He thought Ruaidri had changed his mind about the alliance and came here to challenge him. He didnae expect to see three Templar knights freshly arrived from France. I was sent here to find out… to find out if…"

"What?" Ewan's nostrils flared. "To find out what?"

"If you brought, um, gold with you, or any other kind of… of treasure."

"Treasure?" Ewan stared at her for a moment and then scoffed. "Do you jest?"

Cristie shook her head. "N-nay. Alastair heard you'd arrived with a loaded cart, but no one had seen it since then, and no one knew what was on it. He thought maybe you'd smuggled out some of the Templar wealth and brought it with you. He wanted me to… to get close to you and find out if it was true."

"Pfft, well, of course it's true. You only needed to ask." Morag folded her arms and glared at Cristie. "We stashed it all away in a nearby faerie cave, where it's being guarded by the wee folk. By Thor's hairy arse, are you believing this nonsense she's spouting, Ewan?"

"Sadly, aye." Ewan frowned. "It explains all the questions she's been asking me about the Templars. And I'm thinking that's why Tasgall happened by the other day with a bag of clothes and some other daft tale. My gut told me there was more to it. He was there to see if his laird's wee spy had found anything. Am I right?"

Cristie stifled a sob and nodded her reply.

"And if you'd happened to stumble onto this supposed Templar treasure, what did Alastair intend to do about it?" Ewan raised a brow and looked vaguely amused. "Lay siege to Castle Cathan?"

Cristie fingered her shawl. "I… I'm no' sure. He didnae say."

Ewan regarded her a moment longer and then leaned forward, eyes narrowing. "Tell me, Cristie Ferguson," he said, his voice low and menacing. "Did the whoreson kill Ruaidri?"

Morag let out a soft gasp. "Oh, surely not. Please God."

Cristie shook her head. "Nay! Nay, I'm certain he didnae. Alastair is… is quick to anger, but I dinnae believe he'd ever do a thing like that."

Ewan regarded her in silence a moment longer and then straightened. "I still cannae understand why I was sent a false bride. If I'd married Elspeth, the union would have at least been binding, and MacAulay would have had his alliance, Templar treasure or no'. As it stands, our marriage is a falsehood. Worthless. So why did he send you in Elspeth's place? It doesnae make sense."

Worthless? Cristie's heart shrivelled a little. "Because Elspeth refused outright to marry you. So, Alastair said I… I should go instead. But it wasnae meant to be permanent."

"And you obviously agreed," Morag said, with scorn in her voice.

"Aye, but I wish I hadnae." Cristie blinked away tears. "I changed my mind once I got here. I wanted to tell you the truth about everything, Ewan, I swear it."

"You've had almost a fortnight to do so." Disdain hardened his features. "Plenty of opportunity."

"This lass is a jezebel," Father Joseph muttered. "A deceitful whore, who has tricked a Christian man to lie with her out of wedlock."

Cristie's hands flew to her face, stifling her cry as she gazed up at Ewan.

Nay! Tell them I am yet untouched, Ewan. Defend me, please. It has to come from you. They'll never believe me if I deny it.

Ewan regarded her for several moments, and then gave a bitter smile as he shook his head. "The marriage has nae been consummated," he said, tonelessly, prompting a gasp from Morag. "The lass is still an innocent."

Cristie dropped her hands to her side. "Thank you," she whispered, but Ewan merely threw her a look of utter contempt.

"False gratitude from a liar." Father Joseph's voice cut into the silence. "Obviously, some greater power allowed you to resist her evil temptation, Ewan. The truth remains, however. This woman has mocked the sacred vows of marriage and sworn falsely before God. 'Tis blasphemy. A crime. And she should hang for it."

"Aye, she should." Morag's voice shook with emotion. "She has mocked all of us."

A shudder of fear tore through Cristie. The surrounding walls seemed to move, expanding and shrinking as if the room itself drew breath. Thrown off balance by the nauseating illusion, she swayed once more, set straight by Gabriel's strong hand beneath her elbow.

"I have no wish to die," she said, swallowing against an urge to be sick. "But if my death will make restitution for what I have done to you, Ewan, then… then so be it."

"A false lament," Father Joseph muttered. "Dinnae be fooled by it."

A brief expression of sadness flitted crossed Ewan's face. He mumbled something unintelligible and looked away as if pondering. "Nay, I'll no' see her hang," he said, his voice void of emotion. "But we'll leave on the morrow at first light. Till then, she'll stay in her chamber under guard."

"Wh-where are we going?" Cristie asked, swiping tears from her eyes.

"I'm taking you back to your wretched clan," Ewan replied, and shifted his gaze to Gabriel. "Brother, please get this accursed woman out my sight."

"P-please, Ewan." She gazed up at the man she loved. "There are thi—"

"Be silent!" Ewan's lip curled. "Gabriel?"

Gabriel's voice murmured in her ear. "Come, my lady."

"Wait!" Morag stepped forward, hand outstretched. "The ring," she said. "Take it off."

Cristie tugged the ring from her finger and placed it in Morag's open palm. Then, dizzy with grief and fear, she followed the English knight, hardly aware of their silent progression till he opened the door to her chamber. *Ewan's* chamber.

"I must arrange for a guard," Gabriel said. "In the meantime, I ask that you remain here. To disobey Ewan further would not be wise."

She regarded the English knight, whose expression gave no indication as to the direction of his thoughts. "I willnae disobey him, but please, Gabriel, tell him I'm sorry. *Truly* sorry."

"I fear he's not of a mind to hear it right now, my lady," he replied, his tone solemn. "I can only suggest you ask God for forgiveness, and pray for Ewan as well."

The door closed with barely a sound.

Sobbing, Cristie turned, wandered over to the bed, and clambered onto it. She held up her left hand and regarded the fading mark left by the ring.

A holy symbol of commitment, falsely used.

Worthless.

"Dear God, what have I done?" she whispered, dropping her face into the hands. "What have I done?"

Chapter Sixteen

A pall of disbelief had settled over Castle Cathan. Just as the spirit of the place had begun to rally, it had once again been subdued. Ewan had spent much of the night at prayer in the chapel, trying to find some semblance of peace. So far, it had proven elusive.

The ache beneath his ribs remained.

The shock of Elspeth's—nay, *Cristie's*—betrayal still had him reeling. He didn't know what he felt, since he couldn't quite settle on a single emotion. He tussled with several, mostly a nauseating blend of bitter disappointment, absolute anger, and immeasurable sadness.

The constant nervousness she'd displayed, the sense of furtiveness he'd felt, even all the questions she'd asked—they now had new meaning. He should have listened to his instincts. The lass had been hiding a secret all along. The mere thought of it pushed bile to his throat. And as for her refusal to consummate the marriage, that also made sense. Obviously, she feared the risk of carrying his bastard. Then again, she must have known that he might well have demanded his marital rights. Which meant she was willing to risk conceiving his child out of wedlock.

Dishonest. Immoral.

Only two of several sad epithets that might apply to the lass.

By Christ's holy blood, Ewan couldn't wait to be rid of this false wife. He needed her gone, far away from Castle Cathan. Out of his life forever. Only then might he begin, with God's help, to look forward once more.

The night had seemed interminable. But, at last, dawn had dragged itself over the horizon, the horses had been readied, and Gabriel had been dispatched to fetch Cristie. They'd be on their way soon enough.

"I'm glad you didnae take her to *Lorg Coise Dhè,*" Morag said, trotting along beside him. "'Tis too sacred a place for someone like her."

Ewan frowned but said nothing. He wondered, though, why he'd held back from showing her the hidden glen and his Grandsire's church. Maybe, deep down, his instincts had kept him from doing so.

"'Tis as well you didnae bed the lass, as well," Morag added. "Though I confess I'm curious to know why."

Ewan had been waiting for someone to voice the question. He hardened his jaw. "She wasnae willing, and I wouldnae force her. 'Tis that simple."

"Oh." Morag sucked in a breath. "Well, few men would have been as tolerant. 'Tis a blessing you were, and for more than one reason. What if she'd been carrying your bairn?"

The irrelevance of the question riled him. "She isnae."

"But if she was, would you still be sending her away?"

Ewan threw his sister a hard glance. "If she was, would you still wish to see her dangling at the end of a rope?"

"Dear God, nay." Morag blew out a breath. "I was angry yesterday and wasnae thinking too clearly. Today, I'm calmer. Well, somewhat, at least. And will you slow down a wee bit? 'Tis no' a race."

"The lass isnae carrying my bairn, Morag, so your question has no merit. And I'm hurrying because I'm eager to see her gone from here." The ache beneath Ewan's ribs swelled. "Christ knows, I need to be done with this cursed mess."

Ewan felt Morag halt and paused his own hurried stride, turning to look at her. Her eyes full of tears, she shook her head and steepled her hands, prayer-like, over her mouth. "I'm so sorry, Ewan."

"Och, nay," he murmured, approaching her. "Forgive me, wee lass. I didnae mean to make you cry."

She shook her head again and hiccupped on a sob. "'Tis naught you've done. 'Tis your pain I feel. You dinnae deserve any of this. I ken you'd grown fond of the lass. I could see it in the way you looked at her. And, in truth, I thought she'd grown fond of you, too. To be so betrayed is unfair, and especially after all you've been through."

He sighed. "And you've had naught to deal with, I suppose."

She tugged at her shawl. "Which is why I dinnae want you to leave. I'm afraid of being left alone."

"I'm no' leaving you alone, you bampot." Ewan brushed a strand of hair from her forehead. "Jacques will be here, and you couldnae wish for a better protector." He summoned up a half-hearted smile. "Well, except for me, perhaps."

She scrubbed the tears from her cheeks. "I'm no' afraid for my safety. 'Tis the thought of never seeing you again that I cannae bear. You're all I have left."

He groaned. "I'll be back tomorrow eve, Morag, you have my word. I'm no' travelling alone, remember? I'll have Gabriel at my side. Now, come and see me off, and cease worrying."

And the answer is nay. If the lass was carrying my bairn, she'd be staying here.

They stepped out into a ghostly dawn light and breathed in cool, damp air. The cobbles were dry, Ewan noted, and glanced up at a promising sky.

"At least the weather is agreeable," Morag said, voicing Ewan's same thought.

Hammett stood by the gates, where three horses, including the little mare, awaited, saddled and bridled.

"*Bonne journée*, my lord," the lad said. "All is prepared, as you commanded."

Ewan nodded his approval and eyed the saddlebags. "Provisions as ordered?"

Hammett inclined his head. "Aye, my lord."

"Thank you, Hammett."

"You're letting her keep the mare?" Morag stroked the horse's sleek neck.

"Nay, the mare will be coming back here."

"Good. I dinnae like to think of her being in MacAulay's stable." Morag shifted her gaze. "Here they are."

Ewan turned and watched as Gabriel and Cristie crossed the courtyard, with Jacques, Duncan, and Father Jacob behind them. It was a silent and sombre procession. Indeed, the only sounds came from the tumble of waves against the rocks and the occasional cry of a seabird.

Cristie hugged a cloth bag to her chest, as if finding comfort from it. Ewan frowned at her scant amount of baggage and wondered at it. Not that she had brought much with her when she'd first arrived.

"I'll burn the rest of her things," Morag said, her thoughts apparently following a similar path. "I dinnae want anything of hers under our roof."

It was a harsh remark, but Ewan chose not to counter it. He well understood Morag's bitterness. This imposter had betrayed not only him, but also his entire clan. He remained silent as the group approached. Cristie's face appeared alabaster-white against the darkness of her hair.

Condemned. She looks like a woman condemned.

He shrugged the thought aside and steeled himself against feeling any further pity for the lass. Nothing she had done had been accidental. Her actions had been deliberate. Intentional.

That their union had not been consummated now seemed fated. Perhaps Ewan's will to abstain had indeed been predicated by a higher power, one that had given him the strength to resist his physical desires. Cristie Ferguson had proven herself to be the Devil's conduit. A blasphemer and a liar, fooling everyone with her false façade. Her behaviour surely advocated the need for vows of chastity among holy orders.

As for the small voice deep inside, the one suggesting her reluctance to lie with him had stemmed from genuine integrity, and the love he'd seen in her eyes had been honest... well, it merited no consideration. None at all.

Gabriel, his expression sober, greeted Ewan with a slight nod. "She is ready," he said.

Ewan returned the nod and cursed the treacherous clenching of his heart as his eyes met Cristie's. Their dark depths reflected such sorrow, the shadows beneath them a testament to a sleepless night.

"Ewan," she said, her lip trembling, "will you please hear what I have to say?"

"Nay, I'll hear no more of your lies," he replied, steeling his jaw. "You'll speak only when spoken to, or if you wish to stop and attend to your needs. And you'll also address me as Laird. Understand?"

She flinched. "But if you'll just let me—"

"If you disobey me, lass, so help me, I'll gag you. Hammett, help the lady mount up."

Ewan turned away and swung into the saddle. Then he watched as Cristie settled astride her horse, hooked her bag over the pommel, and arranged her skirts.

"Stay vigilant, Brothers," Jacques said. "And may God deliver you safely."

"I'll be gone by the time you return, Ewan," Father Jacob said. "So, I'll bid you farewell now, and I echo Brother Jacques' sentiment. May God keep you."

Ewan nodded. "Thank you, Father. You're welcome here anytime." He switched his gaze to Morag. "Dinnae give Jacques a hard time, wee lass. I'll see you tomorrow."

"God willing." Morag gave him a grim smile, brushed a strand of hair from her eyes. "And dinnae forget to say a prayer for Ruaidri when you reach the spot."

*

They travelled without incident as well as in near—and blessed—silence. Ewan was not in the mood to discuss anything, mundane or otherwise. And Gabriel had always been ponderous, preferring to put words on paper rather than engage in trite conversation. Cristie had obviously taken Ewan's threat seriously and remained quiet.

Ewan tried not to dwell on his torment. Instead, he forced himself to absorb the natural beauty of his homeland, which always uplifted his spirit as much as any manmade house of worship. More, perhaps.

Clouds threatened occasionally, but held onto their contents as they skittered across the sky. A brisk breeze, fragranced by damp earth and snowmelt, swept along the floor of the glen. The burn serenaded them with its song as it bubbled and danced its way to the sea, and the occasional cry of an eagle pierced the air. They stopped only twice en route, for some personal relief and to stretch their stiffening limbs. Both times, Ewan had helped Cristie down from her mare. To touch her felt torturous, but he couldn't ask Gabriel to do it. Both times, Cristie had refused food, taking only a drink.

At last they reined in their horses at the foot of the pass. The track ahead meandered upwards like the toothed-edge of a saw. Ewan eyed it with some trepidation, remembering the last time he had passed this way, and the subsequent horrors he had witnessed. At least the snow had gone from the lower slopes, although it still blanketed the peaks, softening their ragged, granite edges.

Now, with another hour of travel to go and most of it afoot, Ewan twisted in the saddle and scrutinized Cristie, who had stayed behind them for much of the ride. Misery etched on her face, she stared back at him for a moment before lowering her gaze. She was clearly exhausted.

"Not once has she complained," Gabriel murmured, dismounting. "Yet she is obviously suffering."

Ewan resisted a temptation to counter with a suitable retort. Instead, he merely heaved a sigh and dismounted also, grimacing as his muscles objected.

As he had twice before that day, he approached Cristie and lifted her to the ground, cursing the traitorous physical response that touching her invoked. "We lead the horses from here," he said, and released her as if scalded. "'Tis too dangerous to ride."

I look forward to tomorrow, for tomorrow there will come a time when I'll no longer have to touch you, or to look upon your face and feel this damnable sorrow. God give me strength.

"I understand." She appeared discomforted and grabbed the stirrup leather as if to steady herself. "If I may be allowed a moment, Laird?"

"Aye, take a wee respite if you wish," he said, "but we cannae wait too long. 'Tis best to be at the bothy before dark."

"I doubt she'll make the climb unaided," Gabriel observed, as Cristie disappeared behind a boulder to relieve herself. "I suspect she slept little last night, if at all, and she has not yet eaten today."

Ewan's mind teetered between sympathy and apathy. Cristie had brought her suffering upon herself, so surely merited little sympathy. He couldn't help but wonder if her remorse was genuine, or merely a result of being found out.

"What would you have me do?" he said, tasting bitterness. "Carry the lass on my back?"

A brief frown crossed Gabriel's brow. "I understand your ire, Brother, but beware the contents of your heart. 'Tis a vessel that sustains malice as easily as compassion, but the former is far more damaging to the spirit. I suggest you refer to the teachings of our Lord, or ask yourself what He would have you do."

He turned away to loosen his horse's girth, his quiet reprimand leaving Ewan somewhat chagrined. Of course, he would never physically harm Cristie, nor allow harm to come to her. A blatant display of kindness and consideration, though, was asking a bit much of his injured pride.

"I'm ready, Laird," Cristie said, behind him.

Ewan suppressed a sigh and took a moment to collect himself before responding.

"You'll follow Gabriel," he said, turning to look at her. "Dinnae be afraid to speak out if you need to stop, and should your horse startle for any reason, you'll let go of the reins immediately. Understood?"

She glanced at the steep, winding track and gave a hesitant nod. "Aye."

Ewan gestured. "Go ahead, then. I'll be right behind you."

Gabriel set a merciful pace, one undoubtedly meant for Cristie's benefit. All went well till they approached the bend where Ruaidri's horse had stumbled. Ewan fully intended to pause at the spot and offer up a prayer for his brother's soul. But at that moment, for some obscure reason, Cristie's mare shied and stepped sideways, moving close to the precipitous edge. Cristie, caught unawares, stumbled and let out a squeal.

Ewan's breath caught. "Be still, lass," he said, his voice calmer than he felt. "Let the horse settle."

Cristie nodded. "I… I'm fine," she replied, the ashen pallor of her face belying her claim.

Ewan moved closer. "If you can, hook the reins over the pommel, and then come back here to me." he said. "Watch your step and dinnae worry about the mare."

Cristie threw a glance at the edge. "But I dinnae want her to fall."

"She willnae fall. She'll follow Gabriel. Do as I say."

Whispering words of calm to the mare, Cristie did as bidden and then moved back to Ewan's side, looking up at him with wide, questioning eyes that seemed to seek approval. He resisted the urge to commend her actions and merely hoisted her onto his horse.

Colour flared in her pale cheeks. "Will he be able to carry me all the way up?" she asked, grabbing a handful of mane.

"He'll manage," he said, carelessly. "You weigh little and we've gone half way already."

As they moved past the gully, Ewan offered up his promised prayer for Ruaidri. The exercise, however, brought little comfort. Rather, it served to fan the flames of a smouldering suspicion that Alastair MacAulay had indeed been involved in Ruaidri's demise. Morag was right; the MacAulay's could not be trusted. The lass currently perched atop Ewan's horse was proof of that.

Weary of his fluctuating emotions, Ewan endeavoured to soften his shoulders and shifted his attention to their surroundings. Most of the snow lay atop the crags above the pass, though a few errant drifts were scattered here and there, cradled in nooks and crannies where sunlight could not reach. Dusk, meanwhile, had sneaked in like a thief, stealing the light, but apart from an occasional gust, the wind had mercifully weakened.

The climb, thankfully, was nearing its end. Ewan's legs felt leaden, and his breath billowed in the air. Soon, the path levelled out and Gabriel was able to take the mare's reins. The solid outline of the bothy, nestled beneath its protective granite overhang, was a welcome sight.

As they reached the shelter, Ewan turned to lift Cristie down. She winced at his touch, her body rigid beneath his grasp, and her teeth chattered as she found her feet. She was obviously cold, Ewan realized. Chilled to the bone, even.

Cursing under his breath, he pulled the blanket roll from the back of his saddle. He shrugged off the temptation to pull her close and warm her body with his. His compassion, despite Gabriel's short sermon, had its limits. Besides, he mused, the lass had a tongue in her head, and had obviously chosen not to use it. *Likely a ploy on her part. An attempt to invoke my sympathy.* Women and wile had an alliance as old as time, and he would not yield to it.

Instead, he draped the blanket around her and gave her a reprimand.

"You should have said something instead of sitting up there, shivering."

Teeth still chattering, Cristie hunched her shoulders and pulled the blanket tight. "I'm fine," she said, and glanced at the bothy. "B-besides, we're here now."

The lass looked far from fine, in truth. Ewan stifled a sigh. "Get yourself inside. There are candles and tinder on the sill. There should be some kindling and peat for the brazier, too, if you care to get a wee fire going. We'll be in once the horses are settled."

She sniffed. "M-may I have my bag, please?"

Ewan retrieved it and handed it over. Clutching it to her breast, she hobbled off, a corner of the blanket trailing on the ground.

"She is suffering," Gabriel observed, clicking his tongue as he led the horses into the dark stable.

"She didnae have to," Ewan replied. "She could have asked for the blanket."

"That is not what I meant." Gabriel tugged the saddle off his horse and settled it onto the nearby rack. Ewan set about attending to Cristie's mount and waited for his friend to elaborate. The silence dragged on.

"Are you talking about the lass's conscience?" Ewan demanded at last, with a huff. "She didnae go into this mockery of a marriage innocently, Gabriel. She knew exactly what she was doing."

"I don't disagree." Gabriel grabbed a handful of straw and began to rub his horse down. "But I suspect she was not prepared for the outcome."

"Och, she must have known it couldnae last." Ewan felt the familiar bitterness rising once more to the back of his throat. "Alastair MacAulay, curse his balls, had some addled plot in mind, and the lass was a willing part of it."

Gabriel worked in sober silence for a few moments. "Again, I don't disagree," he said, finally, "though I'm not so sure she was ever willing. But that's not what I meant, either."

"Then what? Are you implying the lass has feelings for me?" Ewan's gut tightened. "If that be so, why did she continue with the lie? Because her loyalties have always lain elsewhere, that's why. I'll be well rid of her."

"Will you confront her brother?"

"Tomorrow? Nay. He'll have his clansmen at his back, and I'm no' willing to die for this nonsense. 'Tis enough, for now, to drop his wee spy off at the gate. But I'll be sure to give her a message to pass on."

By the time they'd settled the horses, night had fallen, moonless and bleak. The wind, still gentle, whistled an intermittent tune. From somewhere in the distance came the mournful howl of a wolf, a sound which summoned up more unwanted images. Ewan gazed out over the darkened landscape, offered up another prayer for Ruaidri's soul, and then followed Gabriel into the bothy to be greeted by warmth and light.

Still wrapped in the blanket, Cristie sat on a small stool by the brazier, firelight flickering across her face. She glanced at Gabriel, met Ewan's gaze, and then lowered her eyes. Ewan set the saddlebags down and released a breath he didn't know he'd been holding. "Are you warmed up?" he asked, his tone purposely austere.

She met his gaze again, unflinching this time. "Aye, thank you."

He gave a single nod. "So now you'll eat."

"I'm no' hungry," she replied.

Ewan raised a brow. "Perhaps you didnae understand me," he said, not unkindly. "You've no' touched a morsel all day. You'll eat, and that's that."

Gabriel pulled a bundle from one of the bags and unwrapped it atop the small table. After blessing the contents, he divided them out, handing some bread and cheese to Cristie.

She ate without further protest or comment. Afterwards, hugging her bag and wrapped in her blanket, she curled up on her pallet of dry bracken and fell asleep.

Later, and as he had on many other nights, Ewan lay on his back and listened to Cristie's soft, rhythmic breaths. Over the past while, he'd become accustomed to hearing the gentle cadence. God help him, he'd even found comfort in it. No longer. Now, resentment soured his thoughts. It irked him that the lass slept so soundly.

She should be tossing and turning, plagued by guilt, and...

Remembering Gabriel's warning, Ewan closed his eyes and prayed for some peace of mind. He told himself that Cristie's conscience, troubled or not, had naught to do with it. The lass slept soundly simply because she was exhausted.

As he, too, approached the cusp of sleep, a whisper drifted out of the darkness. "Don't pray for yourself, Brother," Gabriel said. "Pray for her. That is where you'll find your peace."

The creak of a door, followed by a sudden waft of cold air across his face, roused Ewan from sleep. He sought out the hilt of his sword as he looked to the doorway, where Cristie's blanketed silhouette stood poised on the threshold as if hesitant to step into the darkness beyond. A moment later, she obviously capitulated to whatever need possessed her and ventured out, letting the door swing shut.

Ewan thought about the wolf he'd heard earlier. The creatures were emboldened at this hungry time of year, driven to recklessness. Unbidden, the image of Ruaidri's mangled horse came to mind. The scent of the horses alone, he knew, might have drawn them near. He sat up and cast his blanket aside, grimacing at the stiffness in his limbs as he rose to his feet.

"The heat of the Levant had its benefits," Gabriel muttered. "It helped to keep the body limber, for one thing."

Ewan's mouth quirked as he picked up his sword. "Aye, the Highland climate can be harsh on both man and beast, and 'tis the presence of those beasts which concerns me right now."

He stepped outside and looked about, ears cocked. The chill wind, blowing with a little more vigour than before, nipped at his face. The clouds were threadbare, exposing patches of bejewelled blackness. To the east, a thin ribbon of light stretched across the horizon, promising dawn, but Ewan knew the darkness would endure a while yet.

A footfall to his left had him spinning on his heel. Cristie halted at the sight of him, the look of surprise on her face quickly supplanted by a wary expression.

"There are wolves about," Ewan said. "'Tis nae wise to linger out here over long."

"Aye, I heard them earlier." She brushed a strand of hair from her face. "Th-thank you for your concern, Laird. I'm sorry if I woke you."

"I was already awake," he said, feeling no guilt in the lie. "Get yourself inside and break your fast. We'll be leaving soon."

The descent to the MacAulay glen was easier, the trail snaking downwards in a wide and elongated series of twists and turns. By the time the horses set their hooves onto flat land, the sun had risen, but as yet remained hidden behind the surrounding hills. Sheltered from the breeze by those same hills, patches of mist swirled around them as they followed the trail alongside the loch.

Ewan kept Cristie shielded to his left, by the shore. An attack, though unlikely, would have to come from the stands of birch and pine to their right. Despite Alastair MacAulay's deception, this was not officially enemy territory, but Ewan's spine tingled with vigilance nonetheless. He kept his eyes skinned and sword hand at the ready. Gabriel's quiet demeanour undoubtedly belied a similar attentiveness. His white Templar mantle, ghostly in the morning twilight, would be sure to capture interest if seen.

So far, however, all indications of life had been passive. The pungent aroma of peat-smoke teased Ewan's nostrils from time to time. Apart from a variety of bird-song, he also heard the distant bleating of sheep and the intermittent lowing of cattle.

At last, as the sun reached its apex, Dunraven came into view beyond the trees—a sombre grey sentinel sitting at the head of the loch. Ewan knew any watchman of worth would see them if they cleared the woods. And any bowman of worth could find his target if they moved much closer.

Ewan reached over and grabbed Cristie's reins, halting her horse. "That's far enough," he said. "You can walk from here."

Cristie's eyes widened a little, but she said nothing as Ewan dismounted and reached for her. She slid to the ground but held onto his arms even after he'd removed his hands from her waist.

"Ewan, please." She clutched at his sleeves, her eyes now bright with tears. "You have to hear—"

"Let go, Cristie," he said, the calmness of his voice concealing the turmoil in his soul. "There's naught of any worth you can say to me, but you can tell your brother he's no longer welcome on MacKellar land. I'll pray for him, though. You can tell him that as well." His gaze dropped to her hands. "I'll pray for you too. Now, let go."

A sob erupted from her as she released her hold. Ewan gritted his teeth and climbed back into the saddle. "Dinnae forget your bag," he said, reaching for the mare's reins.

Tears tumbled down her cheeks as she went to tug the bag free. It jerked out of her hands and fell to the ground, spilling its contents. Yet another hit to Ewan's heart, since it appeared all she had brought were the gifts he'd given her; the comb, the shawl... and the seashell.

"I h-hope you dinnae mind me k-keepin these, Laird MacKellar," she said, sobbing as she gathered up the items and pushed them back in the bag. "I v-value them greatly, but I'd gladly g-give them up if you would only f-find it in your heart to forgive me."

Ewan drew a breath, held it, and clung to his stubborn resolve like a drowning man to driftwood. *Christ, give me strength.*

"Ewan." Gabriel's voice, little more than a whisper, broke through his angst. "Find it within yourself. For your sake as much as hers."

Ewan released the breath and took another. "The gifts were always yours to keep, lass," he said, and then cleared his throat. "And you can take my forgiveness with you also. I'll bear you no ill will."

Cristie's dejected expression softened a little. "'Tis more than I deserve. Thank you." She hugged the bag to her chest. "I shall always treasure them."

Sniffling, she turned and set off along the trail. Ewan did not need to see her face to be aware of her despondency. It surrounded her like a shadow, burdening her rounded shoulders and hindering her step. Eager to turn away and kick his horse into a hard gallop, Ewan gathered up the reins, but paused as Cristie came to a sudden halt, and spun around.

"Nay!" she cried and, stumbling over her feet, marched back to him. "There are things I must yet say, Ewan Tormod MacKellar, and you'll hear them, even if I have to scream the words at you as you ride away." Scrubbing tears from her face, she stood at his horse's withers and held his gaze, her chin set in a determined line. "What I did was wrong. Very wrong. There's nae excuse for it, and I'm ashamed beyond words." She shook her head as tears filled her eyes once more. "But I'm no' a bad person at heart, truly. I… I didnae think it through. I didnae stop to consider the outcome, so I was unprepared for the consequences, do you see? I never expected to fall in love with the man I was deceiving. And I do love you, Ewan. With my whole heart, I do! No one has ever treated me with such kindness, and I regret deceiving you more than I can say." A fresh sob escaped her. "I swear I'll regret it for the rest of my life. Please believe me."

Ewan bit down so hard his jaw ached. A saddle creaked at his side as Gabriel shifted. His friend's insight had been correct, it seemed.

But, despite Cristie's professed regret and her declaration of love, there was naught more to be said, no restitution to be made. The sanctity of trust had been violated. And she had not only betrayed him, but also his clan. Ewan could see no way to defend or repair it. Whether the lass spoke true or not, her presence in his life had come to an end.

And it pained him to the core.

"I forgive you all of it, Cristie," he said, his voice ragged. "Away you go, now."

Unblinking, Cristie regarded him a moment longer as if committing his face to memory, and then she set off once more. This time, she did not turn back.

Chapter Seventeen

At one time, Cristie might have worried about the reception she'd receive upon her return to Dunraven. Knowing Alastair's temper, she might even have feared it. Her ruse, after all, had been exposed, and she'd failed to find any evidence of a Templar treasure. But at that moment, she neither cared nor feared what Alastair, or anyone else for that matter, might say or do.

All she wanted to do was seek out her chamber, curl up with her misery, and lick her wounds. Facing Alastair, however, was still a hurdle to be overcome, and the sooner the better. Given the hour, she suspected he'd be in the great hall, and headed that way, almost colliding with Elspeth and Brochan in the doorway.

"Well, well, will you look who's here." Elspeth folded her arms and regarded Cristie with disdain. "What brings you back so soon, *Lady MacKellar*? Did you decide the poor Templar laird wasnae to your liking? Or did he discover you were the cuckoo in the nest and tossed you out on your arse? The latter, I suspect, judging by your sorry appearance."

"Keep your voice down, Elspeth." Brochan glanced over his shoulder and then turned back and regarded Cristie, brows raised. "Did you find anything, Cristie?"

"Dinnae answer that." Tasgall strode through the doorway and stepped between them, his sober gaze sweeping Cristie from head to toe. "You'll come with me, lass."

Elspeth huffed and glared at Cristie. "Our father would be ashamed of the way his daughter," she switched her glare to Tasgall, "and his *clan* is behaving."

Cristie's cheeks warmed. "Aye, he would, true enough," she said. "I should have listened to you, Elspeth. You were right. About everything."

An expression of surprise flashed across Elspeth's face. "How so? What hap—?"

"You'll come with me, lass," Tasgall repeated, a flush of colour also arising in his cheeks, "and wait in the solar while I fetch the laird."

In silence, Tasgall led Cristie up the winding staircase and into the solar. The room failed to live up to its illuminating designation. Deerskins, shielding the windows against the winter winds, denied entry to daylight. The resulting gloom was challenged by a large candelabra that sat atop the table, its twelve flickering tapers casting shadows over the tapestried walls.

"Stay here." Tasgall put his hand on the door latch. "I'll be back in a wee while."

"You should nae have left me there that night, Tasgall," Cristie said. "You should have brought me back with you."

"I couldnae, lass. I'm sorry." He cleared his throat. "Did Ewan MacKellar mistreat you? When he found out the truth, I mean?"

Cristie drew a shaky breath. "Nay. He wasnae well pleased, but I wasnae illtreated, nor even cast out without a care. He personally escorted me all the way back to Dunraven."

A weak smile came and went. "That's… that's good," he said. "Um, wait here."

Cristie continued to stare at the door for a few moments after Tasgall left. She had the impression he'd wanted to say more and wondered at it. Then, with a weary huff, she sank onto a wooden bench, heart and mind united in misery. Every passing moment sent Ewan further and further away. She wondered how far he'd travelled already. *Not that far yet. He'll likely still be on MacAulay land. Maybe he'll change his mind before he reaches the pass and come back for me.*

She released a soft, bitter laugh and cursed her foolishness for the thousandth time. Ewan would not come back. Not that day. Not ever. Such imaginings were as false as their marriage.

Hopeless.

Funny, she thought, how a lack of something could weigh so heavily upon the soul, as if emptiness somehow had form and substance. Of course, Alastair must never know how she felt. He must never know that she'd fallen in love with Ewan MacKellar.

The door creaked open and Cristie rose to her feet, determined to meet Alastair's gaze, but he didn't even look at her. Instead, goblet in hand, he moved past her and went to stand before one of the tapestries, his interest in the textile obviously feigned.

The chill of his displeasure filled the room, and Cristie's empty stomach lurched as the sour stench of his breath swirled in his wake. Movement behind drew her attention, and she glanced over to see Tasgall standing sentry by the door. He nodded and gave her the hint of a smile.

"So." Alastair took a gulp from his goblet and continued to gaze at the tapestry. "You were found out."

"Aye." Cristie suppressed a sigh and hugged her bag tighter. "I was."

"How?" Alastair belched and took another swig of his drink. Fear at last manifested, and lifted the hair on Cristie's nape. The noon hour had barely passed, yet it seemed the man was already in his cups.

"Are you deaf?" Frowning, her brother turned and approached, his stride not quite orderly. "Answer me. How were you found out? Did you betray me somehow?"

"Nay, I didnae. It was a visiting priest," she replied, keeping her voice steady while resisting an urge to back away. "His name was... is Father Joseph. He knew I wasnae Elspeth and forced me to confess everything."

"Father Joseph." Alastair grunted and scratched his jaw. "Aye, I ken the man. May his cock rot. So, what happened?"

Cristie gave him a sardonic look. "Do you need ask that question? I'm here, am I not? Obviously, they threw me out."

Alastair's lip curled as he drew closer. "Mind your mouth," he said, glancing at her bundle. "What's in the bag?"

Cristie knew the worst thing she could do was let him see how much she valued its contents, so she held it out. "A shawl and a comb. I didnae have time to pack anything else. Laird MacKellar wanted me gone as soon as possible."

To Cristie's relief, he grunted and shifted his gaze back to her. "So, tell me what, if anything, you found out about these Templars. They're hiding something, I'm certain of it."

Something deep inside Cristie snapped like a twig. The man had not spared one solitary thought for her, nor shown any concern for her well-being at all. His single-mindedness caused her simmering emotions to boil over in a heated wave of anger.

"Nay, Alastair, you're wrong." She curled her lip and regarded him with loathing. "I found naught, and I saw naught, because there's *naught* to find and *naught* to see. And even if there was, what could you do about it? Declare a clan war? Launch an attack? Ewan MacKellar laughed at the idea of you laying siege to Castle Cathan. Aye, and he said to tell you the MacAulays are no longer welcome on his land as well. So, there goes your cursed alliance! I wish I'd never listened to you. I wish I'd never gone there. It was a foolish venture, and you're daft if you think—"

The impact knocked Cristie off her feet. With no time to even cry out, she fell hard, teeth sinking into her tongue as her head struck the floor. Pain sliced through her skull and speared the depths of her right ear as she tasted blood. She gasped and then flinched as Alastair's formed loomed over her.

"Nay!" Tasgall's harsh cry sounded a heartbeat before Alastair's booted foot slammed into Cristie's stomach. The air burst from her lungs as she coiled into a tight ball. She felt, rather than saw, Tasgall approach. "That's enough, Laird," he said. "Stop, please. You'll kill the lass."

"Daft, am I?" Alastair sneered. "I told you to mind your mouth, y'insolent wee bastard. And speaking of bastards, you'd better no' be carrying MacKellar's. I swear I'll drown it at birth."

Cristie couldn't respond. Winded, she tried, and failed, to inhale. Like an approaching stampede of cattle, the noise in her head grew louder, filling her ears. Alastair said something else, his voice harsh, the words unintelligible;

an outburst followed by a muffled thud. The door slamming, Cristie realized, as she balanced on the edge of oblivion. Abruptly, the noise in her head ceased, as if another door had been slammed shut. Unable to speak, she formed the words in her mind—a futile, impossible, cry for help.

Ewan, can you hear me? Please come back. Please.

"'Tis all right, lass." Tasgall's voice sounded hollow. She felt his hands on her and winced as he sat her up. "Jesus Christ, I swear the man has lost his mind."

Pain spiralled up into her head, prompting her to gasp and, at last, take in air. She leaned against Tasgall and saturated her lungs with great gulps as tears streamed down her cheeks.

"Aye, there you go, that's better. Och, he winded you proper." Tasgall uttered a mild curse as he stroked the hair back from Cristie's face. "You'll have a bonny bruise on your cheek by tonight, too."

Cristie tasted blood and grimaced. "I'm... I'm all right," she said, feeling anything but. "Will... will you help me stand, please, Tasgall?"

"Are you sure you're able? You should wait a wee while, perhaps."

"I… I'll be fine. If you'll just help me, please."

He made a sound of disapproval, but hoisted her to her feet and held her steady for a moment. "There you go. All right?"

She nodded and swallowed against an urge to vomit. "Thank you."

"Might you be?" Tasgall cleared his throat and glanced down at her belly. "Carrying MacKellar's child, that is?"

"Nay," she answered, leaning against him. "'Tis certain I'm not."

"Aye, well, 'tis perhaps no' a bad thing," he said, his expression grim. "You should have known better than to challenge the laird, lass, though he shouldnae have hit you. I fear the man's drinking is corrupting his mind. 'Tis an affliction of sorts."

Cristie didn't care to hear about Alastair's affliction. She just wanted solitude. "I… I just need to go and rest for a wee while, Tasgall. Thank you for your concern."

"I'll escort you."

"'Tis nae necessary." She stood upright and placed a hand over her ear, trying to quell the throbbing pain. "I'll manage."

Tasgall looked unconvinced. "Are you sure?"

"Aye, I'm sure." Cristie hobbled to the door and reached for the latch.

"Cristie, lass." The man cleared his throat again. "There's something I think you should know."

She turned. "What?"

He grunted and scratched his head. "Och, 'tis naught, really. Just… just stay out of the laird's way for now."

As if she needed to be told. "I will."

Sore, weary, and desperate for her bed, Cristie kept her head lowered and made her way downstairs to her chamber, unchallenged by anyone until she reached her door. The sight of Elspeth standing outside made her groan inwardly.

"At last," Elspeth said, wrinkling her nose. "By God, 'tis a dismal corner, this. I cannae think how you manage to sleep down here. I was beginning to think Alastair had… oh, sweet Mother of Heaven, what happened? Did he hit you?"

Cristie frowned and pushed her door open. "I'm tired, Elspeth."

"Och, Cristie, nay! He shouldnae have done that."

"It doesnae hurt," she lied. "Please go away. I need to rest."

"I dinnae doubt it." Elspeth followed Cristie over the threshold. "Lord save us, do you have a taper? 'Tis darker than the Devil's arsehole in here. Tell me what happened with Ewan MacKellar."

Cristie tossed her bag onto her narrow bed and opened the single shutter a crack, giving entry to some daylight. "I told Alastair what happened," she said, unhooking her cloak and tossing it onto her clothing chest. "So, you can ask him."

Clucking her tongue, Elspeth peered at Cristie's face. "Dear God above, I cannae believe he hit you. You must have said something to set him off."

Cristie kicked off her shoes and fumbled with the laces on her robe, an exercise that would always remind her of Ewan. "Will you please leave, Elspeth? I dinnae wish to talk anymore. I just want to lie down."

"Here, let me do that. You're all thumbs." Elspeth pushed Cristie's hands aside and loosened the laces with deft fingers. "There you go. Now tell me what happened. I'm curious about what you said earlier. About me being right. What did you mean by that, exactly?"

"Why should you care?"

She shrugged. "Maybe because I was supposed to be the one marrying into the MacKellar clan. Just tell me what you meant."

Cristie stepped out of her robe and lay it atop her discarded cloak. "Simply that the whole idea was foolish, and that I regret being a part of it," she replied. "Just as you said I would."

"But how were you found out?" Head cocked, Elspeth regarded her with a frown. "Did you confess?"

"Not voluntarily." Cristie didn't mention she'd intended to tell Ewan the truth. Instead, she explained about the priest. "He said he knew you, and I couldnae deny it, so I had no choice but to own up. Ewan brought me back here and said to tell Alastair he's no longer welcome on MacKellar land. And that's it."

"So much for his precious alliance," Elspeth said. Then her mouth twitched. "Tell me, did you find a pile of hidden treasure?"

Cristie threw her a withering glance. "I've answered your questions, so you can go now."

Elspeth waved the remark aside. "Was Ewan MacKellar unkind to you?"

"Nay." Wincing at the soreness in her belly, Cristie sat on the edge of her bed. "I've naught else to say. I just want to rest a while."

"But I have more questions."

"And I dinnae care to answer them."

Elspeth grunted. "What's in the bag?"

"Some personal things, and I'll thank you to leave them be."

Elspeth shrugged, picked up the bag, and shook the contents onto the bed, her eyes widening. "Oh, what a bonny shawl!" She held it up to the meagre light. "The colours are glorious, and it feels so *soft*. I never saw such a fine weave. Is it silk? A comb, too. How pretty." She frowned. "A seashell? Why would you bring a dirty old seashell back with you?"

Cristie let out a cry and snatched the shawl from Elspeth's hands. "Are you deaf? I said to leave them be. I'd really like you to go now."

Elspeth raised her brows. "Are they gifts from him? From Ewan MacKellar?"

"What does it matter?"

"Are they?"

Cristie sniffed as she put the things back in the bag. "Aye."

"He was good to you, then."

"Aye, he was." Cristie's throat tightened. "They all were."

Elspeth fell silent. Unsettled by her sister's obvious scrutiny, Cristie kept her eyes lowered and her hands folded in her lap. In truth, she longed to speak of her heartache, to lay bare the raw pain of her emotions. To unburden her soul, even a little. But did she dare trust Elspeth?

"Ah, shite," Elspeth murmured, "you've gone and fallen in love with him. You've fallen in love with Ewan MacKellar. Am I right?"

Cristie released a shaky sigh and closed her eyes. "Please, Elspeth. I… I just need to rest."

"Oh, Cristie, pet, I'm so sorry." Elspeth sat beside her and took her hand. "I never thought for a moment that you might fall in love with the man."

The unexpected display of compassion brought Cristie's fragile emotions to the surface. She swallowed a sob and met Elspeth's gaze. "Well, it doesnae really matter anymore, does it? Ewan MacKellar can no longer bear the sight of me."

"Was he very angry?"

"Or course he was. And hurt. I betrayed him. I betrayed *everyone*." Cristie sniffed. "But before that, I... I felt certain he was falling in love with me too. The way he looked at me, the way he spoke to me. He's a stubborn man, mind. But, oh, Elspeth, no one has ever treated me as kindly, or with as much respect. I hated deceiving him. I meant to tell him the truth the day the priest arrived, but I never got the chance." She bit down on her lip. "Not that it would have made any difference. The result would have been the same. So, aye, you were right, and I wish I'd listened to you. Please dinnae tell Alastair any of this, I beg you. He'll only torment me with it."

"I'll say naught to anyone, I promise." Tears in her eyes, Elspeth heaved a sigh. "I suppose the marriage will be annulled."

"I dinnae believe it was ever legitimate." Cristie's lip trembled. "Ewan said... he said it was worthless."

"Did you have to use... I mean, you're not, um... is there any chance you might be carrying?"

For some reason, Cristie couldn't bring herself to admit that she was still an innocent. She shook her head. "Nay, I dinnae carry his child. I tossed the wee packet into the privy before I left."

"Well, that's a blessing for sure, all things considered." Then, to Cristie's great surprise, Elspeth leaned in and kissed her bruised cheek. "Get some rest, pet. We'll talk again later."

*

Cristie opened her eyes to darkness and confusion, the latter dissipating as her sluggish mind became aware of her surroundings. With consciousness came the familiar sense of despair, pressing on her heart like a stone. She wondered at the hour. Obviously late, she thought, judging by the absence of light and the silence beyond her door.

Her parched throat resisted an attempt to swallow. Wincing, she sat up, feeling rather like she'd been flung against a stone wall. But, driven by thirst, she slid from her bed, dressed as hurriedly as her pain would allow, and stumbled out into the unlit passageway.

Spurred on by a tell-tale scuffle and squeak from a dark corner, Cristie felt her way up the stairs and into the kitchen. A faint gleam from the banked fires cast a feeble, but welcoming glow into the room. She glared at the tabby cat who was stretched out by the hearth, licking its paws.

"You lazy wee beastie," she whispered. "There are things down those stairs needing your attention."

The cat responded with a brief, disdainful glance and continued with its ablutions. Cristie lifted an ewer from the table and filled a goblet. She downed the contents in several greedy gulps, her sore tongue making her wince.

Still craving, she wiped the drips from her chin and went to lift the ewer again, but froze, the hair on her neck rising. From the hallway beyond came the sound of men's voices. Although hushed, one of them was quite distinctive.

Alastair.

Panic knotted beneath her ribs. Holding her breath, she set her goblet down and scurried back to the stairwell, pausing at the top. The thick darkness below did not lend itself to a swift, or safe, descent. With no time to spare, she shrank into the shadows at the top of the stairs. Then, heart rattling, she waited.

And listened.

"The man is close to death anyway," Alastair said, in gruff tones. "You'll be doing him a kindness."

"'Tis murder, nonetheless," came the sombre reply, the identity of the second man now clear to Cristie. *Tasgall.* "I'd kill to defend you, laird, you know it. But to kill an innocent man in cold-blood? You demand much of me."

"I demanded it once before and you persuaded me to wait. I shouldnae have listened then, and I'll no' listen now. This time you'll obey me, Tasgall, with no argument. 'Twill be a swift end, and you dinnae even have to spill his blood to do it. A wee dram in a wineskin of ale is all." There came the sound of a lock turning. "Fergus used some of it on wolf bait last week. I hope he didnae use it all. Ah, here it is. Good. There's more than enough left."

Tasgall let out an audible sigh. "Are you sure about this, Laird? You could always try negotiating for *something.*"

Alastair huffed. "Such as? I only wanted Morag. Ewan MacKellar's untimely return wrecked that wee plan. And sending Cristie in Elspeth's place was a risk that didnae pay off, thanks to the damn priest." He huffed again. "I still refuse to believe the Templars left France empty-handed, mind, but I cannae prove otherwise. So, nay, there'll be no more negotiating. 'Tis unfortunate, but Ruaidri MacKellar's life no longer has any value. You'll ride out at dawn and finish it. With any luck, he may have succumbed already, and you'll have only to bury him."

Cristie clamped a hand over her mouth, halting the involuntary gasp that wanted to emerge. *Ruaidri MacKellar?* Shock deadened her brain, suffocating all coherent thoughts. Except one.

Ruaidri MacKellar is still alive? How can that be?

She shivered as the answer came at her in a sickening rush. Alastair's deceit went beyond treacherous. It was heinous. A cruel deception, worthy of the Devil himself.

The MacKellar's had mourned the death of a beloved brother. Their clan had mourned the loss of a beloved laird. And Alastair had feigned sympathy, pretended to search for a man who, he knew, would never be found.

What of the horse's remains and the bloodied clothes? How far had Alastair gone in this journey of deception? Hate, like Cristie had never felt, welled up inside. She tried to calm herself, for she needed to think. And she needed to act. She also needed to be careful.

Where is he being held? Not at Dunraven, for sure. Alastair could never have kept such a terrible secret quiet. So, where then?

Still shivering, Cristie cocked an ear, all at once aware of the silence. *Have they left?* Hand still clamped over her mouth, she dared to peek around the corner. The kitchen was empty, and her gaze flicked to the small cupboard by the rear door. The one Alastair had evidently opened. She knew it was kept padlocked for a reason, its contents being of a perilous nature. Deadly tinctures like belladonna, foxglove, and…

'Fergus used some of it on wolf bait last week…'
Wolf's bane?

Her hand dropped, freeing her voice. "Oh, Alastair," she murmured, her throat constricting. "How could you? How could you be so… evil?"

She willed herself to stop trembling and tried to clear her befuddled brain. She had to stop Tasgall somehow. But how? He'd sounded reluctant to kill Ruaidri. Unwilling. Perhaps she should seek him out right away and plead with him. *Nay. Too risky.* His loyalty had always been to Alastair.

'You'll ride out at dawn…'

"To where?" she murmured, closing her eyes. "Where would Alastair hold a man prisoner, if not at Dunraven?"

In her mind, she gave herself imaginary wings and soared aloft, searching the glen for a likely place. Like a mirror, the loch stretched out below her, reflecting the surrounding hills. At one end, Dunraven stood watch as it had for over a century. But other than the farms and cottages belonging to the tenants, there were no other buildings. Certainly, none of a defensive sort.

Cristie held her breath. *As it had for over a century.*

Of course! There had been another fortress before Dunraven. One built and occupied by the Norsemen. In her mind, Cristie looked to the far north-western shore of the loch, where a stand of silver birch clustered around the ruins of an earlier and much older castle, one that had burned in a skirmish long ago.

She couldn't remember its name. She only knew that little of it remained above ground. *But what about below? It likely had a cellar or dungeon. Is it still intact? Could a man be kept prisoner there?* She cursed her uncertainty, yet it seemed like the only feasible location.

'*The man is close to death anyway*'...

"God, please, help me," she whispered, opening her eyes. "I dinnae ken what to do."

There was only one other person she could turn to. Did she dare? Aye, she had to. What other choice did she have?

Chapter Eighteen

Breathless from her covert flight up the stairs, Cristie stood before Elspeth's door and took a deep breath. *Please dinnae be locked.* She lifted the latch and pushed. To her boundless relief, the door swung open with a weary groan. She entered and closed the door behind her.

"Elspeth?"

No reply. Cristie blinked as her eyes adjusted to the dark.

"Elspeth, please." She approached the bed. "Wake up."

"What?" Elspeth gasped and rose up on an elbow. "Cristie! God's teeth, what are you doing creeping about? You scared the life out of me."

"I'm sorry, but I need your help."

"With what?" Elspeth sat up. "Is something wrong?"

Cristie shivered. "Aye, terribly wrong, and I fear I dinnae have much time. The old ruined castle at the far end of the loch. Do you know if there's a cellar? Or a dungeon? A place where a man might be held captive?"

Elspeth snorted. "What, in God's holy name, are you prattling about? Did you have a nightmare?"

"Nay, but I fear I'm facing one," she replied, her voice breaking. "Please, Elspeth. I swear this is no jest. 'Tis a matter of life and death."

Elspeth fell silent for a moment. "I'll no' talk to someone I cannae see," she said, at last. "There's tinder on the table. Light the candle, and then explain yourself."

Cristie, near frantic with desperation, bit back a curse. Her hands trembled as she struck the flint, but at last she managed to light the taper and turned back to Elspeth.

"Better," Elspeth said, her eyes wide in the candlelight. "Now, tell me what this is about."

"Ruaidri MacKellar."

A frown appeared. "What about him?"

"He's still alive."

The frown vanished as Elspeth's jaw dropped. "What? Have you lost your mind? Why would you declare such a thing? You must have dreamt it."

"It was no dream, Elspeth," Cristie said, clasping her hands at her breast. "I overheard Alastair and Tasgall just now, talking about *him*. About Ruaidri. He's being held captive somewhere, but they didnae say where, only that he's to be killed in the morning. Poisoned with wolf's bane, I think. Alastair said..." She choked back a sob.

"Alastair said the man was close to death anyway. That killing him would be merciful. I have to do something to stop it, but I dinnae ken where he's being held, and we dinnae have much time."

Fidgeting, Cristie waited. "Elspeth?"

Why did she not answer?

Elspeth continued to regard Cristie with a stunned expression, and Cristie let out a soft cry of desperation. "Elspeth, please! I swear this is no jest."

Elspeth blinked. "Aye, there is."

"What?"

"A cellar," she said, tears filling her eyes. "There is a cellar at Ravenstone. A place where a man might be held. But I cannae believe… God in Heaven, Cristie, what has he done? What has Alastair done?"

"Do you think that's where he's being held?" Cristie wrung her hands. "I need to be certain, or close to certain. Is there anywhere else you can think of?"

Elspeth pondered a moment. "Well, there's no way to be certain," she said, "but nay, I cannae think of anywhere else they might have hidden him. The place is said to be a lair for evil spirits, which means no one ever goes near.

'Twould be the ideal place to hide someone they dinnae want found."

Cristie nodded. "How far is it on horseback?"

"An hour's ride at least."

"At a gallop?"

"Nay, but at a good pace anyway."

"And on foot?"

"Two, three hours." Elspeth gave an incredulous laugh. "But you cannae go on foot, Cristie!"

"I have nae choice," Cristie said, her voice edged with frustration. "I cannae take a horse, because I'll be seen. Which means I'll have to leave now to get there before Tasgall."

Elspeth scoffed. "'Tis the middle of the night, and you're exhausted before you even begin. By the time you get to Ravenstone—*if* you get to Ravenstone—you'll be on your hands and knees. And *if* you get there in time, which is most unlikely, then what? You'll just break down the door and let Ruaidri out? Or do you intend to wait for Tasgall and demand he hands over the key? Aye, and he'll just hand it over to you without a fight, I suppose. Nay, Cristie. 'Tis a mission bound to fail."

Cristie clenched her fists. "I realize it's probably hopeless, but I cannae just stand by and do naught while a member of our clan murders the laird of another. I have to at least try and stop him."

"Tasgall is Alastair's hearth-hound. He'll no' disobey his master's command. And if Alastair finds out about this..." Elspeth's expression softened. "Look what he's done to you already. You'd risk your life for a stranger?"

Cristie gave a bitter laugh. "Ruaidri MacKellar is no stranger to me, Elspeth. I've spent time with those who loved him and listened as they shared their memories. I have to try to stop this anyway I can. I'll... I'll even throw myself in front of Tasgall's horse if need be." She turned to leave. "I must go. Please, dinnae say anything to Alastair."

Elspeth made a sound of desperation. "Nay, wait. Just let me think for a moment. Maybe there's a way we can get a horse past the gate without..." She drew a sudden breath. "Odin's bollocks. Of course! I swear there are times when I'm dafter than you!" She threw back the covers and slid out of bed. "Help me dress. Quickly."

"What? Why?"

"You're right." Elspeth tugged off her nightgown and tossed it aside. "A horse would be seen, but 'twould be folly to go on foot."

"So?" Cristie's teeth chattered. "Like I said, I have no choice."

"Aye, you do. There's another way. A third way. A path as smooth as a piece of slate and straight as an arrow's flight." Stark naked, Elspeth bounced on her toes and nodded toward a large oak chest at the foot of the bed. "God's teeth, I'm freezing. Pass me my shift and be quick."

Cristie did as bidden. "A third way?"

"Aye, a quicker and easier way." Elspeth pulled her shift over her head. "Have you ever rowed a boat, Cristie?"

*

They sneaked out of the rear postern gate and crept along the outer wall, keeping to the thickest shadows. Cristie, wearing one of Elspeth's cloaks, carried a blanket, and a small linen bag containing food, a dagger, a tinder box, and a taper, also supplied by Elspeth.

"Assuming, by some heavenly miracle, you manage to escape into the mountains, you'll need a blanket," Elspeth had said. "The food, tinderbox and taper need no explanation. Nor does the blade, although I'm curious to know if you're prepared to use it, if that's what it takes."

Her query had not been answered. Not then, and not since. A dozen different scenarios had played out in Cristie's mind, none of them ideal. Until the time actually came, she wasn't sure what she'd do. At this point, she wasn't even sure she'd find Ruaidri, alive or dead.

"There," Elspeth whispered, pointing to the water's edge. "In that wee cove over by the trees. Do you see it?"

The small boat formed a black shape against the paler, rocky shore.

"Aye, I see it."

"It belongs to Fergus. He'll be as mad as a hellhound when he finds it gone."

"He'll get it back," Cristie said. "Eventually."

"The night couldnae be better, either," Elspeth continued, glancing about. "No moon, clear skies, calm water. 'Tis perfect."

Cristie gave her a reproachful glance. "If I didnae ken any better, Elspeth MacAulay, I'd venture to say you're enjoying yourself."

"Well, nay, not *enjoying* exactly." She raised her hood. "But I confess, I do find all this rather stimulating. Cover your head, Cristie, and follow me. And watch your step, for Christ's sake. Dinnae fall and hurt yourself."

They scurried across the open space without looking back. Cristie stumbled once, stifling a cry, but kept from falling. Her heart drummed in her ears—a frantic accompaniment to her rapid breathing as she moved further away from the castle walls. Despite wearing a dark cloak and being under cover of night, she felt utterly exposed, certain to be spotted at any moment by those keeping watch.

But a call of alarm, thankfully, never came.

At last, they reached the small cove and Elspeth turned to Cristie, eyes bright even in the darkness. "So far so good," she whispered, on a laboured breath. "But we must still be very quiet. The loch carries sound, especially when it's calm, like tonight. Help me push this thing, will you?"

The small boat slid into the water with little difficulty. Elspeth grabbed hold of the bow rope, holding the vessel steady. "In you go," she whispered. "Sit in the middle. Aye, that's it. Do you ken how to steer?"

Cristie took hold of the oars and set them in the oarlocks. "Aye."

"Good. And do you ken how to swim?" She frowned. "Not that it makes much difference, mind. The water is frigid. If you fall in, you'll no' last long."

Cristie wrinkled her nose. "Aye, I ken how to swim, and appreciate the reassuring words."

Elspeth shrugged. "Just dinnae fall in, and you'll be fine. All you have to do is keep the wee boat on a diagonal course from here to the opposite corner." She lifted her eyes to the sky and pointed. "See that star, there? Hanging over the horizon? That's the mariner's star. It doesnae move across the heavens like the rest. Keep it just over your left shoulder as a guide."

Cristie huffed. "I'm rowing across the damn loch, Elspeth, not sailing to Ireland. Throw the rope in, will you?"

Elspeth hesitated a moment. "Cristie?"

"Aye?"

"I think you're dafter than a duck. But I also think you're very brave."

Cristie smiled. "I'm terrified, in truth."

"Just save the poor man." Elspeth tossed the rope into the boat. "And Godspeed."

Chapter Nineteen

Darkness surrounded her. Above, on all sides, and most terrifying of all, below. Cristie tried not to think about the frigid black depths beneath her small boat. She prayed as she rowed, begging for the courage and strength to endure. It had been a while since she'd set out on her dubious quest. Now, each pull of the oars tore at her shoulders and burned her blistered hands. But she didn't dare stop, not even for a moment. To do so would mean she had failed.

The eastern horizon would soon brighten, and Tasgall would be on his way to carry out his evil objective. Cristie winced as she looked over her shoulder, relieved to be able to make out some faint detail on the distant shore. It occurred to her that she had been within a short ride from Ravenstone the day before. As had Ewan, of course.

She bit back tears. Would she ever be able to think of him without crying? Undoubtedly, her love for Ewan MacKellar was part of what fuelled her determination to save Ruaidri. But she also saw it a chance to atone for the terrible wrong she'd done, to ease some of the burden on her conscience. She told herself she did not aspire to any kind of romantic reconciliation with Ewan and then silently berated herself. Of course, she aspired to it but, fearful of an unbearable disappointment, she did not dare hope for it.

A sudden, nearby splash made her jump. A fish, perhaps. Or an otter. Wrenched back to awareness, she glanced about again, this time noting a faint glow in the eastern sky. At that same moment, as if to confirm the imminent arrival of a new day, a robin chirped out its sweet winter refrain.

The sound pulled Cristie's attention to the shoreline once again, where she could now make out more details; a stand of thick pine, a small reed-choked cove, and a rocky outcrop jutting out into the water.

The proximity of the shore weakened Cristie's resolve to continue rowing. Her shoulders burned and her blistered hands felt as though they had been stripped to the bone. It was still too dark to make out her actual location, but she felt sure she could not be far from Ravenstone. Close enough, certainly, to continue on foot. Decided, she began to look for a suitable place to land and found a small inlet a little further along.

It took all she had to turn the boat towards the shore. A few more pulls, and the wooden hull scraped to a halt on the loch bed. Cristie unfurled her sticky hands from the oars and gritted her teeth against the searing pain. Even in the gloom, she could see the bloody mess coating her palms and fingers.

"You've come this far, Cristie Ferguson," she muttered. "Dinnae quit now."

Toes to heel, she levered her shoes off and made a somewhat graceless exit from the boat. Ankle deep, the frigid water made her gasp. Seeking relief for her hands, she bent and plunged them into the loch too, the sharp shock making her yelp.

Unbidden, a fierce tremble shook her body, and it was all she could do to retrieve her belongings and paddle ashore. As for tying off the boat, she at least managed to drag the bowline onto land and weigh it with some stones. If the boat drifted, so be it. Whatever fate had in store for her that night, she'd not be rowing back to Dunraven.

Wrapped in the blanket, she settled on a small hillock, pulled on her shoes with her torn hands, and gathered her wits as she surveyed her surroundings.

The night was now in solid retreat. The robin's solitary song had swelled into a dawn chorus. Like the previous day, patches of mist were forming here and there. The air smelled of pine but tasted salty, the latter often a harbinger of rain. For now, though, the scattered clouds offered no threat.

Then Cristie turned her gaze to the end of the loch, where a distant stand of silver birch had become visible in the gloom; pale, leafless skeletons that, if her instincts did not lie, harboured a sad and terrible secret.

All at once, her aches and pains seemed inconsequential, her hardship trivial. "Dinnae give up yet, Ruaidri," she whispered, her throat tightening. "I'm coming to take you home."

A raven cawed a welcome—or perhaps a warning—as Cristie approached. The feathered sentinel, perched atop a lopsided column of stone, cocked its blue-black head and regarded her. She hugged her belongings close to her chest and glanced about.

Little remained of what had once been a Norse longhouse. Built of wood, most of it had been consumed by the fire, and most of the stones from the more recent curtain wall had been reused in the construction of Dunraven. Still, the original foundation lines were still visible, and Cristie's gaze followed them, looking for evidence of an underground chamber.

There.

Her attention fixed upon what appeared to have been one of the corner bastions, and the remains of a winding stone staircase that jutted into the air, going nowhere. Did that same staircase continue in a downward spiral, into the earth? Heart pounding, Cristie approached and peered over the ruined walls. Yes, the staircase descended.

Into blackness.

The raven let out another caw, startling Cristie. "The Devil take you," she muttered, blowing out a breath. But the bird's cry stirred her to action. Tasgall was undoubtedly on his way. Setting the blanket down, she took the tinderbox from the bag, lit the candle, and started down the narrow stairs.

At the bottom, she halted and raised the small flame aloft, but its meagre light failed to penetrate more than a few feet ahead. She seemed to be in a narrow passageway, with walls of damp stone and a packed, earthen floor. It was dark, dank, and cold

Like a grave.

A prickle crawled over her scalp. She could not begin to imagine what it would be like to be down here for nigh on six weeks. Alone. Starved of light. She glanced back at the stairwell as if to reassure herself that she had a way out.

"The man is close to death anyway. You'll be doing him a kindness."

"Please, God, let him still be alive." Tears pricked at her eyes as she stepped forward and called his name. "Laird MacKellar. Ruaidri MacKellar." Her voice echoed eerily into the unknown. "Can you hear me? Will you answer me?"

She held her breath and listened, hearing nothing except the thud of her heart. She swallowed her fear and took a few more tentative steps. A space appeared on her right, like a small cave hewn out of the earth, its rotten wooden door hanging askew on its hinges. A storage room, perhaps, and not one she wished to explore.

Several steps later, Cristie felt a sense of space as the passage widened into what had to be the old cellar. An odour—nay, a *stench*—caused her nostrils to flare. It was a fetid brew, a mix of bodily excretions and filth that remained undiluted in the stagnant air.

And it was, most definitely, human.

"Ruaidri?" Trembling, Cristie held her puny candle aloft and squinted into the blackness. "Laird MacKellar? Are you here? Will you answer me? I'm here to help you. I'm here to take you home."

A faint noise came out of the dark; a scuffle, and what sounded like a single, soft breath.

Candle still held aloft, Cristie moved forward again, squinting into the shadows, trying to see detail. The stench intensified, and she swallowed against an urge to retch. Then her light fell upon a metal door, like that of a cage. Square in shape, it sat flush in the wall, its bars rusty but solid. The door was bolted.

And padlocked.

"Laird MacKellar?" Cristie approached and peered through the bars. The candle's feeble light did not clear all the darkness away, but at first glance, the cell appeared to be empty. A layer of filthy straw covered the floor. A wooden bucket sat near the right wall, while a rough pallet lay on the opposite side. The vile stink brought tears to her eyes.

Christ have mercy. How could they? How could they even think to keep a man in such squalor?

But where was the man? She moved closer. "Ruai—"

A hand shot out, grabbed her robe at her chest, and pulled her body hard against the bars. Cristie let out a squeal and dropped the candle, plunging her into darkness. But not before she'd looked into a pair of mad, dark eyes set in a filthy, bearded face that could hardly be described as human.

"Who are you?" he growled, his foul breath making Cristie gag.

"M-my name is Cristie." She tugged at his hand. "I'm… I'm here to help you. Please, let me go."

His grip tightened. "Who sent you?"

"No one."

"I'll ask you again," he said, spraying spittle across Cristie's face, "who sent you?"

"No one sent me, Laird MacKellar, I swear it. I'm here because I heard a conversation I wasnae meant to hear. Tasgall will be here soon, too, and he's coming to kill you. He's going to give you a drink, but it'll be poisoned, so you must no' drink it."

Ruaidri's hot, foul breath continued to wash over her face. "You're a MacAulay?"

"I am Alastair's half-sister," she replied. "But I came here alone, and only mean to help you, I swear to God."

His grip loosened a little. "Who hit you?"

"W-what?"

"I saw your face before you dropped the candle. Who put the bruises on you?"

"Al-Alastair."

"Why?"

Cristie struggled against him. "We dinnae have time for this! Tasgall will be—"

"Answer the question."

"Because… because I challenged him."

His grip tightened once more, and then he released her. "Do you have a key for the padlock?"

"Um, nay."

He laughed softly. "So, what is your plan? Do you mean to tackle Tasgall and take the key?"

"Aye, if… if need be."

He inhaled. "Then you must have a weapon."

"Aye, a dagger."

"Praise God. Give it to me."

"But what—?"

"Just give me the knife, lass."

"What do you intend to do?"

"Given the chance, I intend to slit the bastard's throat. You'll have no trouble taking the key from him when he's dead."

"Nay." She shook her head and stepped back. "I… I dinnae think I can let you do that."

"You said you were here to help me." His breath rattled. "So, give me the damn knife."

"Nay."

"For Christ's sake," he muttered. "What good are you, then? To the Devil with you."

Cristie crouched and groped blindly around on the floor, searching for the errant candle. At last, she found it and dug in her bag for the tinderbox. "Just dinnae drink anything he gives you," she said, trying to get a flame.

Ruaidri huffed. "I'd rather drink his poison than stay in this godforsaken pit another day."

"Dinnae say such things," she said, rising as the wick at last flared to life. She shielded the little flame with her hand. "I mean to get you out of here, but I… I'm no' quite sure how yet."

There came a scuffling sound from behind, and Cristie's blanket landed in a heap at her feet.

"Well, to begin," said a familiar voice, "'tis none too clever leaving clues about your presence lying around outside."

"Tasgall!" Cristie gasped. Candle in one hand, she groped for her dagger with the other, her blistered flesh making her wince. "Dinnae come any closer."

Tasgall scoffed as she pointed the weapon at him. "Aye, and what do you plan to do with that? Clean my fingernails? You're no match for me, lass, with or without a blade. Christ almighty, what are you doing here?"

"She's rescuing me," Ruaidri said, his voice weary, "but so far, 'tis nae going very well."

"Shut your mouth, MacKellar." Tasgall moved forward, scowling as he regarded Cristie. "How did you find out?"

"I was in the kitchen last night and overheard your conversation with Alastair," she said, raising her chin while silently cursing the tremble in her voice. "And I could scarce believe it, Tasgall. 'Tis sickening what Alastair has done, letting everyone think Laird MacKellar dead, and you a part of it. How could you do such a terrible thing? And why? It doesnae make sense. You should be ashamed."

His sword hand curled into a fist. "Who else knows you're here?"

She held his gaze. "No one."

"Dinnae lie to me." He moved closer, his hard features softened by candlelight. His eyes, however, glinted like slivers of black granite. "This place wasnae mentioned last night. So how did you find out about it? And how did you get here?"

Cristie shrugged. "It wasnae hard to guess where a man might be hidden and held captive. There's no other likely place hereabouts. And I came by boat."

He looked perplexed. "Boat?"

"Aye. I borrowed Fergus's rowboat."

Tasgall grabbed her wrist, causing her to yelp and drop the knife. His jaw tightened visibly as he studied her blistered palm. "Shite," he muttered, releasing her. He bent to retrieve the knife. "I cannae believe this."

Still muttering, he snatched the candle from Cristie, went to a metal sconce on the wall, and lit a reed torch, which crackled and snapped as it flared to life. Cristie threw a frustrated glance at Ruaidri, wondering why he'd failed to mention its existence, but the sight of him in the clearer light all but stopped her heart.

What unearthly force, she wondered, allowed this sad vision of neglect to stay upright? Filthy clothes, their colours indefinable, hung loose on Ruaidri's thin, begrimed limbs. His hair, no less hideous, was a matted mess, as was his lengthy, unkempt beard.

Ruaidri stared back for a moment and then smiled through his tangle of whiskers. "Aye, I'm a wee bit untidy," he said, scratching at his chin. "You should have given me the knife. After I'd slit Tasgall's throat, I'd intended to have a shave and make a few beasties homeless."

"How could you," Cristie whispered. "How could you be so damn *cruel*?"

Ruaidri's brows lifted. "You'd no' be so accusing if you had a beard crawling with the wee bastards."

"Nay, Ruaidri, I didnae mean—" She bit back a sob and turned on Tasgall. "Dear God above, will you look at him? He's near starved to death. Could you not have least fed the man?"

"He's given food, but barely touches it," Tasgall said. "And I *am* looking at him, Cristie. I'm seeing a man who's lost his mind and has only hours to live. Alastair's right. 'Twill be a mercy to kill him."

"A mercy, aye." Ruaidri sniffed, stuck a hand through the bars and waggled it. "I'm told you have something for me, Tasgall. Hand it over, then, and let me drink my last. I cannae wait to be free of this hellish shithole."

"Nay!" Cristie dashed away a tear. "Tasgall, please, let me take him home."

"Home?" Tasgall gave a sardonic laugh. "And just how do you plan to do that, eh? You cannae row the damn boat over the pass, and MacKellar isnae capable of walking very far. You really havenae thought this through, have you? And dinnae dare judge me, either, after what you did. You're as much a part of this as I am."

Heat flooded Cristie's cheeks. "The Devil take you, Tasgall," she said. "I knew naught of this vile deceit till last night, so I've barely had time to think things through. And I've yet to fathom the reasons for it."

"Aye, well, he was never meant to be here this long." Tasgall unhooked a wineskin from his belt. "Move aside, lass."

"Nay, I willnae." Spreading her arms, she backed up a step. "I'll no' let you do this."

"Do as the man says, lass, and shift your arse." Ruaidri said, his bony hand pushing at her shoulder. "I dinnae want to be alive when that torch goes out again. If you wish to save me, you can pray for my mortal soul, since it's about to be dispatched to eternal damnation."

"Nay!" she cried again, but despite her attempt to resist him, Tasgall shoved her aside with little effort.

"Here, lad," he said, and placed the wineskin in Ruaidri's hand. "Be sure to drink it all, and quickly."

Cristie let out a wail as she tried, and failed, to snatch the vessel from Ruaidri's grasp. "Nay, dinnae drink it, please! Think about what you're doing, Laird MacKellar. Think… think about Morag."

Ruaidri froze. "Och, now why did you have to go and mention my sister?" His shoulders sagged and his eyes softened with tears. "The poor wee lass. I promised her I'd return."

"'Tis no' too late to do so!" Desperate, Cristie clung to the bars as she pleaded with him. "She would never want you to finish your life this way."

"Nay, she wouldnae, true enough, but since she thinks me dead already, she'll be none the wiser." Ruaidri pulled the stopper from the wine skin and raised the vessel to his lips.

Cristie let out a shriek. "Wait!" she cried "What about Ewan?"

"Odin's bollocks," Tasgall muttered, and pulled his sword. "You'll say naught else, lass."

Brow furrowed, Ruaidri paused and looked at her. "Ewan?"

"Aye, Ewan," Cristie replied. "Ewan Tormod MacKellar. Your brother."

"That'll do, Cristie," Tasgall growled. "I'll no' tell you again."

Ruaidri's frown deepened. "What of him?"

"You mean, you dinnae…?" Cristie turned to face Tasgall. "Dear God. Has he not been told?"

Ruaidri lowered the wineskin. "Been told what?"

Tasgall snarled and lifted Cristie's chin with the flat of his blade. "I'm warning you, lass. The next word from your mouth will be your last."

"Been told what?" Ruaidri asked again, his voice stronger.

Cristie looked along the length of cold steel that was poised to end her life.

"Dinnae make me," Tasgall whispered. "He's no' worth it."

She met his gaze without flinching. "He has more worth than you or me, Tasgall."

Tasgall's nostrils flared. "Dinnae make me, lass."

"Ewan has come home, Laird MacKellar," Cristie announced, her voice loud and determined. "He returned to Castle Cathan six weeks ago."

Tasgall let out a desperate groan as the point of his sword pressed against the well of her throat. "Curse your bones, Cristie Ferguson. You give yourself to one MacKellar, and now you're willing to die for another? Well, here's a wee revelation for you before you leave this world." His face twisted into an expression of pain. "You were supposed to be my bride. Alastair promised you to *me*. You were supposed to marry *me*."

Stunned, Cristie gaped at him. "Tasgall, I... oh, dear God. I wasnae aware. Truly. Alastair never said—"

A haunting cry cut off her response; a primal wail of agony that froze the blood in her veins. She gasped and spun round to see Ruaidri on his knees, head bowed, hands covering his face.

A sudden thrust of panic all but stopped Cristie's heart as she looked for the wineskin. *Och, nay, Ruaidri, you didnae drink it!* Then she spotted it on the ground beside him, its contents leaking out into the straw. *Thank God. Oh, thank God.*

Ruaidri's dreadful lament faded into silence, although his face remained buried in his hands. Then his shoulders began to shake as ragged sobs tore from him, one after another. Tears leached through his fingers, leaving pale tracks as they washed over the backs of his grubby hands. In all her days, Cristie had never seen such wretchedness. This was the epitome of anguish, she realized, a display of utter despair that clawed at her already-broken heart.

"Let him go, Tasgall," she said, turning back to the man who still held his blade in readiness to finish her. This, she knew, would be her final plea, no matter the outcome. "If he must die, let him die a free man beneath an open sky. Please, I'm begging you. If you do naught else good in your life, do this one thing. He probably willnae have the strength to return home, but at least let him try. I'll stay with you if you wish. I'll marry you. I'll do anything you want. Anything at all. But please, let Ruaidri MacKellar go."

Breathing hard, Tasgall stared at Cristie, his knuckles white against the hilt of his sword. Ruaidri's harsh sobs quietened, although he still wept softly.

"If Alastair says you've to marry me, you'll have no choice but to do so," Tasgall said, at last. "Ruaidri MacKellar's fate has little bearing on it."

"That is true," Cristie replied, her throat dry, "but if you kill Ruaidri, I'll hate you forever. If you let him go, I'll... I'll wed you willingly."

"Willingly?" Tasgall gave a soft chuckle and lowered his blade. "Och, I doubt that, lass. See, I ken you care for Ewan MacKellar. I saw the way you looked at him when last I was at Castle Cathan."

Shocked by his insight, Cristie swallowed. "Well, Ewan MacKellar cannae bear the sight of me, so that has naught to do with—"

"I envy the bastard." Tasgall gave her a grim smile. "I cannae imagine you'd ever look at me that way, no matter what happens here today."

"Tasgall, I—"

"Be silent, lass." He held up a hand. "Just... be silent."

The torch spat, and Ruaidri continued to weep as Cristie waited. Tasgall closed his eyes for a moment, drew a slow, deep breath, and released it. Then, to her bewilderment, he slid his sword into its sheath, pulled a key from a pouch on his belt, and moved past her.

"I'll thank you to take good care of Jock," he said. "I've had him from a foal. He's a strong horse, but obedient, and he shouldnae give you any trouble. I'll take the saddle, though. You'll no' have need of it with two of you on his back. And dinnae forget your blanket. Judging by the salt in the air, there's likely some rain moving in from the west. Might turn to snow in the mountains."

The padlock sprang apart as the key turned. Tasgall removed it, slid the bolt back, and tugged the cell door open.

Still confused, Cristie frowned. "Tasgall, what…?"

"Here's your knife," he said, handing it to her. "Where's the boat?"

Was he jesting? Toying with her? Cristie opened her mouth to speak, but merely blinked at him.

"Have you gone deaf, lass?" Tasgall moved toward the passageway. "Where's Fergus's boat?"

Cristie took a breath. "But, how will you explain—?"

Tasgall growled. "Just tell me where to find the damn boat!"

"'Tis… 'tis in a wee cove on the west side of the loch. A short walk is all."

"Right." He grimaced and scratched his head. "When I get back to Dunraven, I plan to tell Alastair the truth, which means he'll likely come after you, so I suggest you dinnae linger here too long. God speed, Cristie Ferguson." A brief smile came and went. "Ewan MacKellar is a fortunate man."

Then he turned and disappeared into the darkness.

Still unable to fully grasp what Tasgall had done—and what it *meant*—Cristie continued to stare at the spot where he'd stood moments before, half-expecting him to return.

A noise from behind drew her attention, and she turned to see Ruaidri standing outside the cell door.

"Is it true?" he asked, his cheeks streaked with dirt and tears. "Has my brother really returned?"

"Aye, 'tis true." The torch spat again, and this time the light dimmed. *Hurry*, it seemed to say. Cristie approached and took Ruaidri's hand, ignoring the pain in her own. His fingers closed around hers, and her spirit dared to hope. "What do you say we get out of this shithole, Laird MacKellar? I'll tell you all about Ewan on the way home."

"Home?" His chest rose and fell. "Aye, I should like very much to go home."

Chapter Twenty

Outside, Cristie watched Ruaidri fall to his knees and lift his face to the sky, drinking in the fresh air like a man dying of thirst. His profound embrace of freedom, his gratitude for something that so many took for granted, drew fresh tears to Cristie's eyes. Also, in the pale, grey light of early morning, his emaciated state seemed even more pronounced.

They had many miles to go and an unyielding mountain pass to navigate. Yet Ruaidri MacKellar barely had the strength to clamber onto Jock's broad back. Cristie wondered if the man would be able to endure what lay ahead. Her hope wobbled a little.

"Settle this around you," she said, handing him the blanket. "'Tis a chill morning. There's some bread in the bag, too, if you'd like it."

"Nay, not right now."

"As you wish." She grabbed a handful of Jock's mane. "I need a stirrup, Laird."

Ruaidri extended his foot and Cristie used it to hoist herself up. Wrinkling her nose, she settled her arse between his thighs. The man's body odour was a problem of a different nature—unpleasant, but not worrisome. Trivial, for now.

"Och, will you look at your hands, lass," he said. "Let me take the reins."

"Nay, I can manage." She gathered them up. "You need to save your strength. Hold onto me."

An arm circled around her waist. "I've never feared anything as much as I fear this might all be a dream," he murmured, a slight tremble in his voice, "and that any moment now, I'll awaken to darkness."

"'Tis no dream, Laird, as you'll soon realize." She regarded the distant mountains. "We've a long road ahead, and I dinnae care for the look of the sky over there."

He gave a soft grunt. "So, will you tell me about Ewan?"

"Aye, I will, and there's a lot to tell." The sudden movement of an overhead shadow drew Cristie's gaze. A raven soared aloft, perhaps the one she'd seen earlier. It let out a harsh cry and drew a wide circle above them. "If you'll allow, wait till this eve when we stop to rest. Then I'll tell you everything. Ewan is well, I'll tell you that much for now."

"If I had my way," Ruaidri muttered, "we'd no' stop till we reached Cathan's gates."

The raven released another harsh call as Cristie urged the horse forward. "That, Laird MacKellar, would only be possible if we had wings," she said. "In the meantime, you can pray we dinnae meet anyone on the road 'tween here and the pass."

His breath rattled against her ear. "What day is it, Cristie Ferguson?"

"'Tis the Lord's day, as it happens," she replied.

"I thought as much," he said, after a moment.

Without mishap or interruption, they reached the foot of the pass a few hours later. Cristie gazed up at the low clouds straddling the mountains and failed to suppress a shiver.

Ruaidri tugged at the blanket and shared it with her. "There." He folded her in his arms.

"My thanks." She continued to observe the skies ahead. "Though, in truth, 'tis more fear than chill. I dinnae relish this climb, nor the descent into MacKellar lands. We'll be blind once we get into those clouds."

Ruaidri gave a soft moan and tightened his hold on her. "MacKellar lands. By all things sacred, I never thought I'd see them again."

"You'll see them again soon enough, and your family." Cristie patted Jock's strong neck. "He'll carry us up, I think, but we might have to shelter in the bothy till the clouds lift. That's if we can find the bothy in the fog. How are you feeling? Do you need to rest here a while?"

"Nay, I'm fine, lass." He shifted his seat. "Unless Tasgall drowned in the loch, Alastair MacAulay is probably already on his way, and at a swifter pace than ours. We need to keep going."

Ruaidri's resolve touched Cristie's heart. She felt his internal struggle, recognized his determination despite his weakened state. His courage helped to shore up her own, for in truth, Cristie was struggling too. Beneath her veneer of fortitude lay a quicksand of fear and emotion. A part of her longed to see Ewan again. Another part of her dreaded it.

She squeezed her thighs and urged Jock onto the upward trail. The horse didn't hesitate, not even when they entered the thick curtain of clouds that hung over the mountain tops.

"I cannae barely see the horse's ears." A knot of fear twisted in Cristie's belly. "We could ride right past the bothy and never see it. 'Tis dangerous—nay, foolish—to carry on."

"All we have to do is follow the trail till we get to Cathan's Cairn," Ruaidri said. "It sits right next to the path, so we cannae miss it."

"Cathan's Cairn?" Cristie shook her head. "That's at the start of the descent, and we cannae descend in this. 'Twould be madness."

"I agree, but we're no' going to descend." His warm breath brushed over her hair. "I'm asking you to trust me. Cristie. I might look like a madman, but I know what I'm doing."

Cristie huffed. "You're just like your brother," she said. "Stubborn as a damn donkey."

"I dinnae think I'm as daft as him, though," he replied, nuzzling her hair. "If you were mine, I'd never have let you go."

"How… how do you—?"

"I heard what Tasgall said to you back there. I know something happened 'tween you and my brother. Once we're settled and warm, you can tell me all about it."

"Aye, then you'll understand why he let me go and likely applaud him for it." She glanced about. "And I cannae begin to imagine where we'll be settled and warm anywhere out here."

"Like I said, you must trust me. This weather works in our favour, methinks, since it'll slow MacAulay's pace too."

They pressed on, the fog like a cold, motionless rain that sank its icy teeth to the bone. Cristie's eyes ached with squinting, seeing little other than odd patches of snow in the gloom. The path levelled out at last, but if anything, the fog thickened. *Have we passed the bothy?* No sooner had the thought crossed her mind than the ground began to slope downwards.

"Almost there," Ruaidri said. "Stop when you see the cairn."

Cristie didn't respond. She had no idea what Ruaidri had in mind, but secretly admitted to feeling a genuine twinge of anxiety. The man had been held captive for weeks, kept in the dark, starved and filthy. He seemed rational, but maybe it had affected his mind. Tasgall had even implied it.

There was nothing up here, after all. Nothing but rocks, dead bracken and patches of coarse mountain grass. Even the heather refused to grow. And was it her imagination, or had it gotten colder? She suppressed a shiver.

"Dinnae give up," Ruaidri murmured, as if sensing her doubt. "Trust me."

A short while later, the familiar cairn loomed out of the fog, and Cristie reined Jock to a halt. "What now?" she asked, glancing about.

"MacKellar land." Ruaidri heaved a sigh. "God be praised. You have to dismount now, lass."

Her heart skipped a beat as she twisted to look at him. "Why?"

"Just do as I ask."

"But, I dinnae…" Her scalp crawled as she glanced about again. "Do you mean to leave me here?"

He muttered a soft curse. "I fear I willnae have the strength to dismount without my legs buckling beneath me, so I'd like something to hold onto. Since we dinnae have a saddle, the horse's mane is my only option. You're in my way, you daft lass, which is why I need you to move your arse."

"Oh." Cheeks warming, Cristie swung her leg over and slid to the ground. "Sorry."

"Nae problem." He shifted forward, grasped Jock's mane, and slithered to the ground. "Christ have mercy," he muttered, breathing hard as he leaned against the horse's flank. "Just give me a moment."

Cristie placed a hand on his back. "Take your time."

"We dinnae have any time." He continued to cling to Jock's mane. "And we should really lead this fellow for a while. He needs a rest."

Perplexed, Cristie glanced around. "Lead him where?"

Ruaidri pointed his chin at an undefined point to the right of the path. "That way."

She peered into the fog. "What's over there?"

"You'll see soon enough." He took a breath. "Look at me, Cristie."

She did so, brows raised in question.

"I need you to swear," he said.

"Swear?"

"Aye. I need you to swear to me that everything you see from this point on will stay a secret. You must tell no one about it, and may the Devil take you if you do."

Cristie chewed on her lip. *Christ save us. Maybe Tasgall was right. He has lost his mind.*

Ruaidri frowned and scratched his beard. "You should know, lass, that your thoughts translate plainly to your face. Nay, I havenae lost my mind. I just need your word, that's all."

She had little choice but to acquiesce. "You have it, Laird," she said, "but I fear Ewan would tell you it's worthless."

"And would he be right?"

She blinked away the familiar prickle of tears. "Nay, though he has good reason to think the way he does."

Ruaidri grunted and tugged on Jock's reins. "I cannae wait to hear the details. Let's go."

Cristie cast a dubious glance in their new direction. "That way, you say?"

"Aye. Follow me."

"But there's no path."

"There is, if you know where to look for it. Come on, lass. We need to get out of this fog."

Despite Ruaidri's assurances, Cristie had doubts. Many of them. Their new direction appeared to be nothing more than a thoroughfare for local wildlife. The sodden grass soaked her shoes and froze her toes. And the fog not only dampened her clothes and hair, it also dampened her senses.

Despite what Ruaidri had said about a path, she had yet to see any real evidence of one. She followed him blindly, although he seemed assured of his direction. She guessed they were heading north, or maybe northeast. But surely that took them away from Castle Cathan. Her uncertainty and growing fear brought her to a halt.

"I need to know where we're going," she called.

Ruaidri paused and looked back. "We're almost there." He sounded breathless. "Just a wee bit further."

"What's our direction?"

"North."

"So, away from Castle Cathan?"

"Not exactly. We're moving parallel to the coast right now. We'll turn west in the morning."

She shook her head and moved closer. "Forgive my fears, Laird. 'Tis just that I'm no' certain where I am, and I cannae see anything."

"Aye." Ruaidri grimaced. "I ken how unpleasant that feels."

A flush of shame flooded Cristie's face. "Curse my tongue, I didnae think afore I used it. Please forgive me."

"Naught to forgive," he said. "Like I said, 'tis just a wee bit further. I'm as eager to get out of this devilish weather as you."

Whether Cristie trusted him or not, she really had nowhere else to go. Bone weary, she trudged after him, wondering at his singular endurance. Where was he finding his strength? Could that also be a result of madness? The answer seemed to come a short while later, causing her to halt again, this time with a soft cry of dismay.

The granite crag looming out of the fog was a natural barricade. A dead end.

"By all the saints of Alba." A sense of utter despair washed over her as she stared up at the rugged, impassable wall of rock. "What is this?"

Ruaidri glanced over his shoulder. "I told you it wasnae far," he said, continuing on. "Come on, lass. Dinnae stop now."

Cristie shivered. "But there's nothing here, Ruaidri," she whispered. "Nothing at all."

Without stopping, Ruaidri continued on up a small rise till he reached the base of the cliff. Again, he glanced back at her, this time with an odd smile on his face. Then, in less time than it took to draw breath, man and horse stepped into the solid rock… and vanished.

For a moment, Cristie simply stared at the spot where she'd last seen them, her startled mind unable to reconcile the fact that they were no longer there. Heart knocking against her ribs, she crossed herself.

What kind of devilish delusion is this?

Maybe, after all, she was the one who had lost her mind.

"Laird MacKellar?" A soft gust of wind came out of nowhere and snatched her words away. Trembling, she stepped forward. "Ruaidri MacKellar, answer me!" The lack of response and a growing sense of panic pushed her forward. Chest heaving, she lifted her skirts and clambered up the gentle slope to the base of the crag.

Only then did she see it. Only then *could* she see it.

The face of the crag was not a single, solid piece of rock at all. A massive slab of granite, a natural monolith, rose up from the earth a few feet in front of the cliff, shielding a large cave entrance. Looking straight on, this separate piece of granite blended faultlessly with its background, its detachment invisible to the eye. It was a perfect illusion, Cristie realized. An astonishing and natural deception.

Ruaidri stood on the threshold of the cave, stroking Jock's nose. "Do you believe me now, lass?"

Cristie gaped up at the crag towering above her. "I swear I've never seen the like. 'Tis incredible."

Ruaidri grunted. "You've seen naught yet. Follow me."

At first, as she might have expected, Cristie stepped into darkness. But as her eyes adjusted, the darkness eased, and she was able to make out some detail. Quite a lot of detail, to her growing puzzlement. The large passage stretched into the distance, seeming endless. The air felt warm, tasted of salt, and smelled like the sea, yet the sea was miles away. But the strange light that lay ahead—a faint bluish hue that reminded her of moonlight—bemused her most of all.

"How far back does the cave go?" she asked.

"All the way through the mountain."

She squinted ahead. "Is that where yon light is coming from?"

"Nay."

"Is there someone else in here?"

He chuckled. "I doubt it."

"So, where is the light coming from?"

"You'll see for yourself in a moment."

And indeed, right then, the passage widened and opened into a massive chamber. At the chamber's heart, a bright, circular pool shone like the moon, its surface covered with a thin layer of undulating silver mist. The light it emitted shimmered on the cave walls and ceiling, filling the entire space with a heavenly glow. Never had Cristie seen such a thing, nor could she ever begin to have imagined it. Her hands flew to her mouth, capturing her shocked gasp. Jock let out a soft whinny and dug his hooves into the ground.

"Easy, lad." Ruaidri's soothing words echoed off the cavernous walls as he stroked the horse's neck. "There's naught to fear."

"Dear God." Cristie stepped forward. "What is this place?"

"It is called *Deòir na Gealaich*," Ruaidri replied. "One of Clan MacKellar's most treasured secrets."

"The tears of the moon," Cristie repeated, moving to the edge of the pool. "I dinnae believe I have ever seen such beauty. Is it some kind of magic?"

"According to legend, aye, but it's more a blessing of nature, methinks. Something in the water, a sediment of sorts that glows. I cannae tell you why or how."

"Harmless?"

"To touch, aye, but the water is salty, so I'd no' recommend drinking the stuff. If you thirst, there's a wee spring yonder that seeps from the rock."

Cristie crouched and dipped her fingers in the water. "'Tis as warm as a bath," she said, turning wide eyes to Ruaidri. "How can that be?"

"I dinnae ken. I've heard of places in England where the waters are permanently warm. They dinnae glow like this, though, as far as I know. Dip your hands in it, lass. It'll soothe those blisters."

"It heals?" She knelt and immersed both hands.

"It seems to speed healing, aye. 'Tis good for aching bones, too." Ruaidri spread the blanket on the ground and sank onto it. "When you're done, can I trouble you for a piece of that bread?"

"Of course." Cristie shook the drips from her hands, dug into her bag, and pulled out the package. "I suggest you eat slowly," she said, handing it to him, "so you dinnae shock your stomach."

Grimacing, he glanced down at his scrawny form. "Being captive in that place, shut away in the dark, slowly defeated me. In the end, I wanted only to die."

"Would you really have drank that poison?"

"Aye, and may God forgive me for losing faith," he said, and then his face brightened. "Learning Ewan had come home was like a miracle. I've prayed for his return many times, but as the years passed, to tell you true, I thought the worst had befallen him and that I'd never see him again. Your news restored my spirit. I swear I cannae stop thinking about it. Tell me about him. Tell me all that has happened since I was taken."

Cristie sighed and settled herself on the ground at Ruaidri's side. "Very well, but you'll likely come to hate me afore I'm finished."

Ruaidri frowned and tore off a small morsel of bread. "God willing, I'll see my brother on the morrow, not to mention my wee sister. 'Tis nae just my life I owe you, Cristie Ferguson, 'tis all the joys I have yet to savour. So, no matter what you impart to me in this next while, I could never hate you."

"We'll see." She gave him a grim smile. "And I'd ask that you ignore my tears, too, when they come, which they will. I fear I cannae help myself."

His frown remained. "As you wish. Though, if it hurts you to—"

"Nay, I promised to tell you." Cristie shrugged off her cloak, arranged her skirts, and drew her knees up to her chin. "Well, firstly, I suppose you should ken that your brother is… was a Templar knight. And he's nae the only one at Castle Cathan."

A slow smile chased Ruaidri's frown away. "Ewan? A holy warrior?" He shook his head. "Just like our grandsire. Och, lass, I have the gooseflesh just thinking about it. And he's nae the only one, you say? How many others? And why?"

"Two," she replied. "And I'll tell you why, but first, I have to tell you, Laird Mackellar, you and your brother share the same smile. I can see it even through all that hair on your face."

"Speaking of which." He nodded toward the bag. "Pass it to me. I'll have that knife of yours and shave once you're done your telling. And I'll no' interrupt you anymore, lass,

I swear. I'll save all my questions till the end. Please, carry on."

And she did, holding nothing back. Though it made her blush to the roots of her hair, she even explained why her spurious marriage had not been consummated. She relived every moment, and in doing so realized just what she had found in Ewan MacKellar—and what she had lost. The tears came, as she knew they would, forcing her to pause at times as she gathered herself. Yet relaying all that had happened also felt like a cleansing. A confession, of sorts, to a man whose veins ran with the same blood as Ewan's, and who also loved him. As promised, Ruaidri said nothing, not even when emotion overcame her, although his eyes often took on a soft glimmer of their own. Otherwise, he simply sat and listened.

"And so, here we are," Cristie said in the end, her voice hoarse. The recounting had left her drained, body and soul. She waited for Ruaidri to speak, praying he could still look at her without feeling contempt.

It seemed not. He frowned and glanced away, his chest rising and falling with a soft sigh. Cristie lowered her gaze and braced herself. Any criticism of her treachery and deceit would, of course, be quite justified.

But then, "Forgive me," he said, regarding her once more. "I didnae realize."

Not what she'd expected at all. "Realize?"

"That's it's only been a day since you returned to Dunraven. For some reason I thought you'd been back a while. You must be bone weary, lass."

She could scare believe it. If anything, Ruaidri's selflessness actually caused her more shame. "There is nothing to forgive, Laird Mackellar," she said. "Nothing at all. 'Tis I who should be asking for absolution. I'm ashamed of what I've done. Of what Alastair has done. Beyond sorry."

"I ken you are." He appeared to ponder. "What is she like?"

Yet more confused, Cristie frowned. "Who?"

"Elspeth. What does she look like?"

Cristie's brows shot upwards. "I cannae… I mean, that's all you wish to ask me?"

"For now, aye. 'Tis a question that has merit. I have others, but they can wait till after we've rested. For now, and for reasons I cannae explain, I'm curious about the lass I was supposed to wed. Describe her to me."

"Um, well, she's a wee bit taller than me, and very bonny. Her eyes are large and brown and she has freckles on her nose but hates them. Her hair is curly and the colour of... of pine cones, and is always neatly kept. She's stubborn, but she also has a kind and honourable heart." Cristie closed her eyes for a moment. *A better person than me, for sure.* "She would be a good wife to you, Laird Mackellar. You're well suited, I think."

There followed a moment of silence, then, "Perhaps at one time, but not anymore." Knife in hand, Ruaidri stepped to the water's edge. "Your brother has destroyed any chance of an alliance between our clans, Cristie. He's yet to answer for what he's done, but he will. Mark my words."

Crouching, he dipped the knife in the water, sat back on his heels, and began to shave his beard. The harsh scrape of blade against weeks of growth usurped the ensuing silence.

But the sound faded into the background as a sense of isolation crept into Cristie's soul. Right or wrong, she was now a traitor to both clans. She had abused Ewan's trust and lost his respect. And, while she would never regret saving Ruaidri, she realized that her efforts in that regard had condemned not only Alastair, but her entire clan to retribution. How was she supposed to reconcile everything? Where was her place?

"Where do I belong?" she whispered, just as something flew past her face and landed on the ground.

Ruaidri's shirt, swiftly followed by the flight of his trews.

Cristie turned to see him standing at the water's edge, his back to her, naked as a newborn. Shadows of light and dark served to accentuate the sad state of his body, carving out the bones of his ribs and spine.

"I need a bath," he said, and stepped into the water.

Cristie held her breath, watching as he waded out till waist-deep, leaving swirls of ghostly mist in his wake. The strange light seemed to rise up, erasing the unflattering shadows and sculpting his body in silver. He turned to face her, splashing water over himself, his roughly-shorn face also lit by a grin.

"It feels heavenly." His voice echoed off the cavern walls. "I havenae had a bath since I was imprisoned, though I'm sure you're fully aware of that. Or, your nose is, at least." With that, he filled his lungs and ducked beneath the surface.

Cristie waited, her initial amusement changing to anxiety as the ripples on the water calmed.

"Ruaidri?" She tensed and leaned forward, willing him to reappear. "Where…?"

Then, like some pagan water-god, he emerged from the depths, sucking in a lungful of air as he shook the silver from his hair.

"Sweet Mother of God, it cleanses body and soul." His grin remained wide on his face. "Come on in, lass. It'll soothe all your aches away."

All of them? I doubt it. Cristie smiled. "Tempting, but nay," she said. "I'll rinse your clothes through if you like."

"Dinnae bother. They're beyond hope." He shook more drops from his hair and waded toward her. "I'll no' be wearing them again."

"But…" Cristie averted her gaze as Ruaidri reached the shallows. "Laird Mackellar, you cannae go home naked!"

"I'd rather do that than put those filthy rags back on. They're fit only for burning." The sound of splashing ceased as he stepped ashore. "I'll keep my shoes, though. Dinnae be embarrassed, Cristie lass. Throw me the blanket, and I'll cover myself."

"Aye, I'd rather you did." She tossed it, blindly, in his direction.

He replied with a huff of breath and the sound of fabric tearing. What was he doing, she wondered?

"There," he announced, not a moment later. "You can look now."

She dared to peek, eyes widening at the sight of him in his makeshift robe. He'd cut a hole in the middle of the blanket and pulled it over his head. Flattering it was not. But it would provide some warmth at least, while also allowing for modesty. And it was clean.

"'Tis a fine solution," she said, smiling.

"Better than those rags, aye?" Mirroring her smile, he looked down at himself. "The laird of Clan MacKellar is now suitably attired for his return… for his return to…"

Other than the harsh, rhythmic rasp of his breath, Ruaidri fell silent, still gazing down at himself as his smile disappeared.

Cristie's smile also faded.

Instinctively, she knew what was happening, what had crippled Ruaidri's mirth and struck down his optimism. He was yet fragile, his battered spirit at the mercy of dark emotions that could rise up and attack without warning.

Cristie struggled with similar demons, for her heart lay in a thousand pieces. But her suffering could never compare to the sheer hell Ruaidri had suffered. His was immeasurable. Unfathomable. His demons would likely haunt him for months. Years, even.

"God, help me," he whispered, closing his eyes. "Please, help me."

"'Tis all right," Cristie said, rising to her feet as fresh sobs shuddered through him. "'Tis all right, Ruaidri. You're not alone anymore. I'm here."

She wrapped her arms around him and held him as he buried his face in her hair and wept. Later, she held him while he slept. She found solace in it, and knew he did too. There was nothing more to it than that.

Yet, at that moment, in that place, it was everything.

Chapter Twenty-One

Prayer and swordplay.

Ewan had partaken of both that day, finding some comfort in talking to God, but a more fulfilling release in trying to kill Gabriel. Not that Ewan actually wanted to kill Gabriel. The sparring, though vigorous and done with real blades, had been totally contrived. The energy expelled while trying—and failing—to best the English knight had been the point of the exercise. A discharge of frustration. A release of emotion. Heaving lungs, aching muscles, and sweat-soaked hair. Aye, it helped ease Ewan's burdened soul.

A little.

Time, he knew, would be the only real cure for what ailed him. Not two days earlier, he had wished for the morrow, when he wouldn't have to look upon Cristie's face anymore. He thought it would be easier on him not to see her.

Well, the morrow had come and gone, leaving behind an emptiness he hadn't thought to feel. The image of the lass's distraught face, streaked with tears as she declared her love for him, refused to leave his mind. Cristie's absence did not placate him at all. It cut him bone-deep. At the same time, he felt angry. At himself. At Cristie. Even, to his shame, at God.

Now, at day's end, with the evening repast over, Ewan sat in his private chamber and stared into the fire, nursing a goblet of warm, spiced wine.

"I see a man and a dog," Morag said, seated beside him. "And a tree."

Ewan gave her a wry glance. "No more wine for you, lass. You've obviously had enough."

She gestured to the fire. "Do you no' remember? When I was little, you used to point out images in the flames. People's faces and animals."

He smiled. "Aye, I remember. 'Tis nae a dog, though. 'Tis a goat."

"Aye, maybe." Morag chuckled and then sighed. "Things are no' always as they seem, are they?"

Ewan swirled the wine in his goblet. "Nay."

"I'm sorry, Ewan," Morag said, after a moment. "If I could take your pain away, I would."

"Thanks, wee lass, but dinnae fash. I'll survive." Behind him, the door swung opened unannounced, drawing Ewan's gaze to the doorway. "I should never have trusted Alastair Mac—" He straightened in his chair, frowning at the sight of Jacques standing on the threshold. The Basque knight appeared breathless, as if he'd been running. "You're needed outside urgently, Ewan." His voice had an uncharacteristic tremor to it. "You too, Morag."

"What is it, Brother?" Heart quickening, Ewan rose to his feet and grabbed his sword belt. He tried, and failed, to recall ever seeing his Basque friend quite so rattled. "What's wrong?"

"Just come with me," Jacques said, already turning on his heel. "Both of you."

"Heaven help us, what now?" Morag muttered, as they hurried to keep up with Jacques, who strode ahead, his white mantle floating out behind him like wings.

Ewan reached for his sword hilt as he stepped outside, a move prompted by the sight of the small group standing by the open gates. They appeared to be gathered around a large, dark horse and two figures, all bathed in shadow. Duncan held a flaming torch aloft, which cast flickering light over the others; Brody, Niall and Hammett, the latter standing beside Gabriel.

Meanwhile, Jacques continued his urgent stride across the courtyard.

Yet, to Ewan's growing puzzlement, there was no indication of panic. No sign of alarm. *So why the urgency?* Only as he drew near did he recognize the horse, the tell-tale white blaze on its face visible even in the gloom. His throat went dry. What might have brought Alastair's henchman to Castle Cathan?

Several possible and disquieting answers formed in his mind, all of them dissipating as he saw who stood by the horse. Ewan's stride slowed as he struggled to believe what his eyes told him.

Morag let out a gasp. "What is she doing back here?"

What indeed?

Cristie, her face pale, hair unbound and lifting in the wind, lowered her gaze as Ewan approached. She was not alone, he realized. A man stood beside her; an oddly dressed, unkempt figure, with matted hair and a roughly-shaven face. Thin to the point of emaciated, he clung onto the horse's mane as if needing support. He was obviously ill. Close to death, even. A wretched sight.

Yet something about him tugged at Ewan's memory. More than that, it stirred an instinctual awareness, taunting him with an impossible truth, one his bewildered mind could not quite reconcile. He regarded Cristie and voiced a question, unsure of why he feared the answer. "What are you doing here?" He turned his gaze to the man. "And who is this?"

As if in pain, the man's face crumpled for a moment. "Do you not know me, Ewan?"

A prickle ran across Ewan scalp. *That voice. I know that voice.*

Then Morag whispered a name. "Ruaidri."

Ewan's heart faltered. *Nay, it cannae be.* But as he stared at the man, he found himself looking into eyes he'd known from birth; eyes set in a gaunt face as familiar as it was unrecognizable. Still, his mind struggled to validate what his heart told him, reluctant to listen to a truth that defied belief. Ruaidri was dead, his bones scattered in the mountains. This wretched soul could not possibly be him. It could not be.

For that would mean…

Fear shifted Ewan's gaze back to Cristie. Fear she'd known all along that Ruaidri still lived. That she'd commiserated falsely with a family who had mourned the loss of a beloved brother. Which, in turn, meant her deceit had extended far beyond the limits of iniquity. Depravity worthy of the Devil himself.

Morag took a step closer, her whisper, this time, in the form of a question. "Ruaidri?"

"Greetings, wee lass." The man scratched his chin. "I'm sorry I'm late."

Morag let out a choked cry and fell on him, burying her face in his chest as she sobbed, speaking his name over and over. The man placed an arm around her and pressed a kiss to her head. "Nay, hush, now," he murmured. "'Tis all right."

Ewan closed his eyes as the final acceptance of truth squeezed his heart. His brother, alive. The realization sucked the strength from his limbs and the breath from his lungs. Yet, even as his heart sang for Ruaidri's resurrection, it also wept for Cristie's deceit. He glanced at her once more, gratified to see her flinch at whatever she saw in his expression. Ewan then turned his gaze back to his brother, his heart breaking anew for what the man had obviously suffered.

"Aye," Ewan answered, his voice grating. "I know you, my brother."

Ruaidri released his hold on the horse's mane and stretched out a trembling hand.

"Seeing you here, Ewan, is the answer to a thousand prayers. 'Tis a miracle. A sight I never thought I'd see again."

Overcome, Ewan surrendered to his emotion and stumbled into Ruaidri's embrace, the feel of the man's emaciated body bringing tears to his eyes. "Tis you the miracle, my brother. We thought you dead."

"Not quite." Ruaidri swayed as he gripped Ewan's shoulder. "Though, if you dinnae mind, I should really like… I should really like to rest now."

He expelled a long, slow breath, his legs buckling as he collapsed into Ewan's arms.

"Ruaidri!" Morag cried, trying to lift him. "Oh, dear God. Help him, please."

Cristie also let out a cry and stepped forward, but Morag turned on her like a snake ready to strike. "Nay, dinnae come anywhere near him," she snarled, through her tears. "You dinnae deserve to live after what you've done. Look at him! Starved and near dead. If he dies, I swear before God I'll kill you myself and take pleasure in it."

Trembling visibly, Cristie opened her mouth as if to speak but said nothing. Ewan's stomach churned as he looked at her, for the first time noticing the bruising on her face. But he thrust a pang of concern aside. That she had apparently found her conscience and brought Ruaidri back could not erase the obscenity of her lies. To think that she'd watched them lament the loss of their brother and laird, knowing all the while that he lived. Aye, she'd no doubt surrendered to her conscience and tried to make amends, but it might already be too late. In any case, this, he would never forgive. The immorality of what she had done—what Clan MacAulay had done—defied comprehension. There would be a reckoning. Swift and fierce.

His hold tightened around his brother's limp form. "Help me get him inside," he said, even as Jacques, Duncan and Niall came to his aid. "Brody, close the gate. Dinnae let the lass leave. Hammett, see to the horse."

*

"Enough." Ruaidri turned his face away from the bowl and collapsed back against his pillow.

"But you need to eat," Morag said, her voice almost a whine.

"Aye, but I cannae eat that." He glared at Ewan. "Who's laird of this damn place? I wish to complain about the food."

Ruaidri's humour gladdened Ewan's heart. His brother's spirit, it seemed, was still somewhat intact. Unlike his body, with its flea-bitten flesh and wasted limbs, the sight of which had made Morag weep as they'd tugged a clean nightshirt over his head.

"Aye, standards have lapsed since the new laird took over," Ewan quipped. "He doesnae have a clue what he's doing. Things will no doubt improve now that the old laird is back."

Ruaidri grunted. "Less of the old, if you dinnae mind. Though I must confess, the laird is glad to be back."

Ewan, perched on the edge of the bed, gave him a grim smile. "You gave us a fright out there, Ruaidri. You look a wee bit less like death now, though."

Ruaidri's eyes softened. "I didnae come home to die, Ewan. I'm back where I belong, with those I love. Those I never thought I'd see again."

"I keep pinching myself," Morag said, sniffling. "I still cannae quite believe it."

"Neither can I." Ruaidri reached for Ewan's hand and gave it a squeeze. "We have many stories to share, Templar."

Ewan smiled and returned the squeeze. "Starting with you," he replied. "What happened in those mountains? Was it an ambush?"

"Of sorts." He drew a breath. "I met Alastair and Tasgall at the bothy as planned. We ate, drank, and the next thing I knew, I woke up a captive. They must have put something in the drink."

"They killed your damn horse!"

"Goliath." He closed his eyes for a moment. "Aye, I ken."

"'Twas all I found. Goliath's remains, your cloak soaked in blood, and our father's pin."

"But why?" Morag shook her head. "Why would they do such a thing? I cannae fathom it."

"I'm no' sure anymore. At first, I suspected it had something to do with Alastair wanting to wed you and take over the clan. That, or I was to be held for ransom. But then I couldnae understand why it was taking so long." Ruaidri's gaze settled on Ewan. "Since yesterday, though, some things have become a little clearer."

Ewan's brow furrowed. "How so?"

"Cristie told me you'd returned." His nostrils flared. "The bastards kept that from me. Your arrival here obviously forced them to rethink their mad plans."

Morag huffed. "Well, I hope you'll no' be letting the lass off easy, despite her change of heart. Hanging is too good for her. For all of them."

Ruaidri gave Morag a puzzled glance. "Change of heart? What are you blabbing about, wee lass? Cristie Ferguson saved my life."

"Aye, and she's to be commended for that," Ewan said, unable to keep the contempt from his tone. "Trouble is, she neglected to tell us you were being held captive in the first place."

"Only because she knew naught of it." Ruaidri's eyes darted from one to the other to the other. "She didnae have a clue about any of it till two days ago, when she overheard a conversation 'tween Alastair and Tasgall. None of the clan knew, apparently, though they will now, I should think. I was hidden away in the dungeon at Ravenstone. Nay, make no mistake, I'm here now only because of that wee lass. Where is she? Is someone seeing to her hands?"

That Cristie hadn't known about Ruaidri's captivity lifted a dark shadow from Ewan's mind. That she'd been injured somehow set his heart racing. "What's wrong with her hands?"

Ruaidri groaned. "Shite. I should have made sure. They're badly blistered. Go find the lass, Morag, and make sure she's been taken care of. And you can take that bowl of swill with you, too. If you want me to eat, bring back a plate of Glenna's oatcakes and a tankard of ale. Some cold mutton as well, if there is any. And dinnae rush back, if you please. I wish to have a private talk with my brother."

Morag, wearing an expression of dismay, nodded. "Right, I'll... I'll make sure she's been cared for, then. Seems I owe her an apology, as well."

As the door closed behind her, Ewan asked again. "How did her hands get blistered, Ru? And which bastard is responsible for the bruise on her eye?"

Ruaidri gave a weak laugh. "So, you do still care about the lass." His gaze settled on the disfigured part of Ewan's face. "'Tis odd. When Cristie spoke of you, she didnae mention anything about that scar."

Ewan felt a tug on his heart. "I cannae think why."

"Maybe she simply doesnae see it when she looks at you. How did it happen?"

"As you said, we have many stories to tell, but not all of them tonight." He fidgeted. "Are you going to answer my question, or do I have to—?"

"I'll answer all your questions if I can, but I need to sit up a little. 'Twill be easier to breathe, and I dinnae care to look at the ceiling as I speak."

Ewan did so, plumping up the pillows while cringing afresh at his brother's frail condition. "On reflection, maybe you should rest a while. We can talk later."

"Nay, we'll talk now." Ruaidri settled back. "The state of my body doesnae reflect the state of my soul. I feel as though I've been reborn. Given a second chance. You and your wee bride are responsible for that."

Ewan grimaced as he retook his seat. "She's no' my bride, Ruaidri. Our marriage was false."

"Aye, she told me. She told me everything that has happened since I left. About you and her. About the reasons why you and your Templar brothers are here. Everything. She emptied out her heart by the light of *Deòir na Gealaich*."

Ewan raised a brow. "You were at *Deòir na Gealaich*?"

"We took shelter there last night." He grinned. "I might look like death, and if no' for *Deòir na Gealaich*, I'd smell like it, too. But this wee tale begins yesterday morning, which is when I met Cristie for the first time." His expression softened. "Just now, I said I was alive because of her. While that is true, you should know, my brother, that I'm also alive because of you."

As Ruaidri continued with his telling, Ewan remained silent, though his emotions simmered inside. His brother's captivity had been a cruel and slow torture, one that had pushed him to the point of taking his own life. Reliving it obviously took its toll. Ruaidri's voice faltered several times, weakening to little more than a whisper as he spoke of the poisoned ale and his intent to drink it. "I ken what you must be thinking, Ewan," he said, closing his eyes.

"I doubt you do." Ewan squeezed his brother's hand again. "You need say no more tonight. 'Tis upsetting you. It can wait till the morrow, when you're rested."

"Nay, 'tis a weight that needs shifting now. Consider it a confession of sorts. Let me finish, so I might rest easier tonight."

Ewan sighed. "I cannae give you absolution, if that is what you seek."

Ruaidri opened his eyes and gave his head a feeble shake. "I seek only your understanding and a promise that you'll say naught of this to our sister. I've already sworn Cristie to secrecy." A pained expression crossed his face. "I had the poison raised to my lips, Ewan. I'd have swallowed it, too, for I'd lost all and any will to live. Cristie mentioned Morag's name, trying to dissuade me. And may God forgive me..." he closed his eyes for a moment, "not even that gave me pause. Then she mentioned *your* name, which was enough to set Tasgall's blade at her throat." Tears came to his eyes. "*Ewan Tormod MacKellar, your brother*, she said, and dared to tell me you'd returned to Castle Cathan. And it was as if a door opened in my mind, and whatever lay behind it flowed out and washed over me. Nay, it flowed *through* me, like a purge. And all thoughts of dying disappeared. In an instant, I wanted only to live. To return to Castle Cathan and see you."

Ewan acknowledged with a smile. "And here you are, may God be praised. But I'm struggling to understand how you managed to overcome Tasgall and make your escape."

Expression thoughtful, Ruaidri regarded him in silence for a few moments. Then, "Cristie was originally promised to him, Ewan."

Ewan's eyes widened. "To Tasgall?"

"Aye, but she knew naught of that, either, till he mentioned it." Ruaidri drew a breath. "She then offered to wed him willingly, but only if he set me free."

The mere thought of Cristie married to Tasgall set Ewan's sword-hand twitching. "So…" He struggled to make sense of Ruaidri's words. "How come she's here, then? And with Tasgall's horse, no less?"

"Because Tasgall let her go."

"Why?"

"I'm no' sure, but I believe it's because he knew where her heart lay, and it wasnae with him." He gave Ewan a pointed look. "Nor will it ever be with him. Cristie's heart belongs to someone else."

Ewan ran a hand through his hair. "I did what I had to do, Ruaidri. The lass lied to me and perjured herself before God and the clan."

"Aye, she did, and she's sorry for it." Ruaidri scratched his chin. "She didnae actually come out and say it, but I suspect Alastair threatened her, which is why she did what she did."

"Threatened her with what?"

"Who knows? But the lass is base-born. At his mercy." He heaved a weary sigh, dropped his head against his pillow, and regarded Ewan through half-closed lids. "I'd say she's more than made retribution for what she's done, so let go of your resentment, if you harbour any. You were always an obstinate wee bastard. 'Tis why you locked antlers with Father all the time, since he was just as bad. Are you still as hard-headed? Or has the Templar discipline taught you some humility?"

Ewan chuckled at his brother's forthrightness. "I'd like to think it has, but I confess I'm no' sure I'd have ever returned home if it wasnae for Phillip's edict." He shrugged. "That said, my reasons for staying away no longer exist. In truth, I'm no' certain they ever existed at all."

And I'll always regret not making amends with my father.

Ruaidri grunted. "'Tis surely providence that you returned when you did. I'd venture to say I'm no' the only one in this room who's been given a second chance. Cristie is a fine wee lass, Ewan. You'd be daft to let her go. Right, I'm done preaching. Where's that sister of ours? I'm hungry."

Chapter Twenty-Two

"**This** will likely pain you some," Gabriel said, about to smear salve on Cristie's blistered palms.

"All right." Cristie managed to smile at the English knight. He alone had remained with her after the others had carried Ruaidri indoors. Then he'd escorted her to the great hall, discovering the sorry state of her hands on the way. He'd left her seated in a quiet corner, returning after a short while with a cup of warm ale and the accoutrements for her blistered hands.

Despite his staid demeanour, Gabriel Fitzalan was, she thought, a compassionate man. A true knight. Not a man to vex, however, according to Ewan. She could believe it, too, having watched him training with his sword. And now, to her mild surprise, he also appeared to have some knowledge of healing.

He didn't return her smile but rather frowned as he dabbed the pungent salve on her cracked flesh. Aye, it stung a little. Nay, actually, it burned like fire. Cristie sucked air through her nostrils and held it.

"The burning sensation will soon cease," Gabriel said, administering to her other hand, "and take the pain with it."

Eyes watering, Cristie merely nodded, saying nothing as he wrapped bandages loosely over her treated flesh.

"Who struck you?" he asked, without looking up.

Cristie drew a breath. "Alastair."

The furrows in his brow deepened for a moment. "We must repeat this treatment tomorrow." He gathered his things and rose to leave. "The skin will probably take a sennight or so to heal. Do naught to aggravate the wounds in the meantime."

"I understand." Cristie gave the man another smile. "Thank you for your kindness, Gabriel."

He inclined his head and left her wondering if she'd even be there tomorrow. Despite bringing Ruaidri back, the animosity shown toward her by those at Castle Cathan had not been tempered. Indeed, it had intensified. And the contempt she'd seen in Ewan's expression had sickened her. No doubt he believed as everyone else did—that she'd known about their laird's captivity and hidden the truth from them. Their assumption, while misplaced, had merit, and she knew better than to try and deny it. Instead, she waited, wondering how Ruaidri fared… and not because she needed him to speak for her. She simply wanted him to live. More than anything, she wanted him to live.

To say she had forged a bond with the laird of Clan MacKellar understated the situation. They had shared a deeply emotive experience that would forever bind them in friendship. She also knew he would never force her to leave Castle Cathan. But she couldn't stay. Not if she had no hope of rekindling Ewan's love. It would be too painful. Again, she wondered where she might go.

"Cristie." The sound of Morag's voice pulled Cristie from her musing. She looked up to be greeted by a fleeting smile, which barely hid the lass's obvious discomfort.

Cristie's eyes widened. "Is Ru— I mean, how does Laird MacKellar fare?"

"He's resting and in good spirits. We can only pray that he recovers fully." Morag glanced down at the bowl clasped in her hands and cleared her throat. "Um, he told me what you did. How you saved his life. I wish to thank you from my heart. I… I'm truly sorry for what I said earlier. I assumed wrongly."

Cristie's throat tightened. "'Tis all right, Morag. I'd have assumed the same. As you say, we can but continue to pray for him."

She was rewarded by a nod and another fleeting smile. "He mentioned you'd hurt your hands. What happened?"

"Blisters." Cristie eyed her bandages. "From rowing across Loch Raven. Gabriel put some salve on them, though, and they feel better already."

"Good." Morag glanced again at the bowl in her grasp. "Well, I'd best go. Ruaidri willnae eat this. Says he wants some of Glenna's oatcakes instead."

"A good sign, I daresay."

"I think so. Can I bring you anything?"

Cristie shook her head. "Thanks, but nay."

She watched as Morag wandered off toward the kitchen, aware of being watched herself by others in the great hall. No doubt, her conversation with the laird's sister had snared their attention. Yet, despite Morag's apology, melancholy still weighed heavy on Cristie's mood. And, if she dug deep enough, she knew she'd find the reason for it.

Ewan.

What might she expect from him now that he knew the truth? A simple acknowledgement also? Or dare she hope for more than that? Would he ever look at her again the way he once had?

Beyond exhausted, and weary of the turmoil in her mind, Cristie folded her arms atop the table, rested her head on them, and offered up a silent prayer.

*

"Cristie."

Ewan's voice, little more than a whisper, drifted through her dreams. It echoed around the snow-capped mountains, across the surface of dark, ominous lochs, and through the silver mist that swirled atop secret, moonlit ponds. He'd spoken her name once before—his voice, at that time, cold and hard. Now it sounded warm and gentle. It was but a dream, though. Destined to end. And she didn't want it to end.

"Cristie, wake up."

She fought against an upward spiral of consciousness and lost the battle as her eyes flickered open.

"You cannae stay here, lass."

"Mmm?" Lifting her head from the pillow of her arms, Cristie squinted at the candle flame held aloft, its golden light dancing across Ewan's face. Her heart first skipped a beat and then sank. Had he actually spoken those words?

"You cannae stay here," he said again, confirming her worst fear. "Come with me."

A chill ran across her skin. It seemed her self-assurances had been wrong. "Right." She straightened and glanced about, her head swimming with fatigue. Other than the soft glow of the fire, the hall lay in near darkness. "I... I understand, of course. Perhaps I might be allowed to stay till the morning, though? I promise I'll leave at first light."

A bewildered look crossed Ewan's face, resting there a moment before understanding took its place.

"Och, nay, lass. You misunderstand. I would never..." He glanced about the hall as he held out a hand. "I meant you cannae stay *here*. 'Tis no place for you to rest."

"Oh." Relief washed over her as she placed her fingers atop his, hardly able to breathe as flesh met flesh. To be near him, to touch him, and to see no sign of contempt in his candlelit gaze, stirred up a horde of butterflies in her belly. "Thank you," she said, as she rose. "Um, how's Ru— I mean, Laird MacKellar?"

"Sleeping soundly." Ewan frowned as he examined her bandages. "I'd have come for you before now, but I was loath to leave him till I saw him settled. Morag told me Gabriel had administered to your hands. Are you in pain?"

"Not much. I doubt I'll be able to row a boat for a wee while, though." She managed a smile. "I'm glad to hear the laird is resting."

"Have you eaten anything?"

"A little, aye."

Eyes narrowed, he studied her face, his gaze resting a moment or two on her bruising. "I misunderstood, Cristie," he murmured. "When I saw you tonight, at the gate with Ruaidri, I assumed, wrongly, that you'd known about his captivity. Please forgive me."

She fidgeted. "Dinnae think any more of it. There's naught to forgive."

His answering smile lingered but a moment. "Come," he said. "You need to rest."

Cristie followed, saying nothing as Ewan led her up the stairs. It was only days ago that they had trod this same path together, before her deceit had been exposed.

Days ago? It felt like weeks.

"Ruaidri is resting in the laird's chamber, which is where I'll also be for tonight at least, in case he has need of me." Ewan paused outside what had been his old room. "You can sleep in my chamber for now. Shall I have someone come to help you undress?"

As he had done, so many times? The memory warmed her cheeks. "Um, nay, thank you. I'll manage."

He looked doubtful. "But, your hands."

"I can still use my fingers," she said, finding a smile.

"As you wish," he said. Then, brow furrowed, he pushed the studded door open, and stood aside to let her pass. Within, a single candle flickered on a bedside table, casting a small halo of light across the wide bed with its blue coverlet.

Cristie met Ewan's gaze and held it, hoping he might say more. Some additional words of kindness, perhaps. A gesture. Something—*anything*—to give her a sign that he still retained some fondness for her. But he merely regarded her, the furrow still etched into his brow. As the silence stretched into awkwardness, she forced another smile to hide her disappointment and moved past him. "Goodnight, then."

"Cristie."

Stomach churning, she turned back to him. "Aye?"

"What you did…" He sighed and moved closer. "What you did was very brave."

She bit her lip. "I didnae act alone, Ewan. It was Elspeth's idea to take the boat, or I'd have been too late. And it was Tasgall who—"

"It was Tasgall who tortured my brother." Ewan's mouth twisted into a snarl. "And who would have watched him die if you hadnae been there."

"Aye, that... that is true," she said, a slight tremble in her voice, "but, by God's good grace, 'twas a combination of blessings that saved Laird MacKellar. I cannae take all the acclaim."

Expression still grim, Ewan trailed his fingertips over Cristie's bruised cheek. "I swear before God," he murmured, "there'll be a price exacted for all the harm Alastair has done."

"I fear your brother is already paying it." Cristie suppressed a shiver as Ewan's fingers trailed down to her jaw. "I'm no' sure what he told you, but I believe his spirit might no' be as strong as it seems. He suffers yet."

"I dinnae doubt it." Ewan dropped his hand. "Wounds to the spirit can be more damaging than those to the flesh. I have seen Templar brothers similarly afflicted. But I have faith Ruaidri will rally. He has the love of his family and his clan to support him."

Ewan's reply prompted a new concern to surface in Cristie's mind as she stammered out a response. "I... I shall continue to pray for him."

Again, Ewan fell silent, his gaze still locked with hers. Cristie had the impression he wanted to say more and she wondered at his hesitation. At that moment, she wanted only to be taken in his arms, to feel his strength and be assured that she still held a place in his heart.

"Get some rest, lass," he said finally, reaching for the doorlatch as he turned to leave.

Desperation forced her to speak. "It was me, Ewan!"

Frowning, he looked back at her. "You?"

She nodded. "I had never seen the sea till that first night with you. And I could listen to your tales of life abroad for the rest of my life without ever tiring of them. It was me who spent time with you. It was me who rode with you, walked with you, and watched the sunset with you. It was *me*, Cristie Ferguson." She drew breath. "Not Elspeth."

Ewan's expression had softened as she'd spoken. "Much has happened this past while, Cristie," he said, after a moment. "Many lives have been touched by misery, not just yours and mine. And there is yet more to come, I fear. 'Tis a time to reflect. A time to pray." He touched her cheek again. "You're exhausted. Get some sleep. We'll talk in the morning."

Hollow inside, Cristie stared at the closed door for a while as her mind replayed Ewan's every word, every nuance, every touch. The exercise gave her no real peace. He had expressed his gratitude, but that had to be somewhat expected. He had also treated her with kindness, but Ewan MacKellar was not, at heart, an unkind man.

His response to her final outpouring had been gentle, but ambiguous. A response that stoked both hope and fear. A response that forced her to acknowledge her new concern.

That Ewan might decide to renew his Templar vows.

Now that Ruaidri had returned, Ewan would be relinquishing his lairdship. He no longer needed to consider political alliances through marriage. Cristie knew how much he valued the Order, how seriously he had taken his vows. How reluctant he had been to surrender the white mantle. And he was now free to resume his allegiance to the Temple, despite the French king's edict.

Cristie glanced down at her bandaged hands as hope yielded to despair.

"Stop this," she whispered, staving off the threat of self-pity. She was indeed exhausted. Overwrought, nerves stretched to the limit, and in dire need of sleep. And, though her weary mind might imagine the worst, she could still pray for the best.

Heaving a resigned sigh, she turned, wandered over to the bed, and got down on her knees.

Chapter Twenty-Three

Unable to sleep, Ewan rose from his floor-bound pallet of furs before dawn and stole from the chamber, being careful not to awaken his brother. Apart from a single, tormented cry in the night, Ruaidri had rested well. That single haunted wail, however, had startled Ewan from his own troubled dreams, leaving him to toss and turn for the remainder of the night.

Now, immersed in the candlelit silence of the chapel, he gazed upon his grandfather's Templar banner and tried to compose his thoughts. The past four days had been an endless deluge of emotions, a flood of truth and lies that had him floundering. With Ruaidri's return, Ewan's obligations had shifted yet again. What he'd been forced to surrender could now be his once more—if he chose to take it.

Choices. He had them. Though in truth, he knew without any doubt what he wanted. Where his future lay. But it would not be met without facing some obstacles. And it would not be embraced without some residual guilt.

He'd gone in search of Cristie the previous evening and found her asleep at the table, head resting on her arms. Seeing her bandaged hands, dark shadows beneath her eyes and that damnable bruise on her face, had all but battered Ewan's heart to a pulp. In saving Ruaidri, the lass had shown courage worthy of any man, let alone a lass. She had shown humility, too, refusing to take all the glory. That she had given some of that glory to Tasgall soured Ewan's stomach, though he could not argue that, without the man's mercy, Ruaidri would be dead.

Later, standing in the candlelit doorway of his room, longing had shone like a beacon in Cristie's eyes as she'd reached out to him. Ewan had stayed his desire to tell her what lay in his mind and heart. At one time, he might have laid bare his intentions without aforethought, but his years with the Templars had granted him a measure of restraint, the ability to curb his impetuosity. Besides, the lass truly was exhausted. What he had to say to her would wait till she was better able to accept it. It—nay, *she*—merited a more befitting hour and location.

The chapel door creaked open, a disturbance that caused the solitary candle flame to dance. A moment later, with near silent footfalls, Jacques moved past him, dropped to one knee before the altar, crossed himself, and whispered a quiet supplication.

"How is your brother?" he asked, taking a seat beside Ewan. "Has he rested well?"

"Aye, well enough, I think."

"Good. And Cristie? What of her?"

"I must assume she is still asleep." Ewan fidgeted. "In my chamber."

"Ah."

Ewan threw him a sideways glance. "I slept on the floor in Ruaidri's chamber."

"Clarification was neither expected nor necessary, Brother."

"Nevertheless."

Jacques drew an audible breath and seemed to ponder for a few moments. "I believe we witnessed a miracle last night," he said, finally.

"What we witnessed was the result of several miracles," Ewan replied, recalling what Cristie had said. "But those responsible for Ruaidri's torture must still pay."

"I understand only Alastair and his henchman were involved."

Ewan threw him another glance, this one questioning.

Jacques shrugged. "Morag told me."

Ewan suppressed a smile. "Did she, now."

"She is of the same opinion as yourself. That your brother should be avenged. I do not disagree. My sword is at the ready, should you have need of it."

"My thanks."

The door creaked open again, this time with a little more urgency, and the candle flame danced yet again.

"Here you are," Morag said, sounding breathless. "I thought you were going to stay with Ruaidri, Ewan."

Ewan shot to his feet. "Is something wrong?"

"Not precisely. He's up, dressed, and wolfing down oatcakes in the great hall. And he's asking for you and Cristie."

"Good morn, brother," Ruaidri announced, as Ewan approached the laird's table. "Where's the wee lass? Still sleeping?"

"I assume so," Ewan replied, nodding a greeting to Duncan and Gabriel, as well as a few others who called Castle Cathan their home.

"Shall I go and wake her?" Morag asked.

Ewan mulled. "Perhaps let her sleep a while yet," he said, after a moment. "She was exhausted last night."

As he spoke, he cast a critical gaze over his brother's gaunt form and felt the familiar rise of anger. At the same time, it gladdened his heart to see a slight flush of colour on Ruaidri's cheeks. The man's eyes seemed sharper somehow, too, their bright depths reflecting the candle and firelight that warmed the room.

"You can take that scowl off your face, Ewan." Ruaidri lifted an oatcake from a plate and waved it at him. "I might look like death, but I'm feeling fine."

Ewan grunted as he took his seat. "Aye, well, I'm no' sure you should be up and about this soon."

Morag snorted and sat down beside him. "I agree. You should still be resting."

"My arse is in a chair, in case you havenae noticed." Ruaidri eyed his oatcake. "Dinnae fuss. If I feel the need, I'll away to my bed."

Ewan reached over and grabbed an oatcake for himself. "Before they're all gone," he said wryly, taking a bite.

Ruaidri grinned, sat back, and regarded Jacques and Gabriel. "My first official duty, since returning to Castle Cathan, is to bid our Templar guests a belated welcome." He tipped his head. "Let it be known, if you're able to spread the word, that any of your brethren will be well received here."

"Our thanks, Laird MacKellar," Jacques said, his response echoed by a nod from Gabriel.

A wistful look came to Ruaidri's eyes as he regarded Ewan. "How I should like to have witnessed your arrival at our gates." He shook his head. "It must have been a sight to behold. My brother, returned after so many years and wearing the Templar garb, no less."

"It was." Morag heaved a sigh. "I could scarce believe my eyes."

Ewan gave a sober smile. "A no more wondrous sight than seeing you last night, Ruaidri, resurrected from the dead."

Jacques unfastened his cloak and rose to his feet. "Stand up, Ewan."

He did so, and allowed Jacques to settle the mantle across his shoulders. Odd, he thought, how a symbolic scrap of fabric could stir both heart and soul. The familiar weight of it felt good.

"*Et voila*," Jacques said to Ruaidri. "*Notre frère*, Ewan Tormod MacKellar, a soldier of Christ."

"It looks well on you, Ewan," Ruaidri said, emotion evident in his voice. "You'll spare some time for me this afternoon, aye? I should like to hear more of what you've been up these past twelve years." His mouth quirked. "Though I confess I'm more curious about what happened in those two years *before* you became a Templar."

"Nothing to be proud of, I'll tell you that much." Ewan touched the cross adorning the white fabric. "I was on a path to damnation. The Order brought me back to God."

"Now that your brother has returned, there is naught to prevent you from taking the mantle again," Gabriel said. "Should you so wish."

"Until such time as I marry and have sons, Ewan is still the heir," Ruaidri said. "But I'll support whatever decision he makes."

Ewan smiled. "As it happens, I've already given it fair consideration."

Ruaidri, frowning, leaned forward. "And have you made a decision?"

"I have," he replied, finding a certain comfort in admitting it. "It was an easy choice."

*

Cristie stepped out into the chill of an autumn dawn, each measured stride a triumph of self-restraint. It took all she had not to break into a run, to demand the gates be flung open that she might leave this place. For she could no longer remain.

How deluded of her, to imagine she still occupied some part of Ewan's heart and mind. She'd been foolish to hope, foolish to lay her feelings bare and open herself to him the previous evening. His guarded response now made perfect sense. It had been a gentle prelude to a truth she had suspected. A truth she had feared.

A truth she had just witnessed.

Ewan was a Templar knight, sworn to serve God and Rome, two indomitable powers. And she was naught but the base-born daughter of a weaver. A sinner who had deceived him. Betrayed him. Lied to him.

And fallen in love with him.

After a restless night filled with disturbing, nonsensical dreams, Cristie had risen and dressed, shivering in the damp air as she struggled to fasten the laces of her robe with bandaged hands. She'd tried to re-braid her hair, but the tightness and pain had defeated her attempt, and she'd allowed her dark tresses to fall free. Shrugging her cloak over her shoulders to hide her failed efforts, she'd made her way down to the hall.

Anticipation had growled in the pit of her stomach. The day promised to be pivotal. Which direction might she be facing at the end of it? She had wondered about Ruaidri, and prayed he'd had a restful night. And she'd wondered what Ewan intended to say to her. Straightening her shoulders, Cristie stepped into the hall—and discovered that Ewan didn't have to say anything at all.

At the sight of him wearing the mantle, she'd halted. Her heart had momentarily halted too, as if a cold hand had squeezed the life from it. Then, before anyone noticed her presence, she'd turned on her heels and fled.

She felt no resentment. No animosity. More than anything, she wanted Ewan to be happy. But she couldn't bring herself to tell him that. He had remarked on her bravery the previous night, but this… this was beyond her limit. With all hope gone, she simply didn't have the courage to look into his eyes and wish him well. She couldn't bear the thought of seeing sympathy in his expression, or hearing an apology in his voice.

All she wanted to do was take her leave. A cowardly decision, perhaps, but seeing Ruaidri seated at the table made it easier. The expression of pride on his face as he regarded his brother had set Cristie's arrested heart beating again. The man still looked thin, of course, but his pallor had brightened noticeably. He would live. She felt certain of it.

Humility be damned. She would take comfort, at least, from knowing she played a large part in saving Ruaidri MacKellar's life, returning him to home and family. It offered her something good to hold onto in a future that appeared bleak. Something to keep her spirit from sinking into a thick fog of despair.

The gloom of early dawn gave her some cover as she scuttered around the back of the keep, heading for the postern gate. She slipped through the small portal unseen, and then watched as the door closed, shutting her out of Castle Cathan.

"Where to go, Cristie?" she asked, gazing out across a cold, grey sea, still shadowed by a night in retreat. The wind brought tears to her eyes. At least, she blamed the wind for them as she tugged her cloak tighter. For a moment, she considered returning to Dunraven. But nay, there'd be no welcome awaiting her there. She'd burned that bridge when she'd saved Ruaidri. For a brief moment, she wondered if Alastair had ever pursued them. A failed attempt, if so.

Where to go, then? Cristie struggled to straighten her thoughts. Not an easy task, when both heart and mind were in turmoil. She had neither food nor coin, but, as a weaver, she was not without desired skills. Surely, she would find work somewhere… once her hands healed. She held them up and tried closing them into fists, but they were yet too painful.

"The skin will probably take a sennight or so to heal. Do naught to aggravate the wounds in the meantime."

From an obscure place at the back of her mind, a small voice dared to suggest the potential folly of her exodus, but she ignored it. She wouldn't—*couldn't* go back. So, keeping to shadow as she skirted the castle walls, she set out. It was yet early. Her absence, then, would likely not be noticed for a while. And, in truth, she didn't expect anyone to come looking for her. Why would they? She was not one of them. She had no place in the MacKellar clan. She had no place in the MacAulay clan, either.

With no clear direction in mind, she decided to take the coast road, heading south. There were surely villages along the coast, fishing villages, farming communities—places where she might find shelter, if only temporary. As Castle Cathan shrank into the pale remains of the night with no indication she'd been seen, Cristie breathed a little easier. She lifted her chin and walked at a good pace, resolute in her decision.

Unfortunately, she soon discovered that the burden of a broken heart weighed heavy on her determination. As the miles passed beneath her feet, she grew more and more despondent. Where once the coastal beauty had touched her soul, it now seemed to heighten her sense of desolation.

The dark waves reflected the gloomy expanse of sky. The cries of seabirds leant a sense of loneliness and melancholy. And the wind, biting cold, swept in from the sea and buffeted her without mercy. So far, though, the clouds had held onto their contents. A blessing that likely would not last.

She quenched her thirst from the small burns that criss-crossed the land. But hunger gnawed at her stomach and her hands throbbed with pain. She'd seen a few cottages dotted here and there with smoke leaching from a hole in their thatched roofs. How she envied the crofters their shelter and the warmth of their fires.

And then, at last, another human soul crossed her path—
a leather-skinned, elderly man driving a pony and cart, the
latter stocked with three, large barrels. The man, dark eyes
glinting beneath a pair of bushy white brows, had regarded
her with some curiosity and nodded a silent greeting as he
passed.

She lifted a hand. "Please sir," she called out, "can you
help me?"

He reined in the shaggy pony and cast another glance
over her, one of his bushy brows raised in question. "What
is it ye need, lass?"

The question drew tears to her eyes, for what she truly
needed she could never have. "Um, I… I wondered if you
know of a place ahead where I might find shelter for a wee
while. And… and something to eat, perhaps?" She
fidgeted. "I have no coin."

The raised brow descended into a frown as the man
scrutinized her, his gaze lingering a moment on the bruised
part of her face. The stink of fish wafted through the air,
turning Cristie's stomach. She swallowed bile and fiddled
with her skirts.

The man's gaze dropped to her bandaged hands and his
frown deepened. "There's a wee village a few miles further

along," he said, gesturing with a toss of his head. "Ye'll see a wee cottage standin' apart from the rest, overlookin' the harbour. Knock on the door and tell my wife I sent ye. Gunna is her name. She'll give ye somethin'."

"Thank you!" Cristie's heart quickened. "Thank you kindly. And may God bless you."

He responded with a single nod, slapped the reins against the pony's rump, and went on his way.

Chapter Twenty-Four

It made no sense. None. Why would Cristie leave? And she must have left, for she had not been taken, which had been Ewan's first fear. But nay, Castle Cathan had not been breached. The main gates had not been opened, nor had anyone seen the lass leave. All of which pointed to a single, undeniable conclusion—that Cristie had left voluntarily and covertly. The lass had, in effect, run away.

And Ewan could not begin to imagine why.

Had he said something the previous night? Something she'd misconstrued? True, he had not told her of his intentions, despite hearing the longing in her voice when she'd spoken. And despite seeing the familiar light in her eyes, the one he'd doubted when her betrayal had first been discovered.

Now, he doubted it all over again.

A shout went up as he and Gabriel approached the castle gates. They opened moments later, and both men spurred their lathered horses into the courtyard. Obviously, their imminent arrival had been announced, evident from the welcoming party

"Any sign?" Ruaidri asked, as Ewan slid from the saddle.

Chest heaving, Ewan shook his head. "Nay. We rode a good way along the burn before turning back. She couldnae have got any further than that on foot. And we came back via *Eaglais Chruinn*, but Father Iain has seen no one." He touched Ruaidri's face. "I told him you'd returned. He declared it a miracle and was still weeping when we left. Says he'll be here on the morrow to see the miracle for himself."

Ruaidri gave a wistful smile. "Something to look forward to, but in the meantime, we need to find Cristie."

"Maybe she doesnae want to be found," Morag said, tucking her arm through Ruaidri's. "Why else would she leave in such a manner?"

Ruaidri grimaced. "Nay, something prompted it. The lass wouldnae leave without good reason."

Ewan shook his head. "Well, I cannae think what that reason might be."

"We should check the coast road," Gabriel said, sliding from his saddle. "'Tis the only other path she could have taken."

"But she'd have no cause to go that way," Ewan said, watching a leather-faced old man steering a pony and cart out of the still-open castle gates. "'Till she came here, the lass had never even seen the sea."

"On reflection, I must agree with Gabriel," Ruaidri said. "I truly doubt she'd have considered going back to Dunraven. She fears Alastair, and with good cause. He'd likely kill her if got his hands on her again."

"Dinnae say that." Still watching the pony and cart, and with the faint stench of fish in his nostrils, Ewan wrapped a hand around his sword hilt. "The bastard might still be lurking out there somewhere."

"Aye, he might. And assuming she also had that in mind, she may well have chosen to take the coast road," Jacques said. "A lesser known, but safer route."

Morag pulled her shawl tighter. "'Tis a desolate, windy path with little shelter," she said. "But you know that. You came that way yourselves but a few weeks ago."

"Who was that man?" Ewan asked, as Niall began to close the gates. "The one who just left?"

"His name is Sim." Ruaidri followed Ewan's gaze. "He's a fisherman and older than the rocks. He delivers barrels of salted herring to us a couple of times a year. Why do you ask?"

A flutter of anticipation arose in Ewan's belly. "Where does he live?"

"He lives..." Ruaidri eyes widened with apparent understanding. "He lives about a half-day south of here."

Ewan drew breath. "Niall," he bellowed, "tell Sim to halt!"

Morag gasped. "You think he might have seen Cristie?"

"I pray so," Ewan muttered, and strode toward the fisherman, who had halted and was looking back over his shoulder. "Dear God, I pray so."

A short while later, riding two fresh horses and leading Cristie's little mare, Ewan and Gabriel set out once more. The fisherman had not learned the lass's name, but his description of her matched Cristie, down to her bruised face and bandaged hands.

"If the wee lass did as bid," he'd said, "she'll be fed and rested when ye find her."

Relief had flowed through Ewan like sweet wine, lifting the burden of fear from his shoulders. Still, the unanswered question remained.

Why did she leave?

The afternoon light had begun to wane by the time they reached the small village. Ewan found the fisherman's cottage easily enough, rode up to the door, and dismounted. The door opened before he had time to knock, and a woman stepped out. If Sim was as old as the rocks, this woman had to be as old as the earth. The deep lines on her face gave testimony to her advanced years, as did her shrunken frame and the strands of fine, white hair poking out from beneath her veil. With one hand holding a staff, she shaded her brow with the other and squinted up at Ewan through milky eyes.

"By Christ's blessed bones," she said. "This wee house is busy today."

"Mistress Gunna?" Ewan had learned the woman's name from Sim. "I seek the whereabouts of a lass. Your husband said he sent her to you."

She peered past him. "Where is he?"

"Your husband? He's on his way home. Is the lass still here?"

Gunna sniffed. "Well now, good sir, that depends."

Ewan frowned. "On what? Is the lass here or nay?"

"Are ye the one who struck her? For I'll no' tell ye where she is if ye're the one who struck her."

Behind Ewan, still seated astride his horse, Gabriel cleared his throat.

"Who's there?" Gunna peered past Ewan again and her pale eyes widened. "Why, 'tis a Christian soldier, as was our auld laird."

"The auld laird was my grandfather," Ewan said, his patience thinning. "And nay, Mistress, I didnae strike the lass, nor would I ever lay a rough hand on her. Is she still here? Answer me."

The woman squinted at him anew, her gaze resting a brief moment on Ewan's scarred flesh. "The auld laird was your grandfather?"

Ewan forced a smile. "Forgive me. I should have said. Aye, my name is Ewan MacKellar. I'm the younger brother of Laird Ruaidri MacKellar."

"Och, well, aye, ye should have said. I heard you'd returned." Gunna shook her head. "Nay, the lass isnae here."

Ewan cursed under his breath. "Then, where is she?"

"She's—"

"Ewan."

He turned to look at Gabriel who nodded toward the shore. Ewan followed his direction to see a small, familiar figure standing at the water's edge, gazing out across the waves.

"Thank Christ," he murmured.

"Said she wanted tae watch the sunset." Gunna gazed up at the clouds. "I fear she'll no' see much o' one tonight, though."

"You have my gratitude, Gunna," Ewan said, turning back to the woman. "Your kindness willnae be forgotten."

"Och, she's a nice wee lass," Gunna replied, retreating back into her cottage. "Doesnae deserve tae be ill-treated. Ye'll see her home safe, then?"

Ewan inclined his head. "You have my word."

Gunna responded with a gap-toothed smile and closed the door.

"I'll wait with the horses," Gabriel said, dismounting.

Ewan gave a vague nod and headed down the narrow path to the beach. A fine shale crunched beneath his feet like broken glass, an accompaniment to the solid beat of his heart in his ears. To add to the clamour, the waves, aroused by the wind, rolled like thunder onto the shore. Cristie stood just out of their reach and appeared to be deep in thought as she gazed out toward the horizon. Her cloak lifted like wings, and long strands of her unbound hair whipped around her face.

She looked bereft. Lost. In need of direction.

Ewan slowed his step as he approached and he wondered, again, what had prompted the lass's exodus. What kind of response might he expect from her? Had he been so mistaken the previous night, hearing the plea in her voice and seeing the want in her eyes?

At that moment, a gull screeched overhead, and Cristie stirred as if waking from a dream. She turned and looked directly at Ewan, her benign expression turning to one of absolute shock.

"Ewan!" Eyes wide, she took a step back. "What… what are you doing here?"

He halted. The lass had the look of a feral creature, one that might turn and bolt if he dared to approach. A frown flitted across his brow. "'Tis a question I should be asking you, lass."

"But, how…" Disbelief etched on her face, she glanced about wildly "How did you find me?"

"By the grace of God and an auld fisherman," he said, moving a little closer. "I've been searching for you all day. What possessed you, Cristie? Why did you leave without a word to anyone?"

She looked at him aghast, as if trying to make sense of his words. "You've… you've been searching for me?"

"Aye." He ran a hand through his hair. "And I cannae fathom why that appears to surprise you. Why, lass? Why did you leave?"

"Because I…" Uncertainty showed on her face as her gaze wandered over him. "Because I couldnae bear…"

"What?" he demanded, moving to within an arm's reach of her. "You couldnae bear what? Did someone threaten you? Hurt you?"

"Nay!" She shook her head. "Naught like that."

"Then explain." Ewan dared to cup her cheek, gratified that she didn't flinch or draw back. "Because right now, I cannae decide whether to kiss you or shake you. To leave as you did, with no warning, no explanation. What, under God's great sky, would make you do such a thing?"

"Because I'm a coward." Her lip quivered. "Truly, Ewan, I didnae expect you to come looking for me. I'm sorry if I've caused you some trouble."

"A coward? What do you mean? What are you afraid of?"

"Facing the truth." She released a tearful laugh, a sound void of humour. "I left because I no longer had a reason to stay. I am happy for you, though, and I mean that from my heart. I just didnae have the courage to tell you to your face."

"*Happy* for me?" Beyond confused, he rubbed his forehead. "I'm adrift, Cristie. I swear I dinnae have a clue what you're talking about."

"Um…" She frowned. "The Templars?"

"What about them?"

"Well, you've… you've decided to take your vows again."

His confusion grew. "What makes you think that?"

"Because I…" A look of bewilderment settled on her face. "Because I saw you this morning, in the hall. Wearing your mantle."

And, in the space of a single heartbeat, everything made sense. "Och, Cristie, nay." Relief flooded through Ewan like an elixir. Her flight had been the result of a simple misunderstanding, a misconstrued moment of time. Of course, if not for the kindness of some simple fisherfolk, things might have been much worse. But she was safe, thank God, and he'd had not been mistaken about her love for him. Quite the contrary. He threw another prayer of thanks Heavenward and drew her close. "It was not what it looked like. It was not what you think."

She trembled against him. "But I saw you."

"Aye, but you saw me wearing Jacques' mantle, not mine." He pulled back and stroked her hair from her face. "Ruaidri said he wished he'd been there the night I returned, wished he could have seen me as a Templar. Jacques took off his mantle and put it on me, but only for Ruaidri's sake. It was an unplanned thing. If you'd waited a wee while, you'd have seen me take it off."

She worried her lip and looked away as if absorbing what he'd said. "So, you're not...?" Eyes bright with tears, she gazed up at him once more. "You're not retaking your vows?"

"Nay." He smothered an urge to smile—not easy, considering his heart now felt as light as thistle down. "At least, not my Templar vows."

She blinked, sending a tear tumbling down her cheek. "What do you mean?"

"Please dinnae cry, Cristie." He brushed the tear away. "I was tempted to tell you last night, but you looked so exhausted, I decided I'd wait till today. A bad decision, in hindsight. I'd prayed for decent weather too, because I'd planned to take you down to the shore to tell you." He glanced about. "Well, we're at the shore, right enough, though a wee bit further south than I'd anticipated. The weather's no' too bad, either, so I suppose I can tell you here and now."

Cristie fidgeted. "Tell me what?"

"That I'd like to take my marriage vows again." He sighed and gazed into the blue depths of her eyes. "And I'd like to take them with you, Cristie Ferguson. I love you. 'Tis as simple and as complicated as that. I love you and want to spend the rest of my life with you."

"You would?" A cautious expression of hope crept onto her face. "I mean... you do?"

"More than anything."

"But I… I am base-born."

"I dinnae care."

"And after all that I have done." She shook her head. "The way I deceived you, Ewan."

He placed a finger atop her lips. "You speak of things past. 'Tis the future that concerns me. Will I remain close to the Templar brotherhood? Aye, of course I will. They'll forever be a part of my life, and if they ever have need of me, I'll try and answer their call. But I…" Ewan paused, unsure of how to proceed. He'd never even shared his innermost thoughts with God. At least, not verbally. But he needed to do this. The regrets that plagued him stemmed from words not spoken and feelings not shared. Opportunities had been forever lost. A harsh lesson to learn, and he had learned it. He took a steadying breath, and continued.

"When I took you back to Dunraven, I confess I never had any intention of seeing you again. But if you think it was easy for me to leave you there, to watch you walk away, you are mistaken. It near killed me, Cristie. I wanted to believe you'd meant to tell me the truth and that you loved me, but—"

"I did mean it, Ewan," she cried. "I do mean it!"

"I ken, lass. The problem was, I couldnae reconcile heart and conscience. I couldnae begin to defend or justify what you'd done. The deception—the damage—was too great. Or so I thought. Then, last night, you show up at the gates with Ruaidri, who looked to be at death's door. At first, I feared you'd known of his captivity all along, till I learned the blessed truth of it. And in learning that truth, I was able to reconcile what I felt for you." He swallowed over a sudden tightness in his throat. "You're brave and bonny, and I want you by my side always. Say you'll marry me, Cristie. Make a stubborn, battle-scarred knight happy."

"Oh, Ewan." She laughed even as her tears fell again. "Of course I'll marry you! I swear there's naught I want more. 'Tis the answer to my prayers."

"Then God be praised." Ewan lifted her chin and lowered his mouth to hers in a tender caress. A soft whimper escaped her; a sweet sound of delight that sparked a flame of desire deep in his belly. "I'm blessed," he murmured, against her lips. "So very blessed."

"As am I." Cristie gave him a sheepish smile. "Though I must confess, I also feel a wee bit foolish now I know the truth of it. I should have waited instead of running off like that."

"Aye, well…" Ewan assumed a stern expression and brushed an errant strand of hair from her forehead. "Dinnae do it again."

"I willnae."

"Ever."

"Never, ever." She smiled and drew a cross over her heart. "I swear it."

"Good." He lifted one of her bandaged hands and eyed it with concern. "Still sore?"

Cristie wrinkled her nose. "A little, aye."

"Gabriel will tend to them." He glanced briefly over his shoulder to where his friend still waited. "Come on. It'll be dark soon. Let's go home."

"Home," Cristie repeated, as if savouring the word.

"Aye." Ewan bent and kissed her again. "From now on, *mo chridhe*, your home is with me."

Chapter Twenty-Five

"**I, Cristie** Elena Ferguson, take thee, Ewan Tormod MacKellar, to my wedded husband…"

Ewan gazed at Cristie as she made her vows. The furtive shadows had gone from her eyes. In their place, a soft glow of honesty, trust and love. She spoke without hesitating, though her voice trembled a little.

Once again, he placed a ring on her finger—a small silver band, hastily hammered and shaped that same day by the castle's blacksmith. Because of her blistered hands, he could only push the ring on partway. But Cristie heaved a sigh, and regarded the meagre trinket as if it was the most precious thing under Heaven.

Ewan hadn't thought to wed the lass that day, but since Father Iain had arrived to see Ruaidri, he saw no point in delaying the ceremony.

"A miracle and a marriage," Morag said as they gathered in the great hall later that afternoon. News of Ruaidri's resurrection must have been carried on the wind, judging by the small army of well-wishers who had been traipsing through the gates since the noon hour. That, in itself, had given rise to added security, since Alastair MacAulay's whereabouts remained a mystery.

"He wouldnae dare show his face here," Morag said.

Ewan grunted. "I'd put naught past him, and I dinnae want to take the chance."

The day had been busy but trouble-free. Ewan had kept a watchful eye on Ruaidri, aware that the man's spirit was much stronger than his body. Now, as the afternoon wound down, dark shadows sat beneath his brother's eyes.

"You'll be retiring to your chamber shortly, Ruaidri," Ewan said.

Ruaidri gave him a weary smile. "Is that a question or an order?"

"An order. And I'll no' hear any argument."

Ruaidri waggled a brow. "You'll probably be retiring to yours as well."

"Aye." Ewan glanced at Cristie, who sat patiently as Gabriel administered to her wounds.

"I would speak with you beforehand," Ruaidri continued.

"Och, dinnae trouble yourself," Ewan said, his tone purposely serious. "I have some idea of what to do. I wasnae always a Templar."

Ruaidri chuckled and leaned forward. "I wouldnae presume to offer my brother any such advice. 'Tis a different sort of information I wish to pass on."

"Is that so? I'm intrigued."

Ruaidri's eyes flicked to Cristie. "In private," he murmured.

Ewan frowned. "What's so private that it must be kept secret from my wife?"

"It willnae be a secret once I've shared it with you. After that, you can share it with whomever you wish. 'Tis just that I'd prefer to share it with you in private."

"Very well." Ewan rose. "Come on, then, Laird MacKellar. Let's get you to your bed."

"Now?"

"Aye, now."

Ewan turned to Cristie, who gave him a smile that went straight to his heart. The lass still had bruises on her face and likely would for a few days yet. The green robe she'd worn for the ceremony belonged to Morag. And her wedding band was naught but a thin piece of silver that only sat half-way onto her finger. Maybe he should have allowed the lass to heal, arranged for a proper wedding ring, and had some new clothes made for her before he'd married her. Despite all that, she looked far from miserable, but he asked the question anyway.

"Are you happy, *mo chridhe*?"

"Very happy, Ewan," she said. "'Tis like I'm floating on air."

That went straight to his heart as well. "I'll be back in a wee while, lass."

She glanced past him at Ruaidri and nodded her understanding.

*

"So," Ewan said, as they entered Ruaidri's chamber, "I confess I'm itching to hear about this secret information of yours."

Frowning, Ruaidri unbuckled his sword belt. "I'll be glad when I get some meat back on my bones. Everything just falls off me."

Ewan scratched his chin. "Is that it?"

"Nay." The bed creaked as Ruaidri clambered onto it and settled back against the pillows. "Oof, I confess I'm ready for a rest."

"Aye, you've overdone it a wee bit today." Ewan raised his brows. "So, what is it that you cannae say in front of Cristie?"

"'Tis not me who wishes to say it, Ewan," Ruaidri replied. "'Tis someone else."

A burning candle atop Ruaidri's desk crackled, drawing Ewan's gaze for a moment. "What do you mean?"

Ruaidri also looked toward the candle and gave a soft laugh. "By Odin's accursed eye. Almost makes me believe the man is still with us."

"What man?"

"Our father."

Ewan fidgeted. "I wish he was."

"That surprises me. You did naught but argue all the time."

"Aye, I ken. But looking back…" He shook his head. "I have a wee bride waiting for me. Can we maybe do this on the morrow?"

"Nay, we'll do it now." He gestured to the desk. "If you run your fingers under the edge on the right side, you'll feel a wee lever. Pull it toward you. It doesnae take much effort."

Ewan chuckled. "Secret compartments, Ru?"

"A laird should never be without them."

Ewan pulled the lever and a small drawer shot out. "There's a scroll in here."

"Aye. Remove it and look at the seal."

He did so, moving into the candlelight to better inspect the circle of blood-red wax. "I dinnae understand," he said. "This is our father's seal."

"I ken it is, Ewan." Ruaidri smiled. "He always said you'd return one day."

Ewan's throat went dry. "Are you saying this is for me?"

Ruaidri nodded. "He asked me to give it to you when you came home. You'll notice I said 'when' and nae 'if'. Read it here if you wish. Or if you'd rather do so in priv—"

The wax snapped under Ewan's thumb and he carefully unfurled the scroll. His father's familiar writing leapt out at him as he sat on the edge of the bed and started to read.

To my son, Ewan Tormod MacKellar.

Written on this ninth day of September

The year of our Lord 1306.

May the Lord have kept you in good health, Ewan.

To me, then, is given the last word, and spoken from the grave, for if you are reading this, then I am gone to the Lord. But, praise His name, you have come home, which means my mortal prayers have been answered.

I find I cannot leave this world peacefully without laying bare my heart. Hence this missive, for there are things I wish to say to you.

Firstly, we are alike, you and I, each with a good measure of pride and stubbornness. How many times did we lock antlers? Too many to count. Have you ever tried to recall what we fought about? I have. And the answers continue to elude me.

I wonder if, like me, you have regrets. If so, then perhaps by sharing mine, I can allay yours. I pray so, for regret is a merciless burden to bear.

I regret not telling you how much I admired your tenacity, your skill with a sword, your horsemanship, your chivalry. You were a knight, Ewan, long before you won your spurs. You made me proud always.

I used to watch you with Morag. The wee lass pestered you constantly, demanding your time and attention. Not once do I recall you losing patience with her. And not once did I commend you for your kindness and tolerance. But I was aware of it. It reminded me of your mother, may God rest her sweet soul.

I know you blame yourself for her death, and use guilt as both sword and shield. And though I never laid blame at your feet... to my eternal shame, I did naught to disarm you. Made no effort to dispel your misplaced guilt. Please forgive me.

Your mother died of childbed fever, but not before she had seen you, held you, and loved you. She is the one who chose your name - Ewan. Named for her grandfather. You are not responsible for her death. If blame must be placed at all, place it with me, for you came from my seed.

I regret letting you leave without trying to make amends, may my pride be damned. But of all the things I did and should not have done, of all the things I said and should not have said, my biggest regret is not telling you how much I loved you.

'Tis not always easy for a man to say what lies in his heart. To profess such sentiment is oft seen as weakness, better left to poets, bards and women. But I can tell you, Ewan, that when a man faces death, all that remains to be said seeks freedom.

For some, there is never enough time. For others, it is already too late.

So, I am giving freedom to what lies in my heart now, while I still have time, and I pray my words will find you before it is too late.

I love you, my son. I always have, and I always will.
Your father,
Calum Ruaidri MacKellar.

Ewan raised tear-filled eyes to Ruaidri. "I dinnae ken what to say."

"I do, if it isnae too late to say it." Ruaidri held out a hand. "Welcome home, my brother."

Chapter Twenty-six

Later, alone in their chamber, Ewan read the letter to Cristie.

"May God bless and keep his soul," she said, with tears in her eyes. "'Tis a legacy without price, Ewan."

"Aye, it is." He set the scroll aside and drew her close. "And in sharing my legacy, *mo chridhe*, I am reminded that I ken little of yours."

She shrugged. "I barely knew my father as anything other than a laird. He took care of us, but from afar. We were never hungry or cold. We had a couple of goats for milk, and a pony and cart. I loved my mother, Ewan. And she was a fine weaver. After she died, I found out Malcolm MacAulay had left instructions for me to be moved to Dunraven."

"Do you ken how to weave?"

"Aye, I do. I love it. I have… *had* my own loom."

"Then I'll add a loom to the list of things you need."

Her eyes widened. "You have a list?"

"Most certainly."

"But all I need is right here, Ewan."

"'Tis very sweet of you to say so, lass. But I'll no' have my wife running around in my sister's cast-offs, and wearing a piece of silver wire on her bridal finger. When you sit at your new loom, you'll be dressed in silken finery with gold on your fingers."

Cristie's laughter faded, and she gave a wistful sigh. "I left my gifts behind at Dunraven. The ones you gave me?"

"Nae problem. A silk shawl and tortoiseshell comb have just been added to the list."

"And a seashell."

"Aye, of course. And a seashell. I might have to search a wee while before I find another like that." Chuckling, he leaned in and kissed her. "I love you."

"I love you too. More than anything."

"'Tis our wedding night, Cristie."

"Aye, I havenae forgotten." She turned her back to him, and bowed her head. "Will you help me, please?"

"With pleasure." Ewan placed his hands on the smooth skin of her shoulders and kissed the nape of her neck. He smelled her sweetness, felt her shiver, and heard her soft intake of breath.

The laces surrendered easily to his touch. It felt symbolically sensuous somehow, and he hardened. The exercise had always aroused him, but tonight the familiar routine would be a little different. Tonight, he was free to anticipate fulfilment.

Lastly, he pulled the pins from her hair and loosened it, letting it tumble to her waist

"Turn around, Cristie. Look at me."

She did so, her face aglow with candlelight. Only now, seeing her unmasked, did Ewan realize how much she had hidden from him. A deception driven by fear.

The bruising around Cristie's eye stirred a familiar anger within him, but he tamped it down. Such feelings had no place here. Tonight, he would know his wife. Every part of her.

His hand first went to the graceful line of Cristie's throat, resting against it with the lightness of a feather. Her pulse tapped against his fingers as his thumb traced an idle line along her jaw. With a little more boldness, he slid his fingers through her hair and cradled her head. Then he lowered his mouth to hers, tasting and exploring her lips in a tender, but commanding caress. Seeking to explore further, his tongue probed the seam of her mouth, nudging it open. She allowed him entry and he deepened the kiss, pulling her tighter against him. Her muffled whimper of pleasure turned his cock to steel.

A rush of desire, like none he had ever known, burned through him, setting fire to his blood. For years, he had been starved of carnal fulfilment. His appetite, unshackled and ravenous, now demanded repletion. Somewhere behind his disintegrating control, he told himself to slow down. To restrain himself.

It took no little effort to break the kiss. Breathing deep, he regarded Cristie. Lips slightly parted, cheeks flushed, she gazed up at him with what looked like a question in her eyes. *Why did you stop?*

Ewan ran a hand through his hair. "You should ken, *mo chridhe*, that I'll no' be sleeping on the floor tonight."

A slow smile spread across her face as she shrugged her robe from her shoulders. She stepped out of it and kicked it aside, and then tugged off her shift and let it fall. Enchanted by the vision before him, Ewan stood unmoving and silent

"I am yours, Ewan," she said, "and that is all I want to be."

"And I am blessed." Every nerve in his body tingled with desire. He first touched her face and then moved his hand down over her heart to cup her breast. His thumb brushed over her nipple, and it pearled beneath his caress. "Very blessed."

Cristie stood on tiptoes and kissed him. "I would see you too, Ewan. I would touch you and feel your strength."

As much as she was able, Cristie helped him undress, and when at last he stood naked before her, she moved without hesitation into his arms. Ewan groaned, slid his hands down the curve of her spine, and pulled her against him. The feel of her belly pressed against his cock almost finished him.

She laughed as he picked her up and placed her on the bed, and then melted against him like liquid silk, eager and reaching.

"My wee wife, bonny and passionate as well." Ewan's hand travelled down over the curve of her waist. "We might be in this bed for days."

She chuckled and kissed the spot at the base of his throat. "I have dreamed of this, Ewan. I have imagined your bare skin against mine, your lips on mine, your hands touching me. I wanted to please you. I *want* to please you."

"You do, *mo ghràidh*." Her familiar scent now carried a hint of female arousal that further stoked his desire. His cock twitched against her. "The 'pleasing' is near driving me mad."

"Yet I fear I cannae touch you the way I would like because of these bandages. The way *you* would like."

"A temporary hindrance. Besides, 'tis no' just the hands that can do the touching, lass. The mouth is a fine instrument of pleasure too."

"It is?"

He grinned. "Aye."

She gasped as he took a nipple in his mouth and tugged it gently into a hard peak. Her spine arched, and he smiled against her flesh, delighted by her unabashed response.

"Ewan. Oh… it feels…" Another gasp. "Oh, sweet heaven!"

His hand moved over the gentle rise of her abdomen and sought out the soft curls at the juncture of her thighs. There, he paused his exploration, taking the time to massage the soft mound as he fought for control. His long abstinence from intimacy had him teetering on the edge of climax. Cristie's unabashed responses to him, so incredibly arousing, didn't help either.

Aye, but the night is young, he told himself, throwing all caution to the winds of passion. Drunk on desire, he slipped an exploratory finger between her wet folds. Urged on by the sweet chorus of sounds coming from her, he inserted a second finger. The two digits mimicked the thrusts of a cock as his thumb teased the hard little nub at her apex. She was slick and hot. And he was past the point of going in any direction except off the precipice.

"Ewan, please." Her hips lifted against his hand. "Please!"

"Aye, *mo chridhe*." Readied at her core, he watched her face as his penetration began, stopping his advance when he felt the resistance of her virtue. "Cristie—"

"It doesnae hurt." Her chest rose and fell. "I want this. I want *you*. I love you. I love you more than... ah!"

With a single, firm thrust, he penetrated her fully, drawing a gasp from her.

"Dinnae move," he said, as much for his tortured self as for her. "Allow your body to adjust to mine."

She released a soft little whimper. "I cannae help it." Her hips lifted. "I cannae help it, Ewan."

"Cristie, I swear..." Ewan withdrew and pushed into her again, and again. He covered her mouth with his, his entire body tightening as he approached fulfilment. As tight as she was, he felt her clench even tighter around him.

And then the heavens exploded and pulled him apart. Ewan heard his name being cried out in passion, and surrendered to a blessed release.

Chapter Twenty-Seven

Five days had passed since Ruaidri's return. There had been no sign of Alastair MacAulay or Tasgall. No news at all, in fact.

Till now.

"I cannae decide if you're brave or foolish," Ruaidri said, eyeing the two people who stood before him in the great hall. "Whichever the case, I'm sure you can understand if I dinnae extend a warm welcome to Clan MacAulay. What do you want?"

Cristie looked on in disbelief, wondering what on earth had brought Brochan and Elspeth MacAulay to Cathan's gates. Brochan's pallor reflected his shock at the sight of the emaciated man before him. Elspeth's hands were clenched, prayer like, over her mouth, and had been like that since she'd first seen Ruaidri. She stared at him in blatant horror, her eyes bright with tears.

"Laird MacKellar." Brochan glanced at Cristie, the slight tilt of his head acknowledging her presence. "We… Christ have mercy, I dinnae ken what to say. I knew naught of your kidnapping or confinement till Elspeth told me of it. And I didnae… I mean, I didnae expect to see you so…"

"Close to death?" Morag spat, not hiding her contempt.

Brochan shifted on his feet. "Aye, in truth."

"Thank God Cristie got to you in time, Laird MacKellar," Elspeth said. "And Brochan speaks true. We had nae knowledge of your abduction. None at all."

Ruaidri's gaze swept over the lass. "Cristie told me what you did, my lady. For that, I owe you a debt of thanks. But answer the question, and tell us what brings you here."

"Our brother." Brochan straightened. "We would know what became of him. We'll understand, of course, if... if you've hanged him already, given the circumstances."

Ruaidri raised a brow and cast a quick glance at Ewan. "Hanging would be too good for Alastair MacAulay. Chained in a dark dungeon and left to starve to death might be a wee bit more appropriate."

Brochan cleared his throat. "Is that where he is? Chained in your dungeon?"

"Nay," Ruaidri replied. "Unfortunately, we havenae had the opportunity."

"What do you mean?" Brochan frowned. "Are you saying you havenae seen him?"

"Neither hide nor hair."

Brochan threw a puzzled glance at Elspeth. "Then, where is he?"

Ruaidri huffed. "I'd like to know the answer to that as well."

"Burning in Hell, I hope," Morag said.

"Where's Tasgall?" Cristie asked. "Was he with him?"

"Tasgall is dead, Cristie," Elspeth said. "Alastair put a blade through him the night he returned from letting you and Laird MacKellar go. Alastair left right after. We just assumed he'd gone after you."

Ruaidri uttered a curse under his breath and turned away for a moment. "Be seated," he said, gesturing to the table, "and tell us everything."

Brochan inclined his head. "Thank you, laird."

Elspeth approached Cristie. "You did it," she murmured, glancing at Ruaidri. "But, Cristie, the poor man! I still cannae believe what Alastair has done. And these are yours, by the way." She held out a cloth bag. "I thought I'd bring them, though I'm no' sure if you mean to stay here."

"My gifts! Thank you. And, aye, I'll be staying here."

"I see." Elspeth looked past her, raising a brow. "You must be Ewan."

Ewan inclined his head. "My lady."

"You've forgiven my daft sister, then? For pretending to be me?"

Cristie gasped. "Elspeth!"

"I have, aye." Ewan slid an arm around Cristie's waist. "The lass rowed across a loch, offered her life in exchange for my brother's freedom, rode a horse through the mountain fog, and delivered my brother safely home. I had nae choice but to forgive her. I had nae choice but to marry her as well."

Elspeth blinked. "You're *married*?"

Cristie grinned. "For three whole days."

"Well, I'm happy for you, truly." She heaved a sigh. "'Tis nice to have something to feel happy about. The past few weeks at Dunraven have been absolute shite, quite frankly."

*

"I ken you didnae like him, but I have to tell you, I feel sad for Tasgall."

Ewan frowned. "I ken you do, lass."

Cristie, sitting crossed on the bed, leaned over and grabbed her comb from the bedside table. "'Tis as if Alastair is unhinged. Or was, since he's likely dead by now."

A chill brushed the back of Ewan's neck. "Until we find out, you'll no' leave the castle without me for any reason. Understood?"

"Aye." She eyed a strand of her hair and pulled the comb through it. "Though I cannae believe he's still alive, Ewan. He's been missing for five days."

"I dinnae care if it's been fifty-five days. You'll no' step out of those gates unless I'm with you. Swear it, lass."

She grimaced as her comb hit a tangle. "I swear."

"And I'll be telling Morag the same." Ewan held out a hand. "Let me do that."

Shuffling around, she settled herself in front of him and shook her hair back. "What do you think of Brochan and Elspeth?"

"I like them much better than their brother."

"I think Ruaidri likes Elspeth," Cristie mused. "I think she likes him, too. They chatted for quite a while last eve. Did you notice?"

"She was the lass meant for him, so he's curious about her. There's naught more to it than that." But Ewan smiled to himself. He'd noticed Ruaidri's interest as well.

"I think they'd be well suited." Cristie sighed. "And you can cross a shawl and a comb off your list, by the way."

"Do you think Alastair is still alive?" Ruaidri asked, watching Brochan and Elspeth ride out of the gates the next morning.

"Aye." Ewan's hand tightened on his sword hilt. "Though I'm no' sure why."

"Maybe he'll be at Dunraven when they get back."

"Rather there than here." Ewan gazed up at a dawn sky. "I'm going to *Lorg Coise Dhè* this morning."

"Taking Cristie?"

"Aye, though she doesnae ken yet. I only said we were going for a ride."

"'Tis putting her at risk. And I'm no' talking about Alastair MacAulay."

"No more at risk than Morag, Ruaidri. Given what's happened, I dinnae want any more secrets between us. She's my wife. She has a right to know."

Ruaidri nodded. "I understand. Tell Father Iain I'll get there myself when I'm feeling stronger."

"I just wish we had news from France." Ewan grimaced. "Then again, maybe I dinnae."

"It'll come." Ruaidri put a hand on Ewan's shoulder. "But I fear it willnae be good news, Ewan. Here's Cristie. Stay vigilant, brother."

*

A look of wonder on her face, Cristie gazed out over the small glen. "What is this place? 'Tis incredible."

"'Tis called *Lorg Coise Dhè*," Ewan replied. "And the church down there is called *Eaglais Chruinn*. It was built by my grandfather. The glen and the church are pledged to the Templars."

"But, why would he build a church here?"

"'Twas a dream of his, apparently. One he carried with him from childhood." Ewan pressed his heels to his horse. "Come and say good morn to its sole resident. You already know his name."

As usual, Father Iain stepped outside as they approached. Ewan dismounted and lifted Cristie down.

"Father Iain." She glanced about. "What a fine place to live."

"Good day, to you, my lady. And to you, Ewan. Aye, I'm a fortunate man."

"But, do you no' get lonely?"

"Nay, lass. God is always with me. And if I fancy some mortal company, my wee donkey and I head on over to Castle Cathan."

Ewan cleared his throat. "I'll be showing Cristie around, Father Iain."

The man's brows raised. "I trust she'll find it enlightening, Ewan."

Ewan nodded. "I trust she will."

The priest nodded, the hint of a smile on his face. "I'll leave you to it, then."

Ewan tethered the horses and then took Cristie's hand. "The white heather is over here," he said, leading her toward the loch. One or two sprigs still had flowers on them. Ewan picked one and gave it to Cristie.

"'Tis a bonny place," she said, gazing about. "Now I'm here, Ewan, I can understand why your grandfather built his church. 'Tis the perfect place to build one."

"It pleases me to hear you say it, *mo chridhe,* for I always feel the same." He kissed her. "Come and see his legacy."

They climbed the church steps and passed beneath a carved stone archway. "Hewn from an English oak," Ewan said, pushing the heavy door open, a groan from the hinges resounding through the church. It faded to silence, and Ewan felt the familiar sense of peace as he set foot inside.

"I have never seen the like," Cristie whispered, crossing herself as she glanced about. "The carvings are incredible."

"The masons were chosen with care," Ewan said. "Most of them had worked for the Templars previously. The symbolism represents the Holy Land and Scotland. You'll see carvings of olive and palm leaves as well as heather and thistle."

She turned a circle. "Yet there is little adornment elsewhere. 'Tis very plain, otherwise."

"The Templars are no' given to ostentation," Ewan replied.

Shafts of daylight tumbled through the windows, lighting the way till Ewan and Cristie came at last to the apse. Here stood the altar, covered by a green altar cloth, and lit by three slender candles. A large wooden cross hung on the wall.

Cristie glanced down at her feet. "What does this say, Ewan?" she asked, seeing letters carved into a flagstone.

"'Tis from the book of Psalms, and is written in Latin." Ewan crossed himself. "'Not unto us, O Lord, not unto us, but unto thy Name give glory'".

Cristie crouched, and traced the lines of one of the letters. "Do you think you could teach me to read? It must be wonderful to understand such words."

"Of course, *mo chridhe*." Ewan helped her to rise. "Come and see where my father lies."

He led her, then, to the side chapel, where the effigies of two knights lay side by side.

"At certain times, when sunlight pours through yon window, it reflects the cross onto their tombs," Ewan explained. "My father was not actually a Templar, but all and any future lairds of my clan are allowed to rest here if they wish."

Cristie bent and placed her sprig of white heather on his father's tomb. "I wish I could have known him," she said. "If, as you say, you were much alike, I'm sure I would have loved him."

Moved, Ewan lifted her hand to his lips. "You honour me, lass. I'm certain he would have loved you too."

"I am the one honoured," she said. "Thank you for bringing me here, Ewan."

"We're no' quite done yet." He gave a sober smile. "There's one more thing I'd like you to see before we leave. Come."

They returned to the altar and the carved floor stone.

"Stand here," Ewan said, moving her to the side, "and dinnae move."

"Why?" Frowning, she glanced about. "What are you doing?"

Ewan didn't answer.

Instead, he unsheathed his sword and anchored it, point first, into the second Latin 'i' that had been carved into the flagstone. The weapon stayed upright, swaying slightly. Ewan waited till the blade stilled and then knelt before it, head bowed as he prayed. Then, he crossed himself and rose to his feet.

"I'm trusting you, Cristie," he said, and pushed down on the hilt of his sword. A moment later, a soft rumble sounded beneath his feet. He watched as an unmarked flagstone at the foot of the altar sank below the floor and slid of sight beneath the altar steps.

The air fell silent.

Ewan looked over to where Cristie stood, an expression of shock on her face. He could almost hear the rattle of her heart as she stared at the opening in the floor. "What is this?"

"My grandfather was a man of vision," Ewan said. "He studied history, and in doing so, came to the conclusion that the powerful are always doomed to fall. 'Tis the way of the world. The way of God. So, he decided to prepare, certain that a day of reckoning would one day befall the Templars. That day, it seems, came on October the thirteenth this year."

Cristie stepped forward and peered into the blackness. "What's down there?"

"The means to survive, perhaps." Ewan shrugged. "The Templars are the richest military order in Christendom."

She gasped. "Are you saying Alastair was right?"

Ewan went to the altar and lifted one of the candles. "Come and see for yourself, *mo ghràidh.*" He extended a hand. "And mind your step."

The candle flame cast a halo of light across a half-dozen boxes that had been neatly stacked on the earthen floor. Ewan went to one of them, took his dagger, cut through the binding, and threw back the lid. Inside, a dozen or so burlap bags, the outlines of their contents bulging against the fabric.

Ewan cut a small slit in one of the bags, just big enough to see the silver coins inside.

"We had an entire night to prepare, Cristie." A sigh escaped him. "We were never going to leave France empty handed."

"All these boxes contain silver coins?"

"Nay, dinnae be daft." He grinned. "Some have gold in them."

"Oh!" She laughed, and glanced about. "Truly, this is incredible."

"Silver and gold only have practical worth, lass," Ewan said. "'Tis the holy artefacts that have true value."

"They are here too?"

"A few, aye." He lifted a small, leather-bound chest from atop one of the boxes. "This is the most important one. Hold the candle for me."

He flicked the small brass latch, lifted the lid, pulled out a yellowed scrap of linen, crossing himself before he opened it.

"What is it?" Cristie asked. "It looks like a piece of wood."

"'Tis part of a cross," Ewan said, "a cross that once stood in a place called Calvary."

*

Later that night, Ewan quietly admitted to himself that there were few things in life better than holding a soft, warm, lass in his arms. That he had come to love the lass beyond measure surely added to the pleasure of it.

Yet his visit to *Eaglais Chruinn* had churned up fresh feelings of frustration and anguish. His heart ached for his Templar brothers. Despite his father's prediction, it seemed impossible to believe that this might truly be the end for the Order. Ewan's future seemed set, but for Gabriel and Jacques, it was still uncertain.

All they could do, for now, was wait for news.

Epilogue

Christmastide had come and gone. Ruaidri had continued to gain weight and renew his strength. Alastair MacAulay remained missing.

And Cristie now carried Ewan's child.

Not long into the New Year, news of the Templars' fate finally reached Castle Cathan. It was as feared. Tales of imprisonment and torture. Templar knights forced to confess to crimes of heresy and blasphemy—crimes they had never committed.

Those who recanted were killed—burned at the stake— or tortured till death.

Gabriel, his soul burdened by anguish, stood on the cliffs outside Castle Cathan and looked to the south.

He could almost smell the carnage.

Still, south would be his direction. But not France. England.

Specifically, Furness Abbey, a great, sandstone edifice that sat in a quiet vale at the foot of the Cumberland hills. He knew the abbot—assuming the man was still there. In any case, Gabriel had made up his mind. He would lay down his sword and take up the cloth.

The beauty of Scotland would forever remain in his memory. Those at Castle Cathan would forever be his friends. The Templar code would forever guide his heart.

But for Gabriel, it was time to move on.

To be continued…

Thank you so much for reading The Sword and the Spirit, 'Ewan'. If you have enjoyed the book, please share your reading pleasure with others by leaving a review on Amazon or Goodreads, or both!

Book Two Now Available!
<u>The Sword and the Spirit, Book Two.</u>

Gabriel

Six months have passed since Gabriel escaped the persecution in France and fled, with two of his brothers-in-arms, to Scotland. The upheaval has not been easy for him. A pious and disciplined man, Gabriel now finds himself facing a chaotic and uncertain future. Unable to reconcile all that has happened, he decides to return to his native England, lay down his sword, and take holy vows at Furness   Abbey.

But returning to the land of his birth is not without risks. His destination lies within the border region of Scotland and England, an area long cursed with conflict. Not only that, the Templars in England are now also facing persecution.

Then there's Brianna, the young woman he discovers in the forest along with her rather unusual companion. For the first time in many years, Gabriel finds himself seriously tempted by the allure of a female. Throw in an unsolved mystery from the past, along with its astounding resolution, and Gabriel's life becomes even more complicated!

Will he adhere to his original plans? Or will temptation and conflict undermine his objective?

Prequel to this series: Read about Ewan's grandfather, Calum, and his connection to the Templars: A Sprig of White Heather

To keep up to date with news please subscribe to my newsletter at www.avrilborthiry.com.

Please follow me on Amazon, BookBub, and Facebook!

My Books!

The Wishing Well

Isolated Hearts

The Sentinel

Stolen by Starlight

Return to Allonby Chase

The Cast of a Stone

Triskelion

Beyond Reason

Matthew's Hope

The Christmas Orange

A Night of Angels

A Very Faerie Christmas

Printed in Great Britain
by Amazon